THE Cinderella PRINCE

THE BOYS OF HUDSON BURROW

HAYDEN HALL

Copyright © 2024 by Hayden Hall
All rights reserved.

No part of this publication may be reproduced, stored or transmitted in any form or by any means, electronic, mechanical, photocopying, recording, scanning, or otherwise without written permission from the publisher. It is illegal to copy this book, post it to a website, or distribute it by any other means without permission.

This novel is entirely a work of fiction. The names, characters and incidents portrayed in it are the work of the author's imagination. Any resemblance to actual persons, living or dead, events or localities is entirely coincidental.

Edited by OneLoveEditing
Cover by Angela Haddon
Photo by Edgar Marx (xramragde)
Written by Hayden Hall
www.haydenhallwrites.com
ISBN: 979-8-3344-4335-8

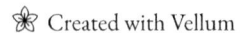

❦ Created with Vellum

Contents

Let's Stay In Touch — vii

1. Hudson Burrow — 1
2. A Wild August Night — 19
3. A Midnight Date — 39
4. The Days That Follow — 55
5. Mama Viv's Burger Bash — 69
6. Lies and Truths — 83
7. Knight In Shining Armor — 103
8. Starting Over — 115
9. After the Dance — 127
10. The Dressing Room — 153
11. To Worship and Honor — 165
12. The Phonecall — 175
13. Confrontations — 185
14. Homecomings — 195
15. A Time of Healing — 209
16. Heroes and Lovers — 227
17. Happily Ever After — 247
    Epilogue — 261

Romeo vs Romeo — 267
Acknowledgments — 269
Also by Hayden Hall — 271
About the Author — 273

Let's Stay In Touch

If you would like to keep in touch with me, the best way is to join my newsletter. As a welcome gift, I'll send you a little digital basket of freebies.

Join my newsletter for a freebie pack.
Follow me on Instagram.
Become a Patron.
Follow me on Amazon.
Visit www.haydenhallwrites.com for more information.

About the Book

All I want is to help those who need it the most. So when a devastatingly handsome stranger lands in Neon Nights, the gay bar where we spend our days and nights, I immediately know he's in trouble. I also know that we share an instant connection that comes once in a lifetime, but our clumsy kiss freaks him out and turns the night into a total disaster.

The truth is that Cedric Philippe Valois Montclair is no random stranger looking for a place to stay. He is a foreign prince about to be engaged to a woman his family picked for him. Facing the prospect of an arranged marriage, the charming prince ran to New York and fell into my arms.

Cedric is a dreamer, an art lover, and hell in a tight shirt. He makes my mouth water and my heart melt.

Can I protect him from his family's pursuit? And can I resist that endless pull of attraction?

I know I can never be more than a friend to him. Even if he didn't have to marry a French marchioness, he couldn't be with me. But every minute we spend on the dance floor, our hands exploring each other's biceps and backs, my desire for him becomes hotter.

I'm about to do something terribly stupid.

I'm about to fall in love with a prince.

CHAPTER 1
Hudson Burrow

Tristan

My best friend's naked ass was low on the list of things I wanted to see before I had my coffee. "Dude," I sighed, turning away from Roman, who was standing flamingo-style on one leg, the other lifted to pull the underwear over it. A wet towel was on the floor of the living room, and Rome's clothes were scattered around.

"Don't kill me," Rome said, bouncing on one foot ridiculously to maintain his balance. I was only glad that he was facing away from me because I didn't need the sight of things flapping up and down this early in the morning.

Rome's foot thumped against the dark, chipped, laminated floor, and the shushing of fabric over legs made me look at him more freely than in short glances. He released the waistband of his dark blue boxer briefs, and they slapped his lower back just above the thick curve of his ass —again, not a thing I was interested in inspecting, but living with four guys made mornings like this far more common than you'd think.

"Is it flooded again?" I asked. Rome could have dressed in the bathroom the five of us shared unless the drain got plugged and water covered the tiled floor.

My friend turned around, arms a little wide in exasperation. "Do you think moonshining you was on my bucket list?"

I exhaled a long breath of air. We couldn't scrape by for a plumber, but YouTube was free. It was also why our plugged drain was a recurring problem. "I'll take care of it."

"You will?" Rome asked, eyebrows rising. "You are a saint, Tris."

I rolled my eyes and shook my head, turning away from the tiny living room section of this one snug area of the apartment. Daylight poured in through the windows facing east, rays of sunshine slanting and filtering through cheap white curtains. The kitchen occupied a quarter of the common space, fully open to the round dining table with six chairs surrounding it. That thing alone took up more space than we could afford, but we had to eat somewhere. The only mark that separated the kitchen from the rest of the common room was a few square feet of tiles replacing the laminate.

"After I've had a lick of coffee," I told Roman.

"Thanks," my friend said, lifting two T-shirts to choose from. "What do you think?"

I inspected them both quickly. "What's the occasion?"

"They're trying to close the youth's art center on Perry Street," Rome said with an edge in his voice.

"The black one," I replied, pointing to the T-shirt he

held in his right hand while using my other hand to search for a coffee filter in the cluttered cupboard. "There's no need to look slutty, but it'll still show off some muscles."

"Yeah? Nobody's gonna mess with me," Rome said, picking the idea and running with it. He tossed the light cream T-shirt that normally revealed his lower abdomen. He pulled on the black T-shirt over his head. It was snug but not too tight. His physique was hard to miss, even when you didn't want to check him out.

I replaced the coffee filter and counted the scoops while Roman finished dressing. Sporty white socks, intentionally torn jeans, and unintentionally torn sneakers. He strapped on a fanny pack that contained his ID, not enough cash to bail himself out, and pepper spray in case he attracted unwanted attention. I knew the contents of his fanny pack because I had forced him to carry these things since he insisted on carrying his head in the bag.

Coffee dripped into the pot, and I leaned back against the small kitchen counter, arms crossed on my bare chest, gaze scanning Roman. "You're ready," I decided.

"Hell yeah," Rome said.

"Don't get yourself killed," I warned him. He still owed me this month's rent. "And give 'em hell."

Roman saluted me. "Sir, yes, sir." With a twirl, he faced the door and marched away.

I washed the dishes from last night's dinner while reminding myself that Roman was just being Roman and that nothing bad was going to happen to him. He'd gotten into scruffs with people countless times, but it had never stopped him from handcuffing himself to a door and refusing to move until someone met with the protestors.

He'd returned home with a split lip or a bleeding nose more than once, brushing it off as the price of doing the right thing. I wondered how many right things he still had left in him. Would one of them cost him more than just a black eye?

The cramp in my stomach clearly came from my vivid imagination. He was old enough to take care of himself. *He's also dumb enough to lie in front of a bulldozer*, I thought. Or brave enough, but I wasn't going to tell him that.

I wiped my hands on my pajama bottoms when the dishes were clear. After pouring myself a big mug of coffee, I grabbed the plunger from under the sink and headed for the bathroom. Rolling my pajamas up, I stepped into the puddle of water and began the grueling process of unplugging the shower drain. Our bathroom was as small as everything else in this place, but it was just enough for us. A toilet, a sink, a ceiling-tall cabinet with enough storage space for five guys, and a single piece of glass separating the shower. Luckily, the floor was at enough of an angle for water not to leak into the rest of the bathroom. Unluckily, the drain was a bitch.

By the time the tiny flood was resolved, I was in desperate need of showering, but my head throbbed with a hint of a headache. I washed my hands, dried my feet, and returned to the kitchen to enjoy my coffee in silence. The other guys were either out already or sleeping off a graveyard shift. My day was only just starting, and it had all the makings of a banger. Whatever troubles came along in the next twelve hours, I had at least a party at Neon Nights to look forward to.

Holding my mug, I walked to the kitchen window, pulled the curtain aside, and opened it to air the space out. Sitting on the windowsill, I looked at the street two stories below me. Framed by brownstone and redbrick buildings on either side, the narrow, one-way Washington Street met the narrower stone-paved Charles Lane at the corner just under my window. Warm air washed over me. People hurried up and down the street, some slipping in through the doors of Neon Nights across the street, which was a perfectly tame and friendly place during the day.

Once my mug was empty, I got ready for my morning run. It was an excellent way to save money on a gym membership, especially with the newly constructed outdoor exercise equipment on Pier 46 on the Hudson River. It was the shorter of the two piers claimed by the residents of Hudson Burrow, and a hard push from the locals got it converted into a place for exercise, leaving Pier 45 to function as a park for families enjoying sunny days on the river.

I was quiet as I got ready and left the apartment, comfortable sneakers on my feet and running clothes sticking to my body. As soon as I descended to the ground floor, ignoring the elevator that had gotten shut down way before my time, the scents of a new day in Hudson Burrow filled my lungs. Freshly baked bread and buns, sizzling hot dogs, roasting corn on a cob, coffee, donuts, the dust of dry streets, sweet summer sweat, cars, and a slightly fishy scent of the river nearby were only just the surface. Hudson Burrow was awake and brimming with people hurrying about their business. Deliveries arrived at cafes, bars, and restaurants, and people shouted, complained, and protested. They laughed, whistled, sang, and greeted you when you walked by.

As I looked around, a figure emerged from Neon Nights. This was a person you'd be hard-pressed to miss in any crowd. Tall, broad, and glamorously curvy, Lady Vivien Woodcock was the stuff of legends in Hudson Burrow. Wearing her tall, purple wig and the finest dark crimson sequin dress at eight in the morning, Mama Viv struggled to hold the phone in her hand, the acrylic nails nearly as long as her fingers.

The grin I put on as soon as I spotted her was wiped away when I realized that mascara was running down her face. Glancing once to my left where the traffic was coming from on Charles Street, I crossed in a hurry. "Mama Viv?"

"...ordered them seven days ago and called yesterday to confirm the delivery time," Mama Viv cried into the phone, her other hand trembling. "What do you mean it was misplaced? Well, how soon can you have it? You do have it? Then what on Earth is the problem?" With a dramatic wave of her free hand, Mama Viv looked at me. She blinked softly as if to signal that everything was alright, but her eyes glimmered with more unspilled tears. "My brunch is starting in two hours. I absolutely cannot welcome guests without them. Will you and will you not deliver these goddamn cupcakes?" Her lower lip quivered. "I see." Mama Viv looked at the screen of her phone, then tapped the red button several times until the call disconnected. "Oh, what a rude man," she said as she leaned over with one arm over my shoulders, hugging me. "Good morning, darling."

"What's up?" I cut to the chase.

"Just the cupcakes for the bar, darling. Their delivery

girl is overbooked and won't be able to bring them. I don't know what to do." Mama Viv spotted someone behind me and lit up a little. "Hello, Zain," she said. "Just put them over there, darling. I'll handle the rest."

"Hello" was all the reply, spoken in a quiet, timid tone. I glanced at Zain, floppy black hair falling over his brow, big brown eyes looking away from me. He carried two carts of fresh produce from his father's little store on the edge of the neighborhood. Zain showed up here every morning with fresh fruits and vegetables for Mama Vivien's snacks, brunches, and burgers, but I never saw him around other than that. He was of average height, skinny, and unmistakably pretty. Dropping off the carts, he handed Mama Viv a paper to sign, then waved shyly and disappeared.

"That is how it should be done," Mama Viv exclaimed. "See that?"

"He's very reliable," I agreed. "What's with the cupcakes?"

"It's a disaster, darling," Mama Viv spoke as she picked up one of the carts. It only contained lettuce, but the nails still got in the way.

"Let me," I said firmly enough for Mama Viv to obey. She held the door open while I picked up the carts and carried them through. There were many, many days when I did odd shifts at Neon Nights when I needed extra cash and Mama Viv needed helping hands. Roman, on the other hand, practically worked here, even if his arrangement was as noncommittal as mine. "I can't be tied to one place," he always said.

Inside Neon Nights, the preparations were underway. Though it had been open for an hour already, the few guests having their coffee were unbothered by the two guys and a girl decorating the place for brunch. The interior was much dimmer than the outside; all the windows facing the street were small and cluttered with decorative stuff. Wooden tables and mismatched chairs were scattered around, and the door leading to the private terrace tucked between buildings was wide open. Servers hurried back and forth. I could see that there weren't any spare hands to deal with the cupcake debacle. "Why don't I pick up the cupcakes, Mama Viv?"

Our matron's eyes grew big with gratitude and relief. "You'd do that?" Mama Viv asked, one hand on her fake large breasts. "Darling, you would save the brunch."

"Of course I'll go," I said. I hadn't exactly had big plans for the day. Besides, it might earn me a free drink tonight at the party. I carried the carts into the busy kitchen, dropped them off, and got a big hug from our favorite queen of drag. Mama Viv ushered me out and handed me the car keys. It was an old Toyota parked in the alley on the other side of Neon Nights, which I knew well since I ran errands for Mama Viv often enough.

She gave me the address of a pastry shop in the Bronx and assured me it was already paid for. "I will call that horrible man and tell him to expect you. Oh, and darling, are you joining us for the quiz at three?"

"I keep telling you, Mama Viv, I'm not a Tina Turner fan," I said with my best grin.

Mama Viv waved that off as irrelevant. "Everyone's a Tina Turner fan. They just don't know it yet."

I was still chuckling when I started the engine and forgot all about my morning plans.

Cedric

I cursed the morning for sneaking up on me. As if jet lag hadn't kicked me hard enough, my first night here was plagued by dreams of running down endless hallways, picking doors at random, and finding myself in identical corridors once again. It was a maze of my own making and very fitting, if I may say so.

The ghastly single bed had not been my friend, either. Its frame creaked every time I turned, and the coarse fabric of the pillowcase that had been washed but not softened had irritated my face enough to wake me up in the middle of the night. That and the nightmares.

I got up, my lower back protesting, my eyelids drooping. I dreaded the mirror, so I avoided looking at it. This small room on the seventh floor was the only place I could find on such short notice without attracting attention. *Do not be seen. Do not be recognized. And whatever you do, don't let them know where you are.* I repeated the mantra I had been reciting to myself for the past seven days. At face value, this room had appeared perfect for my very specific set of needs and circumstances, but I had overrated my ability to adjust.

Maybe Alexander was right. Maybe I was meant for my life exactly as it had been going. That thought was sour enough to make me double desperate to brush my teeth. I hadn't exactly traveled with a valet to account for all my needs, but it seemed, upon the inspection of the small bathroom, that the staff of this establishment had predicted some of those needs. A toothbrush was packed into a plastic wrapper and left on the narrow shelf above the sink. This mirror was unavoidable, and my weary, exhaustion-reddened eyes gazed back at me. They were normally blue, but the days of traveling without being noticed had faded away some of their brightness.

I unwrapped the toothbrush, wondering if the plastic would snap in my grip. The miniature tube left next to the toothbrush, white with plain black letters, must have been toothpaste, but its flavor couldn't prove it in a court of law. I gagged and spat out the white paste, washed my mouth, and splashed my face. Water drops sprayed my neck and bare chest. The bathroom's single overhead light was yellow and weak, the dark brown tiles doing the interior no favors, and the showerhead poking from the wall was as inviting as a bucket in an alley would have been. There was no separation between the shower and the rest of the bathroom. Not even a sheet of glass. Not even a curtain.

I sniffed my armpits and decided it was acceptable until I found someplace with a tad more room. I wasn't entertaining any thoughts of sleeping at the Orbit or any such establishment. I had withdrawn enough cash to last me until I figured out my next move, but I had done that before my flight, muddling the trail for my family and their snoopy spies.

Running my wet fingers through my wild blond hair, I decided not to bother with it. Besides, a perfect haircut would only make it easier for someone to recognize me. As if the airport employees in Amsterdam hadn't made enough fuss over me, I didn't need the locals in New York to catch my scent.

I stepped out of the bathroom and rummaged through my tiny suitcase. I had left my apartments back home in haste. *Not back home*, I reminded myself. *That can't be your home anymore.* My gut twisted, but I kept on searching for something to wear. Everything was a little wrinkled, but I doubted this place offered more than an ancient iron filled with glowing coal. And even if it did, ironing had never been deemed important enough for my handlers to teach me.

I gritted my teeth and settled on a somewhat wrinkled light cream shirt and a pair of universal black pants. I needed to shop for clothes, but I didn't want to spend my money fast. Every time I used an ATM, I set off a beacon for Alexander to find me and bring me to heel. His last message before switching my phone off still burned before my eyes whenever I let myself be foolish enough to close them.

You're acting like a petulant boy. Better return of your own free will, else I will be compelled to handle this matter myself. This is not the end of the world.

I had been sorely tempted to text back, telling him that he was welcome to take my place if he found this situation so light and inconsequential. But that was what Alexander had been hoping for, so I resisted the urge. Instead, I walked around with a dead phone, hoping against hope that they wouldn't trace me to a run-down room in Greenwich Village overlooking the Hudson River.

I shut the door on my way out, causing a cloud of dust to envelop me. Coughing, I waited for the elevator, then strolled out onto the street. The August sun scorched the streets here far more than it did back home on most days. My home... My *former* home, if I had any say in my life, was tucked between France and Germany and the countries of the Benelux, a slice of land that had stood strong for centuries, never changing, never moving forward really, and never dropping some of its sillier traditions, one of which plagued me more than most these days.

This was not a glamorous neighborhood. It was hardly beautiful in the traditional sense. It wasn't new, it wasn't even particularly clean, and it wasn't invested in by the developers that had taken New York into the clouds. Its grunge aesthetic and slightly aged architecture paired perfectly with the colorful people that populated the streets. Graffiti ranged from hateful scrawls, few as they were, to breathtaking portraits and landscapes, to street artists' signatures without any meaning attached to them. Where it lacked refinements, uniqueness made up for it. Where it seemed run-down, soul and charm gave it life. The peeling facade of one building was hidden by a mural of a grassy field, the windows of another were bright pink, and a row of windows of one fairly low, old structure displayed rainbow flags and, pointedly, a bunch of wedding cake figurines, all depicting two men or two women or couples whose distinguishing features made it impossible to assume the gender. I gazed at one figurine couple wearing tuxedos that extended into broad gowns and couldn't stop my lips from twitching into a smile.

The door of this place was wide open, and scents of fresh food wafted out. Like a cartoon child floating toward a hot pie cooling on a window, I found myself in the dim interior of this strange place. Brick, wood, mounted lamps, large, industrial lightbulbs hanging bare over the bar, and wooden tables with mismatched chairs and colorful sitting cushions were only just the beginning. Decorations were pastel and light, in stark contrast with the underground interior.

"Welcome, welcome," a drag queen wearing a purple wig and red sequin dress said. A wave of anxiety rocked me as I assumed she knew my face, but then I noticed a small group of young men wearing all sorts of things, from casual suits and sneakers to crop tops and very short denim shorts and wheeling on Rollerblades instead of shoes.

"Hello, Mama Vivien," one said, glitter practically exploding from every move he made.

This is the kind of stuff I only ever saw on TV, I thought as the eclectic bunch walked and wheeled past me. I stood, dumbfounded, as the boys flocked around the curvy drag queen with intricate makeup framing her eyes.

"Out with you," the queen said. "Out, out there, in the back." She pointed a very long acrylic nail in the direction of a door leading to a hidden terrace. I spotted a stage in the back of the bar, although it wasn't lit currently. Around the interior part, pushed against the walls, weren't just tables with three or four chairs each. There was a sofa with armchairs around it and a longer table, elsewhere was an ottoman with a small, round table before it, and there were taller tables with barstools instead of regular chairs here and there.

The drag queen ushered the boys to the terrace in the back, then turned to me. "You must be here for our brunch, darling," the queen said.

"Er...no, I..." But before I could state my purpose, she lifted a hand politely to stop me talking and gazed at the door. A guy near my age stumbled into the bar, his dark hair falling over his brow and eyes, his feet tripping over one another. He carried a stack of pink boxes that made the queen exhale dramatically and get as close to a run as her heels allowed her. The young man, however, straightened bravely, the pink boxes leaning against the side of his head, his face turned in my direction.

He was breathtaking.

Dark curls had nothing on the bulging biceps that were on full display. Or maybe I was wrong. Maybe it was the wild hair over his handsome face that made my heart miss a beat. When he smiled at something the drag queen was saying, a pair of pronounced dimples emerged on his face. His shiny teeth must have been getting a better treatment than whatever bready paste I had used on mine this morning. And his gaze was as clear and sharp as lasers when he lifted it off the stone-tiled floor. "You never said there were eight boxes, Lady Vivien."

"Oh, but darling, we have a terrace full of guests. I fear eight won't be enough," the drag queen exclaimed as the young man put the pink boxes on the counter. The queen waved someone over, who hurriedly began distributing the pink boxes.

Relieved, the guy ran a hand through his curly locks, revealing his high cheekbones and perfect eyebrows. His face was glowing with heat. If he had noticed me in that one instant when his gaze had crossed the room while unloading the boxes, he didn't search for me now.

"Are you joining us?" the drag queen—Lady Vivien,

apparently—asked. She produced a red fan from somewhere and flipped it open, fanning the guy.

"I'm afraid not," he said. "I'm late for my run, and it's getting hot."

"Try as you might, you *will* love Tina Turner," the drag queen said as though threatening the guy.

"I'll see you tonight at the party," the handsome guy said, giving the queen a kiss on the cheek before spinning away from her and facing the exit.

"You better get here before the crowd does, young man," the queen said in an oddly motherly tone. To that, the guy just laughed melodically and waved. Before his laughter died down, he was outside.

Lady Vivien smoothed her red dress, and then, turning, she remembered me. "All are welcome in Neon Nights, darling. Make yourself comfortable."

"I was just wondering," I said. "Is this a private event?"

The queer lifted her chin defiantly. "There's no such thing as privacy in here, darling."

I laughed bitterly. That was one thing I needed in my life, even if it was just a moment. I might be a petulant boy to some, but I was desperate to be away from my family, even if it was for a short few days.

The queen extended her arm in the direction of the terrace. I shrugged to myself and followed the way she pointed for me. With her trailing me, I stepped onto the terrace that was framed by the walls of different buildings, light pouring from above, shielded by a net canopy from which colorful lanterns and lightbulbs hung. The red brick-paved ground was cluttered with many tables and various kinds of chairs. Some tables, those that were pushed closer to the walls, were long, wooden ones with benches accompanying them; others were wrought iron and glass. There wasn't a matching pair of anything in this place. Potted plants enriched the surroundings, many of which towered taller than I would have imagined.

"And what would you like to drink, darling? We have bottomless mimosas, sparkling rosé, Drag-tinis, rainbow slushies with vodka..." She counted each on an acrylic nail.

"Is Lavander Lemonade alcoholic?" I asked after glancing at the menu.

"Unfortunately, no," the queen apologized.

"I'll have that," I said with a smile, barely able to stifle a laugh. "And there's food?"

"This is your first brunch?" Lady Vivien asked. When I nodded, she beamed a welcoming smile. "I can bring you the menu, but I would recommend Quiche Lorrainbow, Benedict Royale, Avocado on Toast Extravaganza, or fruit salad." She put emphasis on "fruit" as if signaling a deeper meaning. It took me a moment to understand the pun.

My stomach growled, and I picked Quiche Lorrainbow, whatever that might be.

"It's on its way," the queen said. "I'm so pleased to have you in my little establishment. And if you need anything else, just cry for Mama Viv."

My lips stretched into a smile on their own as I nodded my gratitude. Then, just before the queen turned away, I inhaled. "Did I hear it correctly? There's a party here tonight?"

"There is," Mama Viv, or whatever her name was, said mysteriously. "We're never far from a party around here, darling."

I nodded, bending my leg over my knee and watching the queen glide away. She moved with enough grace to be on any stage, commanding the space around her as much with her sharp gestures as her immense aura.

While I might have been on the run, I had no better plans for the evening. And a party here might earn me another look at that handsome guy from earlier. He had promised to be here early.

Around me, queer people chatted and laughed. For all the progressive thinking and policies back home, I had never been allowed near a bunch like this. It wasn't my family's homophobia but their snobbishness that had kept me separated from our people. *Our people*, I thought bitterly while waiting for my Lavander Lemonade and my Quiche Lorrainbow. But even that thought failed to entertain and distract me from the problem at hand.

Sooner or later, I was going to run out of place to run and hide. Sooner or later, they would find me. Pretend as I might that it could be any other way, the second-born son of the Valois Montclair dynasty couldn't go missing forever. The fact that Crown Prince Alexander allowed me to blow off some steam was all well and fine, but I couldn't outrun him forever. Not without suffering some major consequences.

I know I have to return eventually, I thought grimly.

Whenever I directed my mind to the prospect of returning home, my stomach filled with ice. As though I wasn't already sick of having to act all royal and fine for the people of Verdumont. As though it wasn't enough that I had to have my handlers coming after me to all my flings and hookups with nondisclosure agreements. My family now requested—no, they never requested; they demanded—the ultimate sacrifice. But that wasn't even the worst part.

It wasn't just my life they wanted to doom. It would wreck Marchioness Élodie de Beaumont's life as well if I allowed this silly arranged marriage to happen. But Father and Alexander didn't see it that way. Our line had married French nobility for centuries, and sexuality had never been an issue. In their eyes, it hardly mattered who I wanted, even if it was a completely different gender I was attracted to. Even if I would sell my crown for another glimpse at those clear, precise eyes and that dimpled smile.

I'm not going back, I told myself, sounding much more like the petulant boy Alexander had named me. To hell with him. There was never anything beyond or aside from duty for Alexander Louis Valois Montclair. But that didn't have to be the fate I shared.

For once in my life, all I wanted was to have a choice.

My Lavander Lemonade arrived in the hands of a young server with a red sheen in his black hair. He offered help if I needed anything else but otherwise didn't seem to have the faintest idea he was speaking to a prince.

Good, I thought. *At least I can keep that much privacy.*

And with the first sip, I let go of all the nightmare mazes that yanked my attention this way and that. Here, now, for a moment longer, I was just another gay guy enjoying his Saturday brunch.

CHAPTER 2
A Wild August Night

Tristan

Doors around the apartment banged a few times while I dried myself with a coarse white towel, locked in the bathroom, humming to the tunes of Billie Eilish coming from my phone. I could hear the distinct noise of the freezer drawer scraping the mounds of ice I'd never gotten around to defrosting and clearing out. *I wonder if he'll take the peas*, I thought. *I have big plans for the peas*. Then again, frozen peas were the most versatile when it came to taking down the swellings.

I held a sigh, sprayed deodorant over myself, shaved off the hint of a mustache and chin beard that had grown in the last two days, and wrapped up my skincare routine in haste. I dressed for the party just as quickly. The cloud of steam preceded me when I stepped out of the bathroom, but as it dispersed, the sight before me made my heart sink a little. "You scruffy fucker," I muttered, shaking my head.

"Don't get spooked," Rome said. He spread himself on

the sofa, deep in the middle seat, one foot on the cluttered coffee table. The left sleeve of his black T-shirt had ripped at the upper seam, and my bag of frozen peas cooled the right side of his face. His lip had split and was a little bloody. "This is nothing."

"Was it the cops?" I asked in alarm, anxiety fountaining in my chest. I crossed the floor in a hurry and reached for Rome's chin to turn his head around.

Roman grabbed my wrist and thrust my hand away. "Said I was fine," he growled.

The rebuke stung more than I wanted to admit. Catching a breath, I pushed it all away. "Who did this to you?"

"Stop, Tris," Rome said in a no-nonsense tone.

My chest rose as I filled my lungs with air. Baring my teeth, I glared at my friend. "I want to know."

"And do what?" Rome asked in a tone that almost had a hint of helplessness or hopelessness to it. "Kick their ass? You're not getting involved, Tris."

"I just want to know what happened," I said without a trace of defensiveness that was starting to fill my chest.

"No. It wasn't the cops," Roman replied. "And it's done now, anyway. They're moving on with closing the center. We were too late. And too few."

I wondered if he blamed me for not showing up. Had I not gone out to exercise at the park, or to fetch Mama Viv's cupcakes, or to that goddamn class that was never going to get me anywhere, I could have added to Rome's numbers. "I'm sorry," I said.

Roman rolled his one visible eye, the other being covered by the bag of peas. "Here we go again."

"Wh-what's that supposed to mean?" I asked, taking a step back and putting my hands on my hips. Wet locks of hair fell over my brow, but I refused to be distracted by them.

Roman looked at me from under his eyebrow, lips pursed. He held his breath a moment, then sighed. "Nothing. Sorry I said anything."

"No. Tell me what you meant," I demanded, half-aware that I was torturing a guy when he was already down. But it was his fault for making it personal.

Roman moved the peas around his face, flinching once, glanced at me, and promptly looked away. "It's not about you, Tris. You couldn't have changed anything if you'd gone there, so don't act like it's all your fault."

"That's not..." But as I stammered, I knew I had nowhere to take that sentence. Nowhere completely true, at least.

Roman looked at me with that burning passion that never fully left him. "Don't play a failed hero, man. You didn't punch me. And you're not the one destroying the soul of this place. Just...don't act like you could have saved shit."

"Right," I whispered. If I apologized, I might just trigger him more. "Who punched you, though?"

Roman cracked a small smile. "I have no fucking idea," he said. This amused him. He wasn't really a troublemaker, even if certain people defined him that way, but even I had to admit that he didn't exactly run away from trouble. "It was a peaceful protest. The next thing I knew, commotion erupted. Two guys started wrestling. I looked around and spotted a few guys with balaclavas marching in our direction. And..." He shrugged, his words fading away. He removed the peas and revealed the dark red bruise over his sharp cheekbone. "They got me once. The lip's from falling down."

"Fuck," I said in a voice tight with fury.

"Calm down, bad boy," Rome teased, but it didn't take the edge off. "I got worse beatings from my mom."

I didn't laugh.

My friend dropped the peas on the coffee table and hopped onto his feet. "You take things too seriously, Tris. It's not like I can't defend myself."

"You need to go to bed," I said, holding back a sigh. I'd been looking forward to the party at Neon Nights. Mama Viv was going to kill me for missing this one.

"Tris, I can handle myself," Roman said.

I was already moving toward the kitchen. "Liar," I said with a touch of playfulness. "Nobody can handle you, Rome. But I have the most experience."

My friend crossed his arms, biceps swelling with tension even as he seemed unsteady on his feet. "You're dressed for going out."

"I'm dressed like a guy who forgot to do his laundry," I said. My best attempt to sound light was still a little strained. I put water to boil and turned toward the bathroom.

"Who's the liar now?" Roman asked softly.

I ignored him as I walked to the bathroom, opened the medicine cabinet, and rummaged for what I needed. He wasn't badly hurt, but his pride was bruised. Nobody liked losing battles. I collected the items I needed and carried them through the living room, under Roman's firm gaze, into his bedroom. I didn't need to fetch him. He followed when I didn't show up again.

When Roman sat down on the edge of his bed, I poured iodine solution onto a gauze pad and dabbed his lip, then dabbed the bruise on his face just in case there were tiny cuts I couldn't see. I thrust ibuprofen into his hand and brought him water from the kitchen. Sullenly, Roman observed me as I prepared him a cup of chamomile tea and brought it into his bedroom.

"Tonight's the party, right?" Rome asked.

I sucked my teeth. "Is it?"

My friend snorted. "You're really getting on my nerves now, Tris. Go. I'll be fine on my own."

"What if you get bored?" I asked.

"Then I'll stroke one out and watch memes until I pass out," Roman said.

It was my turn to snort. "The usual?"

"Go, Tris. And have fun for both of us," he said.

"Or we could play Scrabble," I proposed.

"For the love of fuck, Tristan. Can't you see I'm busy?" He grinned as I rolled my eyes and retreated. Even if he was lonely and gutted over losing the fight for the center today, he wasn't going to let me in. So I reminded him that he could call me if he needed me, to which he said he could always just ask Oakley or Madison to hang out with him instead.

I returned the medical stuff to their place, washed my hands from the scent of iodine, and debated shortly whether to just stay in the living room. Rome would undoubtedly find me and make a thing out of it. Besides, I was only going across the street.

Cedric

The eighties extravaganza roared within the dilapidated walls of the bar. Today, over brunch, it had hardly delivered on the promise of its name, but tonight, the mood matched exactly what I would have expected from a place called Neon Nights.

I stood at the bar in the furthest, most intimate corner. Before me was a sea of bodies. People moved around, fetching drinks to their tables, passing over the cleared area left for dancing. Some even danced, but most only tapped a foot in the rhythm of the lesser-known samples of the era, swung their hips, or bopped their heads.

My drink of choice was an elderflower spritz with an extra shot of peach schnapps, which the queen running the place had recommended. I was still on my first one when the light-headedness tickled me.

As one song melted into another under the careful mixing of a girl wearing a mix of eighties and punk aesthetics, the atmosphere warmed up.

Although my gaze kept darting to the front door as if I expected someone—truly, I had no reason whatsoever to expect or look forward to a dark-haired, well-built guy I had only ever seen once in passing; that was preposterous—I also scanned the crowd filling the bar. Some of the wall lamps were still on, shedding enough light to reveal the colorful people gathered here.

My whole life, I had been kept from the commonality

of such affairs. In college, attending parties among people closer to my class and status had denied me the experience of simply enjoying myself at a party. Half the time, appearances had been more important than what I felt about the entire affair. *Duty always comes first*, Alexander said in my imagination. *But that is not something you ever understood, little brother.* I could even picture the flexing of the muscles in his face as he clenched his teeth. It was like he clung to his duty by his teeth and nails.

He wasn't the only one I thought of when I thought of the palace. Father's stern, uncompromising features lending strength to our small, proud nation floated before my eyes, too. Even then, amidst their critical stares and their droning, there was something good. There were Sophia and Maximilian, my younger siblings and the mischief twins of the palace. Well, Maximilian was the prince of chaos these days when I was off duty, while Sophia slowly grew more serious and controlled.

My gaze went over the crowd again. Close to twenty-five years of living on this planet, and I hadn't had a chance to be just another guy at a bar until tonight. Young men danced with one another, girls made out in shadowy corners, and more than one drag queen glided through the thickening crowd.

Was there a clearer image of freedom? Not one person here worried about the burdens of duty that would weigh them down tomorrow. They simply existed in the moment, in the movement, and lived more in a single night than I had in a year.

As the beat quickened, I found myself tapping my foot and moving my shoulders, albeit awkwardly, to the rhythm of the music. Lights dimmed, and lasers pierced the air and whisps of artificial smoke. The disco ball sparkled brightly, breaking the lights and spinning at a slow, steady pace.

The front door opened, and a couple more guys entered. My heart stumbled, but it was nobody familiar. *Why isn't he here?* But I pushed that question aside. I was on the very edge of becoming eerie even to myself. That guy was nobody I knew. To be this eager to catch a sight of him one more time freaked me out, but not enough to hold my gaze firmly away from the door.

And when he entered, shoulders swinging to catch the beat before the door shut behind him, I glimmered as brightly as the disco ball. A pool of white light passed over him from a swirling reflector, and I realized his hair wasn't as dark as it had been earlier today. *He was sweaty from the heat and effort, hair matted and face glowing*, I thought. Now, he was in his best, most presentable edition. As he moved through the crowd, his aura beamed like a beacon. He danced like his life depended on it, greeting people along the way between the front door and the bar. It seemed to me he knew every single person in Neon Nights. Except me.

My pulse quickened as the beautiful stranger stood three feet away from me, his hands tapping the bar to match the music. He waited until the bartender looked at him with a bright smile.

I couldn't hear the order over the music, but the two shifted slightly toward me as the bartender began mixing a drink.

"Where's Mama Viv?" the handsome one asked. Truth be told, the bartender was handsome, too, but everyone paled in comparison with the one. His eyes were so warm yet so penetrating. It was like everything he looked at was the most important thing he had ever laid his gaze on.

"Upstairs, getting ready," the bartender replied.

"Oh, that's alright, then," my guy said.

"She was looking for you earlier, Tris," the bartender said.

My heart leaped. I had a name to put to those naughty, disobedient locks of dark. Tris. It suited him nicely, but I wondered what it was short for. Tristan, no doubt. As I formed his name in my mind, he appeared complete before my eyes. Now I hoped to God it wasn't Tristopher.

Tris received a mason jar with a swirly straw; the crushed ice filling the jar was glowing lemony yellow, looking slightly radioactive. He picked it up, his arm flexing slightly. I was in heaven right there and then. Wearing a white ribbed tank top tucked into dark grey pleated pants, he rocked a unique and ever so slightly vintage style. His bare arms were the bane of my existence, sculpted muscles rippling from his forearms to his round, bare shoulders, and when he turned to me on his way to the crowd, his expressive, wide-set eyes met mine. In an instant, I memorized every last detail about him. The medium-length hair parting in the middle and repeatedly falling over his eyebrows and eyes, his strong jawline and pronounced cheekbones giving him the chiseled look, and the tiny pout to his full lips. Every single detail took my breath away.

"And now, my fireflies, give us a 'Yes, Queen' for the mistress of this den, the true American royalty, our Matron, Lady Vivien Woodcock," a male voice boomed from the speakers as if announcing a boxing champion.

Tris spun away from me, losing himself in the crowd closer to the stage at the far end of the bar. Lights beamed in the direction of the stage, where a school piano pressed against the wall. A tuxedo-wearing girl sat before it, her back turned to the crowd, and the immense and captivating presence of Lady Vivien emerged from the shadows. She climbed the stage, then brought the house down with a rendition of "Don't Stop Believin'." To my infinite surprise, Lady Vivien did not lip-sync but sang and danced her soul out in the three minutes that followed. Accompanied only by the piano, this one song alone was worth my escape from Verdumont and the price I would eventually have to pay.

And when the *fireflies* cheered for an encore, Lady Vivien raised her hands dramatically and spoke into the microphone. "Welcome, fireflies, to Neon Nights. This evening, the world ends. This evening is the last evening we are on this Earth. And what do we do when we face the long night? We sing, my darlings, and we dance, and we 'don't go gentle into that good night.'"

If there was something I couldn't have imagined in my wildest dreams, it was a drag queen quoting Dylan Thomas while announcing that the world was going to end. Additionally, the cheers from the bar that followed those words were ten times more than I would have expected.

What bohemian heaven have I entered? I wondered. But my time for asking questions and wondering about my past choices was at an end. The world was apparently ending, and all we had left to do was dance.

Tristan

Mama Viv's hands rested on my shoulders, her long acrylic nails resting on my bare skin. She pressed a kiss to my cheek after I had praised her performance.

"Tell me now, where is Roman? I haven't seen him all day," Mama Viv said. She must have known about the youth center, and she must have known Roman would join the protests.

"He's not feeling like partying," I said. "It didn't go well."

Mama Viv waved her hand as if to tell me she understood every last intricate detail. "Shall I send him cupcakes? I happen to have a few left."

I raised an eyebrow at her.

"Bah! What do you want from me?" She threw her hands up in exasperation. "I may have overestimated the demand by three boxes."

A laugh erupted from me before I could stifle it. Mama Viv was on a mission, sending cupcakes to Roman, and she would have trampled me had I stood in her way. For that reason, as well as this tiny sliver of curiosity, I turned away from her and gazed over the crowd. He wasn't on the dance floor. In fact, the guy with the bluest eyes ever had barely moved from his shadowy nook by the bar.

I closed my lips around the straw as my gaze locked on his figure. Taller than me by a few inches, he was ridiculously blond and as handsome as if he'd stepped out of a fairy tale. As I sucked a sip of my cocktail, something gave me butterflies. *It's probably just sugar in my drink*, I decided, but it had happened at the same moment when those blue eyes noticed me looking.

Playfully, I let my eyebrows quirk in greeting, and I received a very determined nod in return. *Ah, so the game begins*. But this wasn't my first time out at a party. With a hint of a smile, I turned away from him and searched for another target, someone to keep me occupied but not someone so far away that I couldn't see the handsome stranger when I wanted to.

In the far right corner of the bar, directly opposite the blond beauty, were a couple of my friends I hadn't seen in a few weeks. I danced lightly to the Tina Turner tunes, even if I wasn't that fond of them, until I reached Luke. He wore a summer tan under the locks of floppy light hair, and his smile beamed brightly when he spotted me.

"Look who's back from the honeymoon," I all but squealed.

Rafael, officially Luke's husband at long last, spun with an even wider smile. His coppery skin was a shade darker before their two-week trip to the Dominican Republic. "We returned last night," he said, hugging me shortly before letting Luke take his turn.

"And just in time for all this fun," Luke said.

"How was the Dominican Republic?" I asked, practically having to yell over Tina's "Simply the Best." "If you got to see any of it."

Rafael threw his head back and laughed. Luke wore a touch of red on his cheeks. "We saw plenty where we were allowed to explore," he said, but Rafael's continued laughter was the true answer. They hadn't left the room, those lucky fuckers.

"We need to catch up when it's quieter," I said, catching the rhythm of the song despite my best attempts to stay cool. It must have been a whole minute, minute and a half even, since I'd last checked out the hot guy at the bar. "I can barely hear my own thoughts."

Rafael shouted his agreement, but Luke's attention drifted from me to something behind me. That was my moment, then. I could also glance back and search for that hottie without appearing suspicious. But as I did that, I found only empty shadows where he had stood before.

My vision of the rest of Neon Nights was obscured by a towering presence coming into my view. He carried his tall glass in one hand, a wristwatch strapped tightly just above his hand, and white sleeves of his formal white shirt rolled to his elbows. My gaze followed his torso. All the buttons of his shirt were done to the very top. *How do you breathe?* I wondered.

Something shifted behind me, and I heard some snickering. Rafael, no doubt. He soon faded from my mind as my gaze went over the exquisite features of this heavenly face. Long and slender like the rest of him, his face was smooth and chiseled, and his almond-shaped eyes were so blue that they looked to me almost like sapphires or the sea on a clear day in the Gulf of Mexico. Maybe. I hadn't been there to see for myself.

The DJ dropped the beat, and the disco ball sent shards of light over the handsome stranger's face. In the moment of relative silence, he cracked a smile. "Hello."

Something poked the middle of my back, like a stick

herding a reluctant mule to move on. I took a step, then waved my arm behind my back. Rafael was in for a few choice words when I had a moment to spare. Still, I halted a couple of feet away from the guy I'd had my eyes on all night. "Hey." A smile grew on my lips despite my best effort to remain cool.

As the music returned to its deafening volume, the hottie with a sparkling drink in his hand stepped closer to me, moving easily despite the cluster of shifting bodies that surrounded us. "Can I buy you a drink?"

"You're very forward," I replied, basically shouting.

He lifted his chin a little as if to ponder my words. Then he leaned in. "Would you like me to try to be more subtle?" There was a touch of an accent I couldn't distinguish, but it made my heart do backflips.

I thought about it for a moment. "No," I said. "I don't think I'd like that."

His smile carried relief and curiosity in equal parts. He gestured at the bar, and we waded through the sea of people. I threw one glance over my shoulder at Luke and Rafael, who were smirking and observing me as I retreated into the mass of dancing bodies. When I looked at the handsome stranger leading the way, I forgot about everything else. His shoulders were broad, the slightly rumpled shirt snugging his torso tightly, and his waist was narrow. The triangular torso was as close to my ultimate weakness as the disarming smile the stranger wore.

We reached the bar, and I watched him wave one elegant wave at Bradley, who served two girls to our left. When Bradley spotted us, he leaned over the bar.

My sexy stranger spoke with that mysterious accent.

"May I have an elderflower spritz minus the peach schnapps? And my friend will have another round of your finest yellowcake uranium." He didn't even look in my direction when he said the words that dragged a snort-chuckle out of me.

I lifted my nearly empty mason jar of vodka lemon slushie, and Bradley nodded.

The stranger turned around enough to face me while waiting for our drinks. "I saw you delivering cupcakes today."

"Do you always skip the cat and mouse game?" I asked.

His perfect black eyebrows arched in thought. "I don't know. I don't play this game often." He admitted this with absolute confidence, as though plain truth was the fastest, surest way to seduction. His interest was unmistakable in those blue eyes, but I found a glimmer of mischief there. "Do you?"

"Now I sound like a hoe." I laughed out loud, and the charmer joined me.

"You are Tristan, correct?" He wore that continuous smile on his full, defined lips.

I nodded. I didn't ask how he knew. He had obviously been paying attention all day. "And who are you? I've never seen you in the den before."

"Cedric," he said simply, thrusting his hand forward.

"That's a fantastic name," I admitted. His was a soft hand with a firm grip, unlike mine. We held hands for a moment longer than was strictly necessary. I enjoyed the warmth of his touch more than I should have. It wasn't like I was starved for the attention of other men, but the attention of this particular man felt like a much more significant reward.

Bradley set my mason jar and a glass of elderflower spritz for Cedric on the counter. Cedric paid with a large bill and waved it off when Bradley looked for change.

My eyes narrowed. Was that part of the game? Impressing me with his generosity, checking if I'd fall for it? "I like your style," he said before I could think too hard.

"I picked it myself," I said, the heat rising to my face. He was direct, leaving no room for nonsense and doublespeak. "I like your accent."

Cedric's eyebrows wiggled playfully. "I picked it myself."

"Where is it from?" I asked, finding myself a foot nearer Cedric than I had been a moment before. Invisible ropes tied around my wrists and ankles and pulled me in. Fighting them was futile. I better surrender.

"It's French." Now that he said it, it was, although not quite. There was a softness to his words that I couldn't place. He added, "Sort of."

I grinned. It took effort not to lean in and be absorbed by his intense gaze. I could lose myself in the stream of his personality like a tiny twig in a massive river. But I also might stay afloat. "Do you dance, Cedric?"

"I would dance with you," he said, clearly compromising.

We abandoned our drinks to Bradley's care as I grabbed Cedric's hands and pulled him to the dance floor. The lasers cut through the artificial smoke near the stage as we held on to one another and spun. The night swirled around us, the world tilting and spinning and losing focus. When I released him, he caught the rhythm of the music independently. In a few minutes, we danced our hearts out, almost like we tried to show off.

I never saw anyone else. I never noticed the murky, shadowed figures around us. The lights crossed Cedric's smooth face, lit up his fair skin, and made his pearly teeth shine. If he had been a little uncertain at the start, there was no trace of any doubts now. His confidence existed so naturally that he matched my dance skill seemingly by the sheer force of his will.

Our bodies, our heat, and our youth dazzled me as we neared one another and pulled away, always in the movement, never stopping the long game that took us through the night. As though time itself slowed down, I saw things in flashes of blinding white floodlight glimmering, freezing individual moments rather than letting the clock go on. A careless touch, an undone button, a press of my body against his, deep, spicy scent of cologne and sweat, they all mixed into a cocktail of passion I hadn't experienced before. His rolled sleeves and bare forearms became the most intimate and erotic things in my mind. I lost interest in all the underdressed guys dancing on the floor, my gaze never leaving the man who made the undoing of a single top button of his shirt feel like an expensive and exclusive striptease.

And whenever his hand brushed against my arm, his fingers left a blazing trail. His gaze never left me when his eyes were open. His attention was glued to my face, or else his head was hanging back, and our bodies melted together.

Never had I felt as though I was someone's everything. Never until this moment had I felt like a guy I looked at looked back at me and only me.

And when Cedric took my hand and pulled me from the dance floor to get our drinks, the ice had long melted in my mason jar, but I didn't care. We went through the bar and out on the terrace, where a canopy of colorful lights made all his features soft and smooth. "That was surprisingly fun," Cedric said as soon as we were out.

I gazed at the second undone button, his creamy skin taut over his pecs, the interesting part disappearing under the tight fabric of his shirt. He inhaled, and I lifted my gaze to his eyes, burning ice if such a thing was possible. "Who are you, Cedric?" I asked.

"No one," he said, the edge of his glass tapping mine.

I closed my lips around the swirly straw and pulled a mouthful of my lemony vodka and melted ice. "You must be someone," I said after sipping with satisfaction.

Something flickered across his face so briefly that I wasn't even sure I saw it. A tightness of some sort, a concern. "I'm just passing by," he said lightly, even the ghost of worry gone from his smooth features. "And you, Tristan? Who are you? A cupcake delivery guy during the day and a menace on the dance floor at night?"

I threw my head back and laughed. "I'm neither."

"I'm intrigued," Cedric said. Something about him made me believe that he really was. People filed out from Neon Nights, chatting in small groups scattered around the terrace. Tables were occupied by those less interested in dancing. "You're from around here, correct?"

"Correct," I said. "I live just across the street." The

thought of Roman lying in the bed all on his own, licking his wounds—emotional wounds rather than the scuffs he couldn't care less about—made my heart sink. Had he not been so stubborn earlier, I never would have crossed paths with Cedric. Whatever this thing between us was—and it was nothing measurable on any scale I knew—I wanted to see where it would go. He shattered my game of flirting and cut right to the dance. "And I help out when I can. Like the cupcakes."

Cedric smiled and nodded, pieces falling into place, as though I said the most interesting thing ever uttered. I liked this guy.

Chatter grew louder near us, and I glanced at a small group of strangers who'd dropped by for the party. Then, looking at Cedric, feeling my pulse quicken and the heat make my face glow, I took the leap. "Do you wanna go someplace quieter?"

"With you?" He grinned mischievously.

A snort and a nod replied so I didn't have to.

"I would love to," Cedric said.

In an instant, a world of possibilities opened up. I had seen him dance, felt his body up close to mine, sensed his deep and raw interest, and discovered an inkling of something else in him; now, I wanted more. I wanted to put my hand on his waist and get so close that there would be nothing other than the spicy scent mixed with sweat for me to inhale. I wanted to ask him questions until I knew who he was. And I wanted to see where the night took us. A glance from him had been enough to make me want to know the answer to that one question.

I snatched his hand, and we hurried back inside,

dropped off our glasses, and made for the exit. Outside, the residual heat of a New York summer and a breath of fresh air welcomed us.

CHAPTER 3

A Midnight Date

CEDRIC

I TAPPED THE FINGERTIPS OF MY LEFT HAND against my left thumb to calm the trembling. It was a trick I had discovered at the age of eight, having to stand in front of endless crowds of people while my parents addressed our nation. The nervousness of public appearances had never gotten easier on me, but it had also never presented itself when I was alone with a single, incredible human being like Tristan.

He was an adventurer of sorts, it seemed. He led the way down the street and away from Neon Nights. "Mama Viv, yeah," he explained after I had asked him about the drag queen who'd sung at the start of the party. "Her name's Roger when he's out of drag, which is less than you'd think. As Lady Vivien, she's pretty much everyone's cool aunt." He glanced at me as if waiting for something to happen or something to show itself. When I simply nodded, he went on. "She owns Neon Nights and sort of collects lost boys that came through."

"Collects?" I asked, chuckling.

Tristan nodded like it was self-explanatory. "If you need a place to stay, Mama Viv knows someone with a spare bed. If you need a job, Mama Viv will find a vacancy or make one if none exists. And if you just need a shoulder to cry on, she'll be that person." He glanced at me with a hint of sadness before looking away.

"It's very nice to have a person like that in your life," I said softly.

Tristan nodded and cleared his throat. "Yep. She's the rock holding this neighborhood together."

"Are neighborhoods always this self-sufficient?" I asked, switching the topic for Tristan's sake. Perhaps it was a little too early to dig through his past and find out exactly why his voice cracked when he spoke of crying. "I've never seen something like this other than in very small towns."

Tristan rolled his bare, round shoulders, and my heart leaped before I forced myself to focus on his words, not just his looks. "That's what you do in life, right? You make your village."

"You make your village," I echoed, thinking about it.

"It doesn't matter if it's a small town or a metropolis," he said with a bright smile as he gestured for us to cross the street. "It's a buffet, really. You pick your favorite bar, your hairdresser, your classes, your routes and shortcuts. You pick your favorite people. What else is there?"

A palace and a looming threat of an arranged marriage, I thought. "I think you might be right," I said. It was a sweet idea, though not the idea I could ever entertain with seriousness. A chance birth into a royal family had shackled me, defined me, and doomed me. Élodie waited for me, and Alexander either pursued me or was about to start the chase.

"I didn't think this way before," Tristan said. "About having your village. I used to think you had to work with what you got. I thought that life was all about what you were given, and that was the end of the story."

"It can be that way," I said. It certainly matched my situation. "It depends on what you're given, I suppose."

Tristan gave me a significant look, but I replied with a simple smile that made him change the topic. "I really like your accent, Cedric," he said, leading me down a narrow, one-way street onto a wide avenue. Even near midnight, cars moved up and down the double lanes like it was the middle of the day. Tristan led us to the nearest pedestrian crossing. Just across the street, the Hudson River moved like a massive body of water that it was, and on the other side was a glimmering New Jersey skyline.

"And I like your way of thinking, Tristan," I said. It was unquestionably true, even if his thoughts didn't apply to me.

"Do you 'just pass by' a lot?" he asked.

"Around here, no," I replied with a sneaky smile. He knew what he was doing. It was fair, I decided, that he should ask questions. I hadn't consumed the truth serum levels of alcohol to have to be on guard. "I've visited New York twice before, but I was too young to appreciate it the first time."

"And the second time?" Tristan asked.

The second time, it had been an official visit to the Museum of Renaissance Art when Verdumont lent out its incredible collection for an entire year while our museum was being reconstructed. Alexander led the visit, Maximilian and Sophia were here for the fun of it, and I had joined the trip as the only art history aficionado of the family. My studies revolved around the history of fine arts, especially the booming period from the Renaissance to early Cubism.

"It was a work-related trip," I said lightly. "I didn't get a chance to walk the streets like this."

"If walking the streets is what you want, I can absolutely deliver," Tristan said cheerfully. "When you're a broke college dropout, you learn how to find entertainment on the cheaper side."

"Dropout?" I asked. I hadn't expected him to be so forward. Some small part of me felt pity, but I silenced it. A million people were a million unique stories; not all had to fit the expectations my family had placed on me.

Tristan waved it off. He didn't appear embarrassed about discussing it. "Business School," he said. "It took me a year to see it wasn't for me and another to work up the courage to tell my family. That's, erm, where things started going south." He forced a grin to his face, but his eyes no longer glimmered. "It's a long, boring story not fit for a random first date."

"Random first date? I like it," I said. We crossed the street and found ourselves facing a long pier filled with greenery and providing a breathtaking view of New Jersey's lights chasing away the night from its streets and sky.

"You don't do dates like this, I think," Tristan said.

"I don't get a chance," I admitted without explaining that being the third most recognizable face of a country made midnight dates with guys like Tristan a little too difficult. "My life's pretty...structured," I said. It was the only word I could think of using in place of admitting to having handlers lead me through every waking hour of my life. "And the structure doesn't precisely leave room for spontaneity."

Tristan blew a breath of air. "I wish I could have even a shred of structure."

"At the cost of this?" I asked.

He shook his head. "If I had to choose, then no. But believe me, I could use a schedule. Most of the time, I feel like I move around, and things just happen to me, taking me from one to the other. Before I know it, it's bedtime." He moved to a bench that looked over the Hudson River, and we sat down with a couple of feet of distance between us.

Just an hour ago, we had acted in a very familiar way with one another. It hadn't bothered me to feel his hand on my chest. It had been the greatest pleasure to run my hands down his muscled arms. Now, outside the small bubble of wild movement of the bar, it felt like we tried for a bit more control.

"What do you do to have your life so organized?" Tristan finally asked. "And how come you're just passing by?" He lifted one perfect eyebrow to tease me.

Even with the two feet of empty space, I felt his presence. He radiated something beyond heat or any other physical thing. It was his spirit that glimmered brightly and made me feel like I sat next to a furnace. "Oh, it's a family business," I said in an offhand manner. "I'm not sure I see myself doing this forever. So I'm wandering."

"How mysterious," Tristan said, leaning against the back of the bench, his gaze on me like the river and the city beyond it didn't even exist. They were admittedly dim in comparison with Tristan's fiery brown eyes.

I bounced the ball back at him. "So, business wasn't your thing. What is?"

Tristan smiled softly and looked at the starry sky high above us. "I like cooking."

"Really? I like eating. We're a perfect match." The words tumbled over my lips before I could consider their weight. When they were out, I regretted nothing.

Tristan laughed, making all the risks worthwhile. "I might cook for you, then."

"I would absolutely love that," I admitted, then asked him what it meant to him that he loved cooking. Was it a hobby? Was it an aspiration?

"I'm not sure," Tristan said. "Ideally, I see myself having some kind of restaurant, but that might just be another pipe dream."

"I thought you were more optimistic than that," I pointed out.

"The risky thing about optimism is that your heart breaks a little harder when things don't go your way," Tristan said bravely. "In this, I try to be rational. Starting a business like that is hard enough when you have the capital. But hey, if I get to work in a kitchen that lets me experiment, not just stuff buns with hot dogs, I'll consider it a success." He blinked once, his long, dark eyelashes framing his eyes beautifully. "What does your family do, then?"

"Management," I said, the lie forming in my head instantly. "Brand management of sorts."

"Like an agency?" Tristan asked.

"Yeah," I said, my throat tight and mouth bitter from lying. The thing about being a royal was that people treated you differently when they knew who you were. I had met guys who wanted me for whatever influence that would earn them, and I had met guys who were tempted to spit in my face simply for being born into wealth and outdated traditional structures.

Yet I hated the taste of lies on my own tongue.

And I hated that Tristan lived with my lie existing in his brain.

If I tell you now, you'll never give me another chance, I thought. He would rightfully leave and never look back after spending an entire evening with the version of me I had presented to him.

"Oh boy," Tristan said in an amused tone, "you really don't like talking about it, huh? Big trouble?"

I sucked my teeth. "To tell you the truth, they want me to do something that goes against my wishes."

"Something bad?" Tristan asked.

I nodded. Marrying a woman I could never love and denying her a chance at happiness was not exactly the kind of chivalry people sang about.

"Like brand management for an airline," Tristan proposed. "Obviously, you can't tell me the trade secrets." He touched the bridge of his nose conspiratorially, and I chuckled.

"Very well. It's like representing an airline," I agreed. "I don't dislike this airline, but I don't see myself, er, married, so to speak, to her. It. Except that my family has a long tradition of taking on clients in this manner. They want me to continue this tradition even if it goes against my instincts."

"Ah, I see," Tristan said, nodding carefully. "That's a real conundrum."

"I believe the word you're looking for is 'clusterfuck,'" I supplied helpfully.

Tristan snapped his fingers and pointed at me. "Yes. Thank you. You're in a real clusterfuck."

"But I'm not here to talk about that," I said.

Tristan hopped off the bench happily. "Exactly. You're just passing by. You're here to forget about the family business troubles." His smile broadened with each word, his chest rising with bravado. "And I can definitely do something about that."

I didn't need to think about it. I didn't even need to ask. So I simply stood up and followed this happy adventurer to where he was willing to take me.

♛

Tristan

To my surprise, Cedric didn't protest when I took us to the subway. He went along, making conversation about things that had nothing to do with his family and the *airline* client. We left that safely away from our agenda. Instead, he spoke about his previous visit to New York and the museum experience, revealing a profound love for museums. He had majored in history with a minor in art history. He spoke about it while we rode the subway between Hudson Burrow and the Empire State Building.

By the time we reached the observation deck, Cedric told me about his deep love for Goya's later works, the darkness that entered his life and was reflected clearly in his works. Up there, as the light wind chased away the summer heat and ruffled his hair as much as it did mine, we stopped talking. Cedric gazed out at the glimmering lights of New York City.

Cedric's full lips moved for a moment before he spoke. "It's beautiful, Tristan."

There were a few small groups and a few couples moving around the deck. Up here, there was never any true solitude so long as it was open for visits, but that didn't matter. We stepped toward the heavily secured railing that provided clear views of the city lights sprawling in all directions. Everywhere we stood and looked out, more of New York City took our breaths away. The East and Hudson Rivers reflected the shimmering of the city lights, and Central Park was a massive shadow with only a few lights compared to the streets and buildings around it, some parts of it even completely dark, others as shiny as any stretch of the city.

"Thank you, Tristan," Cedric said. "I never saw it from here."

A gust of wind made my skin prickle as I leaned against the railing and gazed out. "It makes you think. We forget how small we really are, how small all our problems are."

"Everyone's problems are the biggest problems," Cedric joked. "But really, they're no less serious just because they're not life and death. If you don't have to worry about what you'll eat tomorrow, then choosing the right place to live and thrive is the biggest thing you need to tackle."

That made me feel better about complaining. I shot him a teasing look, remembering how badly I wanted this night to go on forever. "Keep saying nice things. You make me feel good."

Cedric smiled something that was almost a wolfish grin. *There are so many ways I could make you feel good*, his eyes said before he looked away, some hint of restraint returning to the set of his jaw. "What's your favorite cuisine to prepare?"

"To prepare or to eat?" I asked. "Because you can hardly beat Greek and Turkish flavors, but they're as much an art as a science."

"Shouldn't the same be true of most cuisines?" Cedric asked.

"Probably," I admitted. "And I suppose that's your answer."

"I couldn't agree more," he said, his hands wrapping around the railing, fists tightening and relaxing. "Have you ever been there?"

"No." The answer was curt, but it was cooler than how I spoke so far. I cleared my throat when Cedric allowed the silence to continue. "My family's not exactly wealthy, but they're not as broke as me, either. When I was little, they took us to all the big places here in the States. By the time we were old enough…ah, we just didn't." My throat tightened just as I hastily wrapped up the story.

Jen. I thought of Jen. It was like plunging deep into the icy water, all the way to the abyss of a frozen lake, and feeling every frosty needle stabbing me everywhere at once. Some things were simply beyond anything I could do, yet my mind loved replaying these things just to torture me.

"You're such a happy-looking guy, Tristan, but there's a sadness in you that I can't pretend I don't see," Cedric said softly, shifting to me. He faced me rather than gaze at one of the greatest cities on the planet. He looked at me with those knowing eyes, and I realized why he couldn't ignore my sadness. You knew it when you saw it, but you only saw it when you knew it. There was more that troubled this man than just some airline contract.

"And in you," I whispered. It was almost as though a bond formed between us when Cedric gave a single deep nod.

Few people knew my whole story. Roman knew, and Mama Viv guessed enough, but I kept it shut deep inside my soul. They only knew because they wore the same look in moments when they didn't know they were observed. That distant, wondering gaze of a lost soul that so uniquely said, "I don't want to talk about it. Or think about it."

Cedric licked his full lips and looked at me for an endless while.

I was perfectly content standing there with the most spectacular view of Cedric against an endless flickering background, but the compulsion to reach for him was stronger than I could control. "I want to know more about you," I said.

His eyebrows quirked for the briefest of moments.

"I'd like to know everything about you and that airline

that sent you all the way across the world," I said, firmer. That was what I did. I knew it was so. There never was a stray kitten I didn't take to the nearest shelter or a failed food delivery I didn't volunteer to fix. "Because it must be a helluva contract if it sent you here to me."

"That it is," Cedric said with some hesitation.

"Then tell me, and I'll help you. Somehow, I'll find a way to help," I offered. Or demanded, more like.

Cedric took a step toward me. His body was only a few inches away from mine, his gaze cast down and locked onto my eyes. Those two inches he had on me were significant when we were this close, but I forgot all about it. All I knew was the heat of his body shielding me from the gust of wind coming from the north. "I think I'd rather…" He bit his lower lip softly.

"What?" I asked. Whatever it was, he could have it.

"I think I'd like to kiss you, Tristan," he said.

No way you don't normally do this, I thought, my knees weakening under his words. He had such an easy charm and effortless way of swiping me off my feet. Before I decided on it, I had already licked my lips and found myself rising to my toes.

After so much dancing and flirting in the safety of Mama Viv's blasting music, it felt like the most natural and important end to the night. You couldn't count the minutes down to midnight and not want the fireworks. The intimacy of floating our secrets and discovering camaraderie in one another's sadness was only the final confirmation that I liked this human.

Cedric didn't wait for me to speak my mind. He read it from my body, from the welling desire in my eyes, from my lips waiting to be kissed and my cheeks turning a shade redder. As he placed his hand on the back of my head, I found heaven. But even then, it was more than that. His lips pressed against mine with such thrilling heat that my body glimmered the same as the millions of lights that surrounded us.

Deep in me, some hidden, dormant volcano came to life. The meaningless hookups of my past crumbled into dust, and my blood filled with adrenaline. The urgency I experienced while our lips touched for the first time was such that I grabbed Cedric's shirt with my fists and pulled him close, his torso pressing against mine, his midsection rubbing mine. Whatever excitement I felt his body show was the same as mine, my cock swelling nearly instantly, bulging to press harder against him.

I hadn't realized how badly I needed to be kissed with such dedication until he showed it to me. Nobody had ever made me feel this significant, this unique, this worthy of undivided attention.

So I kissed him harder, proving to him just how welcome his advance had been.

A moan came from one of us, and I couldn't tell for sure which one. I rose higher on my toes, evening our heights and parting my lips so that his tongue could venture playfully into my mouth. I welcomed it for that split moment when our tongues touched.

His hand ran through the hair on the back of my head, and the other one moved all the way down my back until he touched my ass. My cock throbbed hard merely for the touch of his hand on my cheek. I thrust my hips forward, rubbing myself against him and discovering once again just how into me he really was. His cock was as hard as mine.

Cedric gasped the instant after pulling away from me. "That was..." He heaved a breath, his face awash with lust, hope, and a touch of fear.

Thoughts filled my head, but I struggled to translate them into words. I wanted to tell him that I lived with four roommates but that they could assure all the privacy we could need. I wanted to tell him it was only a quick ride back. I wanted to ask him if he wanted to spend the night with me.

Before any of these things left my mouth, Cedric picked one of the feelings to remain on his face. Fear. Pure and chilling, fear froze his features as he stepped back again. "I... I'm sorry, Tristan." He took another step back, shaking his head. Fear was not alone now but in the company of guilt. Was he feeling guilty for kissing me or for scaring me? "I can't do this. I'm sorry."

I didn't have enough time to process the meaning of his words. In the heartbeat that followed, Cedric faced away from me and retreated from the observation deck.

Shame filled me to the brim, and on the surface, there were angry tears blurring my vision. What had just happened? What on Earth could I have done wrong?

Run after him, something told me. *Run and stop him. There must be an explanation.* But I refused to listen to that trickster's voice. I wouldn't be so pathetic and desperate to chase after a guy who kissed and ran.

Except, as I stood on the deck and the wind made my bare arms prickle, hollowness entered me. Had my hope for something happening been so great that I couldn't feel a thing in its absence? Had I been so smitten by one pretty foreigner that I couldn't fathom not being wanted by him?

I couldn't answer any of those questions. My mind was buzzing with alarms. So I stood still, my hand searching the guardrail to hold on to something not for the fear of falling but for the lack of anything else to do. The sense of solitude came at me like an avalanche.

CHAPTER 4

The Days That Follow

Tristan

Even as I turned my key in the lock, I squeezed my eyes shut in mild disappointment. The thing about living with four roommates was that you never had a moment of privacy. Not even when you returned at six in the morning.

Lane poured milk over his cereal when I stepped inside and shut the door. It was a relief that he was the one making noise in the kitchen. Of all my roommates, Lane was the least likely to push his nose into my business.

"Morning," he said over his shoulder, focused on his breakfast and not on my rumpled state. He found a spoon in the drawer and stuck it into his breakfast. "You're up early."

Or late, depending on how you look at it, I thought. "And you."

Lane rolled his eyes as he turned to the round dining

table between the kitchen and the inner wall of Madison's room. "Oakley set an alarm for half past five."

I frowned. "What for?"

Lane lifted his broad shoulders in a deep shrug. "Beats me. All I know is he's been snoozing it for half an hour, and I couldn't put up with it."

"Maybe he's got an appointment," I said, worried that Oakley would miss it. "Shouldn't we wake him up?"

"I'll bet you ten bucks he's trying to build a new habit after some TikToker told him to," Lane said casually.

I snorted. "If I had ten bucks to spare."

Lane agreed with a single nod and began eating. I walked into the bathroom to wash the night off my face and hands, too tired to think clearly. Lane knew Oakley better than anyone in the apartment, even if that wasn't something either one of them wanted. They had to share a double room, and the battle lines had been drawn on the second day of their shared lives. I expected a Peeling Palace meeting as early as tonight to discuss Oakley's use of unreasonably early alarms.

When I finished washing up, I heard Lane's footsteps crossing the living room outside the bathroom, and the door of his and Oakley's room opened and shut. I slipped out of the bathroom and yearned to drag myself to my bed. If I could sleep for a week, it wouldn't cut it. But I could settle for a lazy day in bed and drinks at Neon Nights in the evening.

I walked toward the hallway between my and Roman's rooms, and my heart sank. My friend stood in the doorway of his room, arms crossed on his chest, a questioning arch of his eyebrows reserved for me. "There you are. Busy night?"

"Don't ask," I said dismissively. "How's your head?" The swelling had gone down significantly, but the bruise looked dark and angry.

"Aside from worrying about it, my head's just fine. Where have you been, Tris? I've tried calling you ten times." He shook his head to emphasize his frustration.

A frown creased my face as I pulled my phone out. "It's dead," I sighed. "I wasn't exactly checking my phone." Then, with a slight accusation in my tone, I said, "You were supposed to be sleeping, Rome."

"You're deflecting, Tris," my friend fired back. "But it's fine. You're back, and you're alright."

"And sleepy as fuck," I said. Roman put a hand on my shoulder firmly and gestured with his head toward my room. "Sleep well, buddy."

"Night," I said, fully aware that it was eight hours too late for that word. Even so, I pulled my blinds down and crashed on my bed. For all my desire to fall asleep as soon as my head touched the pillow, that was the precise moment when my eyes opened wide, and every trace of sleepiness abandoned me. My heart pounded, and bitter disappointment filled my bloodstream.

I really thought it was a good kiss, dammit.

And I really thought we had been going somewhere all night.

After Cedric left the viewing platform, I lingered for some time, unaware of how long until fewer and fewer people remained, and I knew it was time to head out. When

I was back on the ground, I walked. I walked aimlessly, visiting Central Park at night, sitting on benches every half an hour, and wandering through the city until my feet carried me back to Hudson Burrow.

The night had replayed itself a thousand times before my eyes before I returned here. And now, it replayed itself a thousand times more. Every careless touch I'd imagined was flirtation could have scared him away. Every time our faces neared as though we might kiss by accident, I could have pushed him further away. And when the explosive cocktail of lust and curiosity led him to want to kiss me...I didn't know where things could have gone wrong.

It was his creamy, soft skin and his impossibly blue eyes that floated before me as I gently drifted asleep.

Cedric

I turned the phone in my hands countless times before I knew I was doing it. When I looked at it, its screen was dead black. The thing emitted no signal anyone with access to sophisticated tracking software could pick up on. Or so I hoped. If they tracked me, they hadn't taken me yet.

Truth be told, I didn't expect the security to flock around me and kidnap me in some badass action sequence. It would be worse than that. It would be so much worse. I could see it. Alexander sitting in front of me, looking at me with those cold, pale blue eyes, his hair freshly cut as *always*, his lips thin and pressed so tightly they turned white, and his back so straight he looked uncomfortable. "Do you truly wish to be the one to break the centuries of tradition, brother? You can't. The thing about the wheel of our fortune is that countless people you haven't heard of have tried to break it, but the wheel simply ran over them. History doesn't remember them. They failed their country and their family. They fell, but we still stand."

Alexander had been raised as the Crown Prince since the moment he opened those pale blue eyes. Ever since then, he acted like he carried the future of the world on his square shoulders. In short, he was dreadful company at parties. He was also the biggest pain in my ass.

My mind wandered to Élodie. What the hell was wrong with her to play along so quietly? I could hardly scratch the surface of that mystery. Élodie de Beaumont was as closed off as a person could be. I wondered if there was anything beneath that facade of perfection. On every occasion when I'd met Élodie, she spoke of vague things nobody could disagree with; she walked perfectly, sat straight, and ate like a lady. It was maddening that her entire being was as bland as a definition of nobility.

I rubbed my face after tossing the phone on my large bed and sprawled on the mattress. This room was far better than the accommodation I had secured on my first night in New York City. A couple of streets away from the original apartment, this was a proper hotel room with a view of the Hudson River and the Hudson Burrow neighborhood. The latter I could have lived without. As it was, it was a constant reminder of the small injustice I had done and the things I couldn't hope to reach for.

I'm sorry, Tristan, I thought, staring at the canopy

above the bed. *My life's complicated enough without roping you into the mess.* Even so, Tristan refused to leave me completely. Five days after that one fiery kiss that had threatened to pull all my threads apart and I still ran my fingers over my lips thinking about it.

But what was I supposed to do? Had I let it go any further, the consequences would have been dire. I would have been a lying liar who slept with the most amazing guy while hiding the truth of my identity. Or I would have told him I was a royal on the run from his own family, which would have scared Tristan away, and I would have exposed myself to a greater risk of discovery.

Why hasn't he found me yet? I wondered, then quickly pushed that question away.

Tristan occupied my thoughts now, so I entertained him. Beneath the two options I'd placed at the forefront of my mind, I knew there was a greater fear. It was a fear I didn't want to poke too much, but it never lifted its claws off my heart.

I wasn't exactly a free man. Although I had never made any promises to Élodie, our implied agreement was clear to all. We were to be married. Eventually. For now, we were to be officially engaged, and there wasn't a better time to announce the engagement than this fall. The confidence in the monarchy has reached its lowest point in Verdumont's history. The coming parliamentary election stirred the talks of reducing the significance of the royal family. There were candidates demanding the abolition.

But I'm not a goddamn pawn, I growled internally.

Although my new room was a suite with all the amenities I could possibly need for a short stay and enough space to throw a ball, it suffocated me so abruptly that I needed to get out. I needed to go outside, even at the risk of being recognized. The upside was that there really was only one royal family Americans knew much about. Few would think to look me up and match me with His Royal Highness, Prince Cedric Philippe Valois Montclair, Duke of Belleval.

Grinding my teeth, I shut the door of my apartment on my way out and descended to the ground floor. A clerk at the front desk stopped me politely as I passed.

I halted where I stood, feeling a creeping anxiety rise along my spine. Slowly, I approached the desk and greeted the man with my finest smile. "Is everything alright, Mr. Erikson?"

"Of course, Your Highness," the man replied. Revealing myself to the hotel staff was unavoidable, but they had very strict policies on keeping their guest lists private. "It is only that you are due to check out today. I apologize if I am mistaken, but it appears as though you are perhaps staying with us a while longer."

I'd forgotten about that. Today. Time was flying when you were on the run. "That would be correct, yes. I would very much like to stay if the room is available."

Mr. Erikson glanced at the screen, dry-washing his hands before calming them down and holding them firmly together. "The room is available, yes. However, there is the matter of your payment. If you still insist on paying with cash, it will be necessary to settle it at your earliest convenience."

I clamped down on the bolt of annoyance that passed through me. My fists clenched, but I quickly forced them to relax and pulled out my wallet. "How embarrassing that it slipped my mind," I said. *Does he assume I will not pay my bills?* The frustration roiled within me as I looked at the cash in my wallet.

Trying to count it discreetly while dividing it by the price for a night was tough business when Mr. Erikson's gaze was politely and firmly set on me.

"Ah, if another five nights is acceptable..." I muttered.

His quick fingers glided over the keyboard, and Mr. Erikson confirmed it. He then proceeded to take most of the cash I still had. Trying not to sweat at the desk, I paid for another five nights, turned on my heels, and marched out.

Had I remained in the run-down room where I'd spent my first night, I would have had twice as many nights for the same price. Three times, perhaps. But it was just as likely that I would have returned to Verdumont to escape the purgatory that place was.

I walked out of the hotel and into the hot August air, traffic congesting the street and people muttering at having to walk around me on the sidewalk. I was set for another five days. My room included food and access to the hotel's spa, sauna, and pool. The knots in my back begged for a massage, but my toes were too antsy to let me lie still for forty minutes.

So I walked aimlessly away from Hudson Burrow, beating myself over my poor financial choices and telling myself how there had never been another way. Eventually, I would have to use the card. Eventually, I would break and slip and fire up a beacon for Alexander.

He could trace me to the States, but I didn't know how

precisely he could pin me down. And if he could, I wondered if this was his plan all along. Was he showing me I couldn't function on my own? That I was doomed without the family's support? If that was his strategy, it was beginning to work. My confidence had never been this low, and I had never felt more trapped. What had begun as a run toward freedom's warm embrace was starting to feel like a self-imposed exile.

You can end this, a voice told me. I wasn't sure whose voice it was, mine or Alexander's.

If he left me to destroy myself, he would have an easy time convincing me that my marriage to the Marchioness was the best conclusion to my story.

"No," I growled aloud, earning a look from a passing woman whose stride quickened soon after. *If you need a place to stay, Mama Viv knows someone with a spare bed. If you need a job, Mama Viv will find a vacancy or make one if none exists.* Those had been Tristan's words. And those words might be my last chance to reach a better fighting ground.

The universe made this decision for me. I turned around and headed back to the heart of Hudson Burrow.

♛

The cigarette in the long, elaborate holder made of ebonite and worked silver was unlit, but that didn't stop Lady Vivien Woodcock from biting her end of the holder. The sound of teeth meeting the black ebonite was sharp and quick, matching the acrylic nails clacking against the wooden surface of the table between us.

"It's wonderful to put a name to that face, Cedric," Lady Vivien said, her voice deep and velvety. She wore a black dress with stripes of white and a rich red lining. Her sleeves were loose, and their edges were worked with lace that also held the hems of her neckline together. With makeup and padding, it was hard to tell that Lady Vivien didn't have a big bosom on the verge of spilling from the dress. "I've seen you here before, haven't I?"

"I believe you have," I said and lifted my lemonade off the table, sucking a sip through a thick straw. After swallowing, I smiled my best smile for Lady Vivien. "You see, it's a pretty bad situation I found myself in."

"I don't doubt it," Lady Vivien said, amusement dripping from those words like melting chocolate. "But I can't imagine a short-term job that will cover the cost of an apartment at Henriette. Why not try Orbit while you're at it?"

I gritted my teeth. I never should have let that slip.

Lady Vivien laughed at her remark and stuck the cigarette holder between her teeth with a loud click. Her eyes were glimmering with curiosity and entertainment. After releasing the holder, she nodded. "If you are searching for cheaper accommodation, I happen to have a spare room."

Muscles in my neck knotted. I had tried living on a budget. It had almost driven me into Alexander's arms. "If you don't mind, we could revisit that later."

"Suit yourself, darling," Lady Vivien said, measuring me all the same. "And what work experience do you have? What can you do?"

"Anything," I said. "By profession, I am a historian." That wasn't exactly a lie.

"A history degree?" Lady Vivien's amusement soared. "That certainly qualifies you to wash the dishes, darling."

I bit my tongue hard. "Art history, to be exact," I said.

"Even better," Lady Vivien said, positively jiggling with laughter. "Oh, don't take things so seriously, Cedric. Nobody's out to get you."

She didn't know how wrong she was, and I wasn't going to tell her. But I forced a smile on my face. "Truth be told, I would be happy washing the dishes. Or serving tables. I've found myself in a complicated situation where I don't have too many choices."

"You can always marry rich," Lady Vivien said with a rapturous laugh.

I could feel the sweat that soaked the shirt on my back. I laughed as joyfully as I could pretend. "Until I can find a wealthy marchioness, I'd very much like to wash the dishes, Lady Vivien."

"Mama Viv, darling," the queen said, waving her unlit cigarette in the holder in a dismissive way. "And if you are certain, I can have you do a paid trial starting this afternoon."

I rubbed my hands against my knees. My fingers moved nervously, and I discovered that my mouth was dry. Only now, I realized that I had been hoping to be turned down so I wouldn't have to do this, and I could still say I'd given it my best shot. But Lady Vivien was inviting me to...work... today. "H-here?" I asked, my voice squeaking.

"Why, of course, darling," Lady Vivien said, spreading her hands around her head as if to encompass the entire bar. "We're throwing a Burger Bash this evening, and I can always use a pair of hands to clear the tables and wash the plates. If you can cut the buns or wash the lettuce, it's even better." She turned away from me and called for someone named Millie. A tall girl around my age with thick curls tied into a bushy tail walked through a door behind the bar, the sleeves of her white shirt rolled, and a black apron covered her torso and legs down to her knees. The apron sported five acrylic nails in the color of a rainbow painted across its front.

"You called for me, Mama Viv?" Millie asked.

"Millie, darling, this is Cedric. Can you make sure there's a locker for him by—" She looked at me, then, "—shall we say four o'clock?"

I inhaled a deep breath of air and held it for what felt like an eternity. I was really doing this, wasn't I? I suppose life could have been worse. I could have been picking flower arrangements for my royal wedding. As I exhaled, I nodded. "Four o'clock sounds perfect."

"And what will Cedric be doing that he needs a locker, Mama Viv?" Millie asked, unmistakably bristling.

"He'll do whatever you need him to do, Millie, darling," Mama Viv replied, one hand moving elaborately to encompass the entirety of the bar and the activities one might be paid to do around here. Then she looked at me again, a challenge in her eyes. "Let's see what you're made of, Cedric."

My smile was locked on my face, frozen and icy, and I nodded. I was ready to play my part. I'd never been allowed anything like this at the palace. "I'm made of harder stuff than it appears, Mama Viv," I promised her, although I failed to convince myself.

In fact, several hours later, I discovered just how soft the stuff I was made of really was. There were many places on the planet that could test your adaptability and endurance, and many jobs could push you to the limit of your sanity, but none other came to mind when you were caught in the hellish twister of your local restaurant's kitchen.

CHAPTER 5

Mama Viv's Burger Bash

TRISTAN

MY KNIFE SLICED AND DICED AND MINCED ON THE cutting board. I was lost in the moment and the movement, like a leaf in a river. It carried me to a happy place as inspiration filled my body and everything else dimmed around me. I was cooking. That was all I needed to be happy. The Culinary Horizons Evening School represented three hours a day in my otherwise empty and directionless life. This was where I felt like I had something to move toward, something to strive for.

And when it was over, I did my cleaning and chatted with other students. A couple of them were respected chefs from the city, perfecting their craft in foreign cuisines. Most were, like me, amateurs with nothing more than a love for culinary skills.

I was about to propose grabbing drinks after the class when my phone vibrated in my pocket. Slipping it out, I wondered what Mama Viv needed. She rarely called unless it was an emergency, normally choosing to type out long, emoji-riddled messages no matter how challenging it was with the long nails clued to her fingers.

"Hello?" I answered cheerfully.

"Tristan, oh thank God, you are my last resort, darling," Mama Viv blurted, clearly upset and out of breath. "It's Millie, darling."

My heart clenched with terror. "What about Millie? What happened to her?" Images of things I never wanted to see again flashed before my eyes. I didn't even know it, but I was moving toward the exit, my stride letting everyone know that I was heading out, even if I had to trample someone to get there. Cold water closed on me and tried to crush me, but a hand around my wrist made my heart leap with joy that maybe this wasn't how I ended. That sneaky, treacherous joy. I had spent a lifetime running away from the fact that I had been *happy* to be pulled out of the wreckage. "Is she alright?" I demanded.

"She'll be fine, darling," Mama Viv said hurriedly, removing the worst of my anxiety. "She was showing this... ah, never mind. She cut her finger. It wasn't much. She didn't even make a sound. I hurried to bring her a napkin to stop the bleeding, but she just turned pale, and the next thing I knew, she was on the floor as good as dead."

I grumbled at Mama Viv's choice of words.

"Millie's getting an IV, darling, but I don't have my chef for Burger Bash," Mama Viv said, voice quivering.

"Of course you have a chef," I said. "I can be there in twenty."

Mama Viv had been floating the idea of employing me permanently in her kitchen, but I had never felt ready to take the leap. Instead, I helped Millie out when there were bigger crowds, practiced when I could, and tried to learn from the best. Millie had a command of the kitchen, but apparently, she had a weakness for something that was all too common when you worked with knives all day long.

I considered getting a cab, but the fleeting thought disappeared as soon as I remembered that my pockets were mostly empty and it was my turn to replenish the kitchen cupboards this week. Another bold of anxiety rushed to fill me, but I used it to fuel my run, halving my time from the culinary school to Neon Nights.

Mama Viv nearly collapsed with joy at the sight of me. She clapped her hands before hugging me.

"I'm sweaty as hell, Mama Viv," I protested.

"You are beautiful," she said. "You beautiful thing. I'll be paying you extra for emergency work."

"Don't worry about it," I said, pulling away from her. "Let me just wash my face, and I'll get on it."

"Don't tell me what to worry about, darling," Mama Viv said, but the words didn't have an edge to them. She had made up her mind. However much I hated special treatment when others could do all the things I could do—and they probably did them twice as well—at least I didn't have to worry about spending the last of my money on coffee filters.

I slipped into the staff bathroom to wash my hands and face, then walked down the white-tiled hallway to where the small locker room hosted employees' things. I took off my black T-shirt and tossed it inside a spare locker that already had some of my things there, kicked off my shoes, stepped out of my pants, and rummaged through the clean clothes I could work in.

The locker room was positioned at the end of a hall that contained all of the bar's inventory that we could possibly need, from spare tableware to packages of herbs and spices to bottles of sauces. There were fridges stacked with fresh produce and meat, freezers brimming with frozen goods, and a row of beer kegs hooked to tubes leading to the taps at the bar. There was no privacy in a place like this. People scurrying over to unhook an empty keg or to fetch items the kitchen ran low on was a constant thing. Truly, there was never a moment to breathe or think when you managed a kitchen. And Neon Nights wasn't a typical restaurant equipped to handle constant volumes of food orders. Its kitchen was modest and compact, so people needed to move in very precise ways, always sticking to their right side to avoid colliding with one another. They also needed to watch their step and be perpetually aware of their place in the space we were all given.

It was something a newcomer wouldn't know.

So when a hurrying newbie bumped into me and sent my nearly naked body slamming into the locker, I only managed to yelp once.

"I am *so* sorry. Christ, did I hurt you? I am..." And his words cut off as abruptly as my heartbeat had stopped.

That voice. That sweet, soft, husky voice. I had almost missed it now that it was speaking in a hurry.

My head had slammed the closed door of Roman's locker, and stars swirled around me for a moment before I straightened and turned around.

"Tristan," he said, all the joy flickering out of his eyes

and leaving them cool and expressionless. His lips pressed into a line. His gaze dropped shortly from my face, and I remembered that I stood there in nothing but underwear and socks.

I licked my dry lips. "What are you…?"

"We need those plates, Newboy," a girl shouted. "Chop-chop."

Cedric stiffened, and his panicked glance shifted from me to the shelves containing five different kinds of plates. "Which ones?" he whimpered quietly.

It was Mama Viv's Burger Bash. She would want the textured black round plates and no others. "Those plates," I said matter-of-factly and pointed to the middle row containing thirty plates.

Cedric looked at me with something like gratitude in his worried gaze. As he stepped closer to the shelf, his gaze dropped over my torso, but he looked away. "I'm really sorry, Tristan," he said clearly and lifted all thirty plates off the shelf. His biceps tensed with the effort.

I was light-headed, although I couldn't tell you why. Maybe the shock of seeing him here in the back, wearing Mama Viv's apron and uniform, or maybe I'd bumped my head harder than I'd realized. Or because his short sleeves revealed how perfectly sculpted his arms were. Whatever the case, my breath was shallow.

Cedric retreated down the hallway, cutting right through the middle.

"Right side," I yelled after him.

He pressed his right shoulder against the row of fridges instantly and stuck to the right side until he disappeared from my view, which was just lucky because Bradley swept in from the bar and would have crashed into Cedric had the sexy fucker not moved.

Bradley greeted me in a hurry. "It's so good you're here," he said while swapping kegs of a particularly bitter pale ale. "Mama Viv underestimated the interest after the lukewarm response to last week's brunch."

It was the Burger Bash night. I could have told her people would show up. "We'll survive," I said, winking at Bradley while yanking a clean pair of pants up my legs. It took me a minute to get ready, strap on my apron, and secure a cap on my head to keep my hair from falling over my eyes or, God forbid, into people's food.

I strode with a purpose when I headed down the hallway and into the kitchen. Bradley scurried before me, slipping to the left and behind the bar, while I took a right turn and entered the hectic mess that a busy kitchen always was. Glancing around, I knew all I needed to know.

"Hello, everyone," I said loudly. "It looks like they're getting slaughtered out there. Be sharp, be focused. Ana, fill up the fryer. Keep it full until I tell you to stop. French fries, chicken wings, fish fingers, and mozzarella sticks. Got it? Raj, start slicing fresh tomatoes, and watch where that knife goes. Cedric, dishes are piling up, start washing." If I felt a sliver of vindication, I didn't let it show.

"What do you have for me, Chef?" Roman asked, popping up out of nowhere.

It took me a second to process his presence. "What are you doing back here?"

"You should know by now that I'm always where the fight's the thickest," he said with a dark laugh.

A spatula was already in my head as I walked through

the small, square kitchen. "Right," I said, scanning. To my left, in the middle of the room, was a cluttered table where Raj was slicing tomatoes as I had requested. He knew how to use a knife. I didn't worry about him. To my right, along the wall, was the assembly and serving station, a grill, and a row of busy fryers. Against the further wall straight ahead, more cluttered surfaces stretched all the way to the ovens. And against the left wall were crates with spare inventory, bread baskets, and clean dishes. A hole in the wall provided me with a view of Cedric's back as he scrubbed the dishes.

"Sauce bottles," I told Roman. "Fill 'em up and start assembling burgers. I'm taking the grill." I tossed the spatula high. It swirled in the air until I caught it. The moment my fingers wrapped around it, an impenetrable bubble formed around me. I was in the zone and in the moment, keeping this thing running, overseeing everyone's work, and measuring the meat patties on one grill, cheese on the vegetarian section, and the constant flow of orders being printed in the corner of Roman's assembly station.

Cedric brought plates to Roman's work table. Raj swapped empty containers with the full ones, and Ana kept the fryers full. Bit by bit, we caught up, and although seeing eleven patties—all with different requests—and eight slabs of grilled cheese gave me a sliver of panic, I knew how to use it to my advantage. Panic was fuel for efficiency, in my opinion.

The shouts of "coming through" and "hot plate" bombarded me, scents of grilled food opened my appetite, and the camaraderie of kitchen staff filled my heart.

Mama Viv showed up once, at some point, to see if there was anything she could do. Her eyes watered over the freshly diced onions on Raj's work table, and she retreated with loud exclamations that Bradley could use some help behind the bar instead.

"Did the class go well?" Roman asked once we caught up to the most recent orders.

I tossed a slice of cheddar over a patty and covered it with a metal bell to melt quicker, keeping the meat juicy and medium rare while getting that lovely cheese softness. "Perfect. But nowhere near as fun as this."

"You really are a daredevil, Tris," Rome said, sticking a skewer into the burger and sliding the plate away to make room for the next one. He rang the bell as soon as the plate was ready for serving.

I scanned the queue of orders hanging above the grill. "Ana, go low on wings, and double the mozzarella sticks. Looks like we got a vegetarian table."

"On it, Chef," Ana said.

I couldn't lie. It felt good to hear that. This was my tribe, and I could only hope to work hard and get to be in this spot by earning it, not just because the real chef had passed out.

A moment of respite came with a flood of thoughts I wasn't in the mood to unpack. But when Cedric finished with all the dishes, he was no longer confined to the dishwashing room. Rushing back and forth across the kitchen with stacks of plates for Rome to use, refilling the sauce bottles, and sweeping the floors, he was an unavoidable presence.

His presence was even more acute when Mama Viv recruited Roman back to the front. "Tris has it under control, darling, and I could use your experience on the floor."

"Yes, ma'am," Rome said, saluting, and winked mischievously at me, eager to be busy.

I had put Raj to mix the new bath of burger sauce, which required both skill and intuition, and Ana was the mistress of frying, so I reluctantly lifted my gaze to Cedric's blue eyes. "Stand there," I said, pointing next to myself. "I have to teach you how to assemble burgers."

Cedric seemed more nervous than I would have imagined. Was he nervous because he needed to stand next to me? If so, he could rest assured I wasn't interested in anything beyond having my burgers assembled. *Why does that sound like an innuendo?* I wondered distantly. I sure as hell wasn't going to do something stupid like flirt with him.

He licked his lips, and my resolve rocked. "Okay," he said in a low voice. "Teach me."

"Er...well, let me get one ready for that," I grumbled, flipping over the patty that was about to be served. Just because he was hot as hell and could kiss the soul out of your body, I wouldn't give Cedric preferential treatment. I recited the instructions as I would have to anyone in this kitchen. "Cut the bun, making sure the bottom half is thicker than the upper half, butter it, put it through the toaster, pour the sauce over the bottom and half as much over the top..." The instructions went on and on, and it was all fairly easy, straightforward stuff. But then we got to the moment when I delivered the patty on the bottom half of the bun, and Cedric panicked.

Holding my breath, I stepped closer to him. He was sweaty

and greasy from a day of work, but I could still make out the spicy scent of his cologne. *Who are you, Cedric?* I wondered. His back was stiffer than anyone's in this room, his chin held higher, and his gaze more contemptuous, especially when he was insecure. I grabbed his gloved hand and turned it over, palm up, put a wrapping paper into his hand and punched it open, then navigated his other hand to put the upper half of the bun containing all the vegetables onto the meat patty, forced his hand to hold the burger firmly together, and thrust it into the wrapping paper. When it was done, I practically carried his hands with the burger to a clean plate, set the meal down, and punched a skewer through the top. "Now, serve that full cup of fries and add two small saucers of ketchup and mayo. Voilà."

Cedric nodded in gratitude, but it was stiff and controlled.

"And when that is done, maybe you can tell me what the hell you're doing here," I muttered. Raj was mixing a massive container of burger sauce in the furthest corner of the kitchen, and Ana had left the fryer full of items to fetch more from the freezer.

"Gotta earn a living somehow," Cedric replied. He moved the plate over to where the servers would pick it from, rang the bell, and looked at me. "Next?"

I glanced at the grill. Was he asking for the next burger or the next question? Well, the burgers needed a couple of minutes longer. "I thought your family ran a successful business. Why would you be a dishwasher in a run-down bar?" *And why would you disappear without a trace for five days after kissing me?* My mouth didn't ask the question, but my contemptuous sneer very likely did.

"They do," he stated plainly.

Ana walked in with two bags of frozen onion rings and stuffed them into the small freezer next to the fryer. I lowered my voice. "So why are you here, Cedric?"

"Maybe I'm proving a point," Cedric said, glancing at the grill.

One of the patties had dripped with grease and now caught fire. I let it burn for an instant before the flames died on their own. "A point?"

"Yeah," Cedric said. "Maybe that's why I'm here, assembling your burgers, instead of..." He sighed and turned away from me. "Never mind."

Instead of chasing an airline contract, I assumed. *Or whatever his airline contract really is.* "Alright," I said quietly. "Get ready for a hot one." I grabbed the piece of paper with the full order and moved it from above the grill to above the station. Soon after, the patty followed. I instructed him on how to butter the bread for a vegetarian burger, as the cheese was somewhat drier than the meat patties, and walked him through everything.

I didn't have to like it. We only had to work together and make sure Mama Viv didn't lose her customers. Whatever Cedric's reasons were for getting a job at the one place I called home, he wouldn't reveal them to me. Something had happened that ripped a gap between us that was impossible to cross.

Something's wrong, an old instinct told me. I always listened to this voice. I always followed where it led and meddled when I had no place to meddle. *But something is wrong here*, it insisted. I couldn't tell why. I couldn't tell what it was that felt off aside from the absurdity of someone very clearly rich settling to peel onions whenever I commanded it.

Orders slowed down, and Raj came around to ask if I could spare him so he could prepare the caramelized onion for the next day, which was the kind of initiative I hoped I exhibited when I was the helper in this very kitchen. "Go ahead," I said resolutely. "I'll manage everything here."

Ana offered to start cleaning from the freezers in the hallway so we didn't have to stay until midnight preparing the kitchen for the morning. Breakfasts were usually another rush hour in Neon Nights, and I wanted Millie to find her kitchen precisely how she would have left it.

A couple of new orders came through, but nothing fancy. I could do them without Cedric's help. Even so, he lingered at the assembly station and drummed his fingers against the polished stainless steel surface.

I avoided looking at him, but he very clearly faced me as he tapped the inox table.

My lips tightened, and I focused on the two pieces of cheese on the vegetarian grill.

"Tristan," Cedric said in a low voice that made my skin prickle and hairs on my neck stand as if he could create an electric field around me. "About the other night..."

I turned my cold gaze to his face. "Don't you have a pile of dishes to wash?"

His mouth remained open for a heartbeat. He closed it quickly and stepped back as if I'd pushed him. With a firm nod and the bravado of a samurai facing gunpowder canons, he turned away from me and marched into the dishwashing room.

My heart clenched, but I growled at myself and flipped

the square blocks of cheese on the grill. Whatever he wanted to say about the other night, he was welcome to keep to himself. I wasn't interested.

Except that night, when all the work was done and when I showered for bed, sleep abandoned me. Worries about the twists of fate that changed our lives on the whims of gods seeped into me. I fretted and sweated and failed to keep my eyes closed, for whenever I closed them, I sank into the depths of icy water, only to retrace all that had led us to that moment, to that bridge, to the truck driver falling asleep at that exact minute...

If something was wrong with Cedric, and if something happened because I'd been too hurt over a rejection, then I would never forgive myself. I would never be able to live with myself after.

CHAPTER 6
Lies and Truths

CEDRIC

DAYS BLURRED IN MY MEMORY. HOWEVER MUCH I tried to remember the sequence of events, it only took three or four days for my mind to mash all of it together. If I couldn't be sure what day it was, I could very well be certain of how tired I was throughout.

My sleep at night had never been more guaranteed. There never was any room for insomnia. My body craved the bed at the Henriette Hotel, and my head seemed to always beg for the pillow.

Mornings always came too early. Spending another minute in bed was always the most precious commodity I had in life. Many moments started to feel more important than they ever had before. Within the first week of plunging into the thick of it at Neon Nights, I moved from total certainty that the work would kill me to appreciating the minutes of calm and quiet that had once reeked of boredom. I valued my breaks and didn't cry when Mama Viv put me to scrubbing floors or hauling crates of beer.

In morning shifts, breakfasts were as hellish as that devastating Burger Bash had been, but Millie was a feisty chef with a sharp tongue and no mercy. She also had a knack for motivating the staff. They all relegated the simpler tasks to me, but the trick was that the simpler ones were usually the same ones that involved carrying heavy things from one place to the other.

Zain Amari delivered fresh produce first thing in the morning. He was younger than any of us working at Neon Nights and had the biggest brown eyes I had ever seen. Perhaps it was the poorly concealed wonder at seeing the glitter that made the bar into what it was. Perhaps he was just a very easily dazzled person. Either way, Zain never lingered for longer than he had to, and there was a shyness to him that added a skip to his stride when he was on his way back to his father's traditional produce store a few blocks away.

Zain's arrival always signaled the beginning of my work. The produce he brought needed to be stacked in the particular ways the chef insisted on. If I ran out of things to do in the back, then I helped Bradley or one of the other servers to clear out the empty kegs, wash the tubes and taps, and bring in the new batches of the many beers Mama Viv served.

"Darling, you're a far tougher nut than I'd given you credit," the formidable drag queen told me one morning after the breakfast rush. "I owe you an apology."

I waved my hand and shook my head. "Not at all. I owe you thanks for giving me a chance."

"I find it odd," Mama Viv said pointedly just as I thought the conversation was over. "You don't look like someone who would blend in so easily and do everything they ask you to do."

"Looks can be deceiving, Mama Viv," I said. A drag queen should know. Mama Viv nodded deeply. Pride told me to insist that I could do more, but the truth was that my legs ached in that sweet, tired way that begged for bed and promised a sense of satisfaction at the end of a long day.

The only real trouble in my life was the looming threat of Alexander coming through the doors one day and finding me sweeping the floors. But I hadn't turned my phone on even for a second, and I hadn't used my card. I spent what I made, thinning the little wad of remaining savings on prolonging my stay at the Henriette. It was not a wise decision, and Mama Viv never failed to remind me that I was living beyond my means. *If only you knew how far below the means I lived*, I would always think and never move to withdraw more cash.

The thing I had once said to Tristan seemed to become truer with every new day. I could be independent if it came to that. I could survive without playing by my family's rules and the centuries of tradition built by those who couldn't have imagined what the world would look like today.

I had a point to prove to myself and my older brother. I'd include my parents in that statement had I imagined they cared enough.

Roman Lowe was one of the workers who swept in every so often to do a shift for a few dollar bills. He wore cuts and bruises the way other people wore jewelry. Scruffy and wiry, he was unmistakably defined under his tight clothes, and he bristled on occasion to scare others away, but he was generally a lighthearted, fun-loving guy. And from what I gathered, he was the closest to Tristan among them all. So when Roman had a sudden interest in how exactly I was doing, I suspected Tristan was behind it.

"Seriously, dude," Roman said on one occasion. "If there's anything you need, don't hesitate to ask me. I know everyone around here."

It's either that, or he's selling drugs, I decided, but the latter hardly fit with the justice warrior and near vigilante that he was when he clocked out.

The only odd thing about it was Tristan's absence.

When I had taken Mama Viv's offer, I had prepared myself for having to live with Tristan. My impression had been that Tristan used Neon Nights as his second home or that he didn't make a distinction between the two whatsoever. I had even convinced myself of all the upsides to that. *You get to apologize and make sure he knows it's not him*, I'd told myself. And then he never showed up again.

And for that reason alone, it was a surprise to see Tristan march in on Friday morning. He wore a loose, sleeveless shirt and tight shorts, visibly ready for a run. The last time I had seen him, he had been standing practically naked, and it had taken me all my strength not to fall apart right there and then. He had been gorgeous. So this morning's look only spiced the image that lived in my memory.

"Hey," Tristan said as soon as I turned to face him. He waved at Bradley behind the bar, but he very visibly marched toward the stage that I had been sweeping. "Got a minute?"

I blinked at him, then looked at the remaining work. "A minute," I said.

Tristan gestured at the door leading to the hidden terrace between Neon Nights and two other buildings that closed around it.

I was reluctant to follow. Mama Viv employed me, so I could respect her telling me what to do and where to go. Tristan, however, presumed a lot. He strode away, and I found myself following while complaining about it quietly.

As I followed Tristan out of Neon Nights, I ran a mental checklist of things I needed to do. I had already accepted Zain's delivery, stocked the fridges, swept most of the floor, and needed to wipe the tables and make sure chairs were all clean before the crowds arrived for breakfast.

Crossing my arms on my chest, I waited for Tristan to turn around. The last time I had seen him, he had sent me away to wash the dishes. I inhaled the air I needed to apologize to him properly. If he wasn't interested in my apology, I wasn't entirely sure I was interested in what he had to say.

"Listen," he began.

Before I could make up my mind, words broke through my sealed lips. "I'd appreciate it if you didn't have a friend spy on me. We're not in seventh grade, Tristan." Regret followed those words very quickly, but I clamped my mouth shut and lifted my head regally.

Tristan's features grew still. I might have been speaking to a rock. "Alright. If that's how you want to be."

A pout formed on my lips before I could stop it.

Tristan inhaled after a moment of silence. "And Rome's not spying on you. I told him you were new here and that maybe you could use someone to watch your back." He shrugged. "Whatever he offered was genuine."

"How touching," I said, fully aware that sarcasm was the lowest form of comedy and yet unable to stop myself. "Then I guess there's nothing to talk about. I should get back to the dishes." If he didn't understand it, it would have surprised me. But this guy saw way more than his face betrayed. It was in his eyes, this depth of knowledge and this skill of observation. He knew I was lashing out, and it only made me feel more petulant.

Angry with myself far more than I could be angry with Tristan, I turned on my heels and stalked off, leaving him behind before he could say whatever he had come to say.

I hadn't known this about myself any more than I had known I could be truly hardworking and enjoy it. It appeared I was a spiteful prick. He hadn't let me apologize, so I refused to be roped into a situation when I might be tempted to try again.

It would have been easy to lean against the rusting bring-and-mortar wall and lose myself in his warm, brown gaze. It would have been all too easy to lean in and inhale the fresh scent of mountain dew and peak of spring that seemed to follow him everywhere. And what then? What would happen on the day Alexander found me here? What would happen when I opened myself a little more to Tristan and found myself utterly consumed by him, only to have to return to Verdumont and marry Élodie?

For my own sake and his, I needed to put Tristan out of my mind.

Tristan

"He's infuriating," I grumbled to Roman over the dinner table after Lane and Oakley took their feud into their shared room. "And he's *not* my boyfriend." That bit, I growled at my friend. Where did he even get that idea from? "I told you. He kissed me and freaked out. That's not a mess I'm willing to touch with a stick."

Roman snorted. "And yet, I need to watch his back."

I narrowed my eyes at my friend. "You don't have to do anything."

"Tsk. Don't be like that, Tris. It doesn't suit you." He got up and began collecting the tableware. He shot me a mischievous look. "I don't mind keeping an eye on him, buddy. I'm just stating the obvious."

"Yeah, well, it's not obvious to me," I muttered, getting up to help with the dishes.

Roman put a hand on my shoulder and pushed me back into my chair. "No way. You cooked, and one of us will clean." He carried the dishes to the sink.

I got up anyway, incapable of sitting down while others worked around me. Instead of helping out, I leaned against the kitchen counter and crossed my arms on my chest. "I feel like something's wrong there."

Roman gave me a semi-sad and semi-knowing look as if to say I always found something wrong around myself. And that may have been the truth, but it didn't change the fact that I couldn't get out of this dead end until I saw it through.

"I know his family's rich, Rome," I said. "You don't need to be a genius to see it in the way he holds himself. Besides, he told me so. And what's he doing now?"

"Stealing jobs from honest Americans," Rome said in that supreme tone of sarcasm that flew over people's heads.

"He's working every day in the one place I don't want to share," I said a bit sulkily.

"Which is just crappy luck when the place you don't want to share happens to be a bar with doors wide open." Rome chuckled at his own wit, then sprayed me with drops of water from his fingers. "Cheer up, Tris. If you really want to know what his deal is, he's across the street."

I shook my head. "Absolutely not." I had tried. I had tried and failed, and that was it. But because Roman couldn't wrap his mind around my sudden stubborn streak, he just shrugged and busied himself with the dishes.

After I realized there was nothing more to say, I turned away and went into my room. Before I knew what I was doing, I pulled the curtain away from my window and looked down. The dusk glow gave the street a vibrant golden look. Everything was dry and begging for rain. Dusty leaves of the few trees dotting the sidewalks and the cracks in the soil around those trees all needed a good rainstorm to wash away the heat of the summer.

But there, just across the street, the door to Neon Nights was shut, and movement through the bar was slow and steady. Sundays were lazy, especially after the heavy hitters like the Saturday night drag show. I'd missed last night's show. Something told me that I would either go there and be disappointed or enter the bar and be distracted from the show altogether.

It's my home, I growled to myself.

I didn't know it until I was back in the living room and Roman yelled, "Atta boy," after me, but I had changed my mind again and headed out. Before it all even sank in, I was downstairs, then in front of my building, then crossing the street.

As I entered the bar, I realized the severity of my mistake. It was Sunday. The bar was practically empty. Even Mama Viv was out. The few tables with people sitting around them offered no friendly faces I could join and get out of the confrontation I'd signed up for. Now, when Cedric looked at me from behind the bar, a cloth and a glass in his hands, a cool look of disinterest in his eyes, I knew I was stuck.

Inhaling a deep breath of air, I pushed my chest out bravely and crossed the bar. *Idiot. You fucking idiot, why did you come here?* But it was too late to berate myself over it. I swallowed and walked up to the bar.

"Tristan," he said as a greeting.

I nodded.

"What can I get you?" he asked.

I glanced at the row of taps. "Stonewall IPA," I said. I could use a bit of Stonewall courage right about now. I sat on a barstool and braced myself for the conversation that I had been having in my head for days.

Cedric foamed up my beer significantly, cursing in a language I didn't understand before grabbing a spoon and taking off the thick layer of foam with it. He poured some more until it was satisfactory in his view and handed me my beer. Without missing a beat, he picked up the glass and cloth he had been polishing and turned away from me.

"I'd also like to talk," I said.

"Oh?" He was so cool and stiff, and it would have been just fair if I let him be then and there. I had only met this guy once, but it had been too magical and too wonderful to erase from my memory. Besides, the night we worked in Mama Viv's kitchen together hadn't been terrible, either.

I wrapped my hand around the glass and took a sip of beer. It was refreshingly cold and only a little bitter. Exhaling, I closed my eyes for a moment, then looked right at him. *Damn. You're too beautiful for my own good.* His gaze was both frosty and melting if such a thing was possible. "Cedric, it's not fair to leave me hanging like this."

He clenched his teeth, a muscle in his face tightening. When he relaxed it, he looked at me with total attention. "I tried to apologize, Tristan."

I shrugged. "Maybe it's too late for that," I admitted. "But that's not at all what I want. Something's wrong here, and I want to get to the bottom of this."

Cedric eyed me for a long time. I watched as his reluctance turned to curiosity, and he finally yielded. "You're really annoying. Do you know that?"

"I've been told," I said, still holding the big breath of air in my lungs. I didn't want to celebrate before we found some common ground.

If the corners of his lips twitched a little as if to smile, I couldn't be sure of it. He set the polished glass down. "Why do you insist something is wrong? I might just be lying low until my family cooled down."

"If this is your idea of lying low while staying at the most expensive hotel in the neighborhood, then we don't understand each other at all," I said in a straight, no-nonsense tone. "Who is your family, Cedric?"

He snorted. "You don't know them."

"That's not why I'm asking," I said.

Cedric narrowed his eyes as if to acknowledge I scored this point. But when he inhaled, there was something like cooling his anxiety in that move. I knew the gestures, the little cues, the forced calm when things bubbled too violently below the surface. "Tristan, if I tell you everything..." He shook his head. "There's no point in it."

"How about you let me decide?" I suggested calmly. "Because we're not total strangers, Cedric. Maybe I did something to spook you. Maybe I was too forward and too eager. I'm like that when I like someone. But even so, even if we can't start over, I don't want to pretend that I don't know you at all. And you can't lie to me forever. I know when someone needs help."

His reply was a clear attempt to deflect. "How so? How do you do that?"

"Experience," I said shortly. "Tell me."

Cedric rolled his eyes when his deflection failed. Then, he closed his eyes and stood like that for what felt like ages. "Fine. I'll tell you." It was a sigh full of surrender. It was like he would soon reveal to me that he was a wanted criminal and his fate was in my hands. Was I sure I wanted that kind of responsibility? I didn't have the time to decide for myself anymore. Cedric spoke. "I didn't lie when I told you my family was powerful. And I didn't lie when I said they wanted me to do something against my wishes."

I nodded and listened intently, never breaking eye contact with him even if Cedric kept looking at his hands, his feet, the bar around us, and anywhere except my eyes.

"But you are correct, Tristan. I am not who I say I am." The softness around his words and the French edge in places grew slightly stronger. "You could say it's a family business, but that doesn't precisely do it justice. We're nowhere near as productive in today's society as real businesses are. If anything, we're sort of big in the entertainment industry."

Something was creeping up my spine as Cedric struggled to get the words out. He was dancing around something, and I couldn't seem to find a way to lift the veil off the truth. "What do you do?"

That seemed to amuse him. "Not much, to be honest."

"Cedric, what does your family do?" I asked again, firmer. Worry that settled in the pit of my stomach was disproportionately large.

"And you are absolutely right, Tristan. I'm in trouble. They're not the sort of people that would treat my escape lightly. God, they probably have someone watching my every step. That's why, Tristan. That's why I can't walk around New York City, hold your hand, and kiss you whenever I wish. I can't let us go there because something else is waiting for me. I don't know if they're moving to force me there even as we speak." He shot a panicked look at the door. "They'll never let me have this, Tristan."

"I can help," I said, tension rising in me, my back straightening just the same. "I have friends who can help you. We can find a safe place for you where nobody will be able to find you."

Cedric snorted as if that was laughable. "You could lock me up in a cellar, but that's not the life I'd choose over them finding me. No, Tristan. You can't help me because I know how this thing is going to play out. They'll sit and let me blow off some steam, then they'll sweep in and take me back."

"Back where?" I asked. I just realized I still didn't know where he was from.

Cedric's eyes glimmered a little. The muscles in his face knotted with tension, and tears glistened in his eyes. "The palace of Verdumont, of course."

"The p...What? Why would they take you to a palace?" I stammered. "Cedric, who is your family?" If worry had filled my stomach earlier, now it only contained a big block of ice. Shivers ran down my arms as I held the bar with both hands. "Who are you?"

Cedric sucked his teeth. "I'm sorry, Tristan," he whispered. "I shouldn't have lied, but you have to believe me that it felt so good to be no one." He must have picked up the horrified expression on my face because he straightened in the next moment, all the rich and cultured posture I'd seen in him in glimpses pouring into that sculpted body and perfect face. "I'm Prince Cedric Philippe Valois Montclair, Duke of Belleval, son of His Royal Majesty Ferdinand Valois Montclair, the King of Verdumont."

It couldn't have been the beer that blurred my vision and made me see double. The black vignette around my field of vision reminded me that I needed to breathe. I had been so scared, thinking his family were terrorists of some kind. As I inhaled and my vision cleared, I barked a laugh. "Okay, um, and I'm the Prince of Wales. How do you do?"

This time, his lips absolutely twitched into a smile. "Seriously?" he asked, entertained, surprised, perhaps a little outraged. "You don't believe me?"

"Erm...what is Verdumont?" I asked. If he was willing to pull my leg this hard, it couldn't all be so serious. I had, perhaps, heard it mentioned in school. Or maybe I was imagining it.

Cedric took a step back, head tilted. "Do you know what France is?" he asked.

I show him a narrow-eyed look. "Yes. Obviously."

"And Germany?" he asked.

I rolled my eyes. "Of course."

"And Luxembourg, Netherlands, and Belgium?" he asked as if speaking to a child.

I pouted. "Yes. Yes, I do." Maybe I couldn't tell the difference between those if you gave me a map, but I'd heard of them. "What's with the inquisition?"

Cedric crossed his arms on his chest, reminding me of his sexy biceps at a pretty inconvenient time. "Do you have your phone with you? I see that we need to cover your geography lessons if you mean to continue offering your services to me. And mind, I am what I just told you I was."

I laughed again. Right. The Duke of Mars. I grabbed my phone and handed it to him. "Don't they have smartphones in what-do-you-call-it?"

"They have very sophisticated tracking software in Verdumont since it's in the heart of Europe. And I can't use my phone if I don't want to be found sooner rather than later." He spoke in a harsh whisper, sarcasm spilling over.

He typed something and returned my phone to me. "There. Verdumont."

It was a Wikipedia article about a country sandwiched between France and Germany, stretching around Luxembourg, bordering Belgium, and reaching as far up as the Netherlands. When I skimmed the top paragraph, his information seemed to be up to date. This place had a king and a queen, and the stern-faced man's name really was Ferdinand something and something. When I opened the list of royals, my heart skipped a beat and then sank all the way through my stomach and into hell's pits of doom. **Cedric Philippe Valois Montclair**. The portrait was dated two years ago, but those piercing blue eyes and that floppy blond hair were unmistakable. His defined jaw and high cheekbones, his straight nose, his full lips. Here, he wore a high-collared crimson jacket with decorative buttons, a white sash draped from his left shoulder to his right hip, a black belt around his narrow waist, and black pants with a gold stripe down the side. Polished black leather boots reached high and seemed to fit him perfectly, not to mention that they made him ever so slightly hotter when he was already a million degrees hot and causing me to sweat. "You...have a Wikipedia page," I said, my mouth dry, my body numb with shock.

I blinked several times before lifting my gaze off the phone and finding Cedric's surprised frown framing his gorgeous eyes. "*That's* what impressed you?"

"Um..." I put my phone on the bar and grabbed my beer, lifting one finger to signal for him to wait until I'd had a few more sips. When I put the glass back and exhaled, I stared at him. "That can't be right. You can't be a...a prince."

"Why?" Cedric asked.

Because I can't be the person who has a crush on a goddamn prince, I screamed internally.

"To be honest, Tristan, you're not taking this the way I imagined," Cedric said.

"H-how did you imagine I would take it?" I asked, my voice so thin and distant it might have belonged to someone else.

Cedric shrugged. "Mainly, I imagined you'd run the hell away and curse me until the end of days. Or to call my brother and tell him where he could find me." He hesitated, but there was more. Biting his lip, he shrugged one more time, but it was a what-the-hell shrug. "Or to bow and scrape like some medieval commoner. I hate that."

"I don't bow," I said. That was only half-true. But I wouldn't bow to him for being born to a royal family, that was for sure. "I'm sorry, I guess I'm just really shocked."

"I can see that," Cedric said. He laughed a little. Then, he laughed a little more. When he saw my bewildered expression, he shook his head and leaned a little closer. "I wasn't going to tell you. Ever. But I gotta say, it's such a relief to share the truth with you."

"I won't tell anyone," I promised.

"Thank you," Cedric said and lifted a glass in need of polishing. He got busy. "My problems remain the same, Tristan. My family is looking for me. I'm half-certain they know where to find me." He glanced out the window. "I feel...watched. Sometimes. Except, when I turn, there's no one there."

I looked at the window, too, but it was too dark outside to see anything except our own reflections. So I looked at His Royal Highness instead. He had the face for the job, that was certain. How it took my breath away... "What's your airline, Cedric?" I asked.

He shot me a sad smile, the saddest I had ever seen. And I was the king of sad smiles. "Marchioness Élodie de Beaumont. I am to be engaged to her this fall. A political and traditional alliance, if you know what I mean."

"B-but you can't be," I said. And it wasn't even that I assumed he was completely gay, but the abrupt possessiveness that poured into me. I wasn't letting her have him. He wasn't livestock to be sold for some kind of profit. "That's outrageous." I tried to cover myself up and hide just how jealous I suddenly was.

"That's what I said," Cedric replied. "But the thing about my family is that they're very loyal to traditions, Tristan. It's all they are. It's all *we* are. Without them, my family has no place in the world."

"So you're marrying some girl? Do you love her?" The demand was strong in my tone, stronger than I'd meant.

Cedric's snort was pure contempt. "And I don't believe she loves me, either. Which, if you ask my parents, has never been a problem in the history of our dynasty."

I heard myself laugh bitterly and shook my head. "This is fucked-up, Cedric." After he gave me an agreeing look, I added, "I guess I see why you would want to keep low, then."

Cedric put a hand on the bar next to mine. I felt as though he had meant to touch my hand and changed his mind at the last second, but I couldn't swear on it. He looked into my eyes, though. "And you see why I couldn't let us do anything more after that kiss."

My throat tightened. I shook my head like it was nothing. "Of course. N-no big deal."

Cedric pressed his lips into a tight line and pulled away from me. "I'm sorry it went so far, Tristan."

Don't, I wanted to say. *Don't regret it when it was the most beautiful thing that happened to me.*

"I was...taken by my feelings. The night was magical. I felt like anything was possible. And kissing you made it all real." There was a heavy tone of apology in there, but I could have sworn I heard some whimsy, too.

"It's fine," I croaked and cleared my throat. "I wouldn't hold that against you."

He nodded thankfully.

Mama Viv barged through the door, fanning herself dramatically, and spotted me sitting at the bar. "Now, do my eyes deceive me, or has the runaway chick returned to his mama hen?"

Cedric appeared very busy very quickly, and I couldn't blame him. Not that Mama Viv would remind him to do more when the hours were so slow. Oh no. Mama Viv would, in complete secrecy, confide in half of Hudson Burrow and ask everyone to keep the truth to themselves. Gossip would spread like wildfire, and Cedric would be outed within two days.

Mama Viv hugged me, and I kissed her cheek. "It's good to see you."

"And you, my darling," she said. "Tell me everything. What's kept you away from your home all these days?"

So I went on to recount all I had been doing in the past

few days. It was true that I had been avoiding the bar and Cedric, but I was pretty sure that was over now. Careful not to spill any of the beans that didn't belong to me, I told Mama Viv I would be here more often.

The truth was there was a lot more to talk about. And Cedric was still in the same mess he had been in an hour ago. But at least I knew the truth. And I could help.

CHAPTER 7
Knight In Shining Armor

CEDRIC

THE VERY FIRST NIGHT I TOLD TRISTAN THE truth, I learned how heavy the burden I had lived with was. Its absence allowed me to fill my lungs with air, to lift my head high, to smile without feeling like I deceived him.

The very next day, Tristan came around while I helped Bradley behind the bar. He asked me when I would be off and then told me to wait for him after the shift. I wasn't in the habit of being told what to do or to wait on people, but I had been making allowances for work all these days, so I figured I might as well include Tristan in my growing list of exceptions.

"I've been thinking about your, ah, situation all night," Tristan said when he came around at three in the afternoon. His skin had absorbed the August sunshine and tanned in such a smooth way, whereas mine needed layers of SPF to save me from burning like a crab. I avoided the sunshine in New York like a vampire.

We carried a round of beers to the terrace under the canopy of lightbulbs that were off at this hour. The shadows cast by the buildings closing around us were thick and as close to cool as could be expected this deep into the summer. "Oh?"

"Yeah," Tristan confirmed.

We sat down in the furthest corner, with cool brick walls extending to two sides. My back faced the buildings that met in this corner, and I had a full view of the terrace and the door to Neon Nights. Nobody could walk out here without me seeing them.

Tristan leaned in conspiratorially and looked at me. "I decided I believe you."

I arched my eyebrows. "Decided?" And hadn't that already been resolved?

He shrugged innocently. "Decided."

"Does your decision have anything to do with the fact that it's all true?" I asked.

Tristan pulled back ever so slightly, eyes narrowing. "It's mostly that you talk like a prince."

"And how is that?" I asked, holding back my smile.

My ally chuckled and took a sip of beer, then wiped the foam from his upper lip with the back of his hand. "You can't believe I needed to check the information for myself. That's how it is."

"Ah, and now we're on the same page?" I tilted my head.

Tristan nodded firmly.

"I still think you shouldn't get any more involved, Tristan," I said, all humor fading out of my voice. This morning, I had seen a stiff-backed woman pass by the bar. She hadn't looked through the window and peeked inside, but she had walked just the same two days ago. The tight, nononsense ponytail, the makeup that defined her face, and the square shoulders told of a lifetime of service. Or I was a paranoid runaway. It was one or the other, but something told me I was being observed. I certainly wouldn't imagine it was out of Alexander's range of tactics. "If you help me, there could be considerable blowback."

Tristan snorted. "This is a free country. What can a foreign king do to me?"

"You underestimate the power of a royal bloodline." It wasn't supposed to be self-flattery. I was glad that Tristan didn't take it that way.

He simply shook his head. "I'm not afraid of your family, no matter how influential they are."

That's because you don't know them, I thought.

"They wouldn't assassinate me, would they?" Tristan added, the bravado in his voice trembling slightly.

I shook my head. "I don't imagine they would. But they could make your life hell if they want to. They could pull strings and have all the best culinary schools reject you for some made-up reason, should you ever apply. They could spread some falsehood about you among their friends in New York, and you'd never be allowed a significant loan to open your restaurant because the bankers would consider you risky and unreliable. That's the kind of influence I'm talking about."

"Oh, boo-hoo," Tristan said mockingly. "I'll never be invited to a black suit gala. Don't you see where I live? I'll never get a big loan regardless of what your father tells some New York banker. And unless they mean to send some goblin to tie my shoelaces so I trip on my next run, I can't imagine them doing anything that'll have significant consequences, Cedric. I'm a small fish."

"You're nothing of the sort," I said before I could stop myself. "Not to me."

He stopped speaking abruptly and looked at me for a few heartbeats. The heat in my face must have become visible because Tristan smiled and looked at his beer instead. "Still," he mused, "I don't think they'll grudge me for making sure their political asset is safe."

"Is that what you're offering?" I asked.

Tristan met my gaze again. He licked his lips. "I don't know if I can keep you from being kidnapped by your own family—if that's what they'd do—but I can watch your back while you're here. And I can help you pass the time when you're bored."

It begged the terrible question that had the potential to open too many paths of consequences. "Why?" I asked, voice dry and cracking.

"You're in my 'hood," he said simply, but that wasn't it at all. He hesitated, tilted his head this way and that, and sighed. "I know, I know. You're a prince. I can't wrap my head around it, by the way, but that's who you are. Still, the person I know is the guy who skipped all the rules of flirting, bought me a drink, and danced with me all night. And...I like you. Simple as that." He shrugged like he'd said something completely inconsequential.

"I like you, too," I replied softly. It was odd to say those words to him. To anyone, really. I'd never had a chance to express something as innocent as that. Sure, I'd done my fair share of hooking up, but it had hardly even been about liking the person the way they were.

I looked at Tristan. His brown hair and strong, defined jawline, and his warm, focused brown eyes. It was too easy to forget about everything else and just gaze at him. His presence calmed me, grounded me, and kept me in the moment instead of letting me roam and lose myself in worry.

My back stiffened. It was also too easy to imagine taking his hand and going somewhere less crowded than the terrace of Neon Nights. I leaned against the back of my chair and drank a little. "To be perfectly honest, having told you everything makes life much easier."

Tristan nodded. "I'm glad it did. Now, if only I could remember the proper etiquette when I refer to you..."

"Don't even," I said, mock horrified. "That's the very thing I'm trying to avoid."

Tristan chuckled. He gazed into my eyes for a little while, perhaps a moment too long, before he asked his next question. "Can it be that bad? Aside from marrying an airline, of course."

"Define bad," I said. "I'm not going to pretend that never having to work for the sake of survival isn't a big perk, Tristan. But I've lived my entire life publicly. Since I was old enough to look at the lens, my life's been in the service of upholding our traditions. It's all stunts. And getting engaged to Élodie is just another performance."

"You think it's unavoidable," Tristan concluded.

"I'm here, aren't I?" I asked. I needed to hear his thoughts, too. Hell, I had no idea what I really believed. I hoped with all my heart that some part of me expected life to go on just the way it was now.

Tristan shrugged. "I don't think you mean to stay." It was a statement, plain and simple, but it carried a hint of melancholy I knew well. "You live in a hotel and work while it's still fun. I don't hold that against you. But you're planning to go back, Cedric. Maybe you were right the other night. Maybe you're trying to prove a point."

Maybe. If I were going to return home, then I would do it on my terms. I needed some bargaining chips before I considered facing my brother and parents. "I'm not going to marry her," I said flatly.

"I can't believe we're actually talking about this," Tristan said, frowning a little. "I mean, think about it. You're being forced to marry someone. What year is it in Verdumont?"

I laughed softly. "Same as everywhere, but that doesn't apply to royalty. This..." I sighed and shook my head. Leaning in, I brought my face closer to his. "To us, this is like a business contract. Or to my brother, at least. To marry someone is to be partnered with a person for a project in the normal world. And it has a certain set of requirements, of course, like the family line and the clean record in the eye of the public."

Tristan snorted with the same contempt I shared. "Does the checklist mention anything about love?"

I shook my head. "Don't get me wrong. They're not completely heartless. My parents love each other dearly, even though theirs was a marriage of convenience. It helps that they're both heterosexual, which I'm most definitely not. Theirs is the opinion that, given time, Élodie and I will build something sort of like a nice life together. And it'll ensure that we remain, for the lack of a better word, employed."

"And what would you do?" he asked. "Sorry, I'm just trying to understand your life a little better."

Something tugged my heart toward Tristan. I rarely wanted to explain myself to people or to share my routine. Those things were available on the website of the royal family for those following us closely, and I fled from the sort of journalists that obsessed over our every move. But Tristan? Yes. I wanted Tristan to know what my life was like. And I wasn't fooling myself; this thing wasn't going to go anywhere. It couldn't, and it mustn't. "Should something happen to Alexander, I would assume the role of the Crown Prince." Tristan blinked. The word must have crossed his mind. "I'm the *spare*." He winced so subtly that I might have imagined it. "Long live the Crown Prince," I said lightly. "And for as long as he is the heir, my job is to support him in the public eye. It might not cross the Atlantic, but we're a big deal in Verdumont. Alexander will need our help when he gets our father's job. The monarchy has never been less stable. My family holds up traditions that, coming from a gay man in this day and age, might be better off dead. If people knew just how much of our lives are staged for photo ops, they'd abolish us immediately. We're a remnant of another time, Tristan."

"Whoa," my knight in shining armor said. "You're very harsh."

"It's not easy growing up knowing you're different," I said. "It should be. Verdumont is a progressive place. We were among the first countries to legalize same-sex marriage, enact bans on non-necessary surgical intervention for intersex children, and legalize everyone's right to self-identification. There hasn't been a hate crime against a sexual minority in three decades. All these rules exist to make everyone equal, but..." My gaze dropped as my words grew too strained.

"They don't apply to you," Tristan whispered, voice tight with unchecked anger.

I shook my head. "Ironically, I could walk you through the entire history of our family and tell you about King Augustus III, who was so smitten by a young French knight that he offered the man lands and titles just to keep him close. Or King Frederick the Tall, who had married a duchess his father had picked, had a single son with her, and sent her to live on their summer estate for the rest of their lives. Meanwhile, Frederick the Tall appointed Sir Louis de Châtillon as his secretary, giving him apartments next to the King's own—with a shared door, mind you—a yearly allowance on par with what the Princess Consort received, and was rarely seen in anyone else's company. They were what contemporary historians would refer to as 'very good friends.'" And there was no missing the sarcasm in my voice. "My father's brother is bisexual. My great-grandfather's brother was gay. Their grandfather had a very public affair with the master of his stables. The list goes on and on."

"Don't stop," Tristan said, a grin splitting his face in half. "Don't ever stop. I love this."

I chuckled. His joyful expression was contagious. "There is a portrait of Frederick the Tall with Sir Louis de Châtillon, which I studied privately in my college days. I wrote a paper on the ill-concealed homosexual subtext in the painting." I asked Tristan to give me his phone, typed in the name of the painting, and handed it to him. "Just look at it. Sir Louis is holding an apple. Grooms used to give apples to their brides."

Tristan snorted. "You wrote a paper about an apple?"

I laughed loudly. He was challenging me. I liked it. "If it were only that, I'd call it a coincidence. Look at their hands."

Tristan frowned. He made the gesture on his screen to zoom it, frowned harder, then let his mouth hang open. "Are these matching rings?"

"When I said 'ill-concealed,' that's exactly what I meant," I said. "And look at the background. That rosebush in full bloom is entwined with thistle. Those are the symbols of love and defiance, sometimes secrecy. Ferdinand's cloak partially covers Sir Louis, which they say shows the impressive height of the king, but it's very clearly a symbol of protection in every other portrait that depicts a king and a queen. And that dove up there on the branch? It's paired with a crow, the bird that represents hidden truths."

"Alright. I'm convinced," Tristan said, chuckling. "Your gramps had a thing for Sir Louis the Hot."

I glanced at the screen of his phone. Sir Louis was indeed very attractive. Dark locks of hair framed his chiseled face, his eyes brown and big, his nose slightly crooked. He was shorter than Ferdinand, of course, but not by much.

"What's with the pomegranate?" Tristan asked.

On the other side of the painting was a small table with a white cloth draped over it and a silver tray containing a single open pomegranate. I snorted. "I asked my art history professor," I said. "It seemed out of place in the context of a gay relationship. My professor insisted it was to symbolize the fertility of the country in their united leadership. Ferdinand the Tall is considered one of the most revered leaders in the history of Verdumont, bringing years of prosperity and peace to otherwise war-riddled times. But I think Ferdinand had a wicked sense of humor. Why else would he commission this portrait? Why else would it hang in his apartment? I think it was a juicy 'fuck you' to his deceased father. He had done his duty, fathered a son to take over, and provided money, privacy, and freedom to his wife—the Duchess lived with several 'very good friends' over the years and wrote fond, friendly letters to Ferdinand, hinting at some spicy secrets of her own—and he could live his life however he chose. I think that's why the pomegranate is sliced open."

Tristan rubbed his face. "This is bonkers. Do you understand that, Cedric? It's absolutely insane that you are a...royal."

"I just want to do the dishes, Tristan," I admitted. "I just want to clean Mama Viv's kitchen and dance at her shows and get a little drunk." I was tired of always worrying about where the lens was and what face I needed to show it. I was tired of living like a goldfish in an aquarium.

"I can do that much for you," Tristan said.

It was still beyond me why he would want to. He was an odd one.

"There's a party the day after tomorrow. Make sure you're off that night because we're going to dance," he said with a big grin that wouldn't take no for an answer.

My heart clenched. Or maybe the reality clenched my heart when it tried to leap. *Yes*, I wanted to say. *Yes. That's all I want to do. To dance with you, to touch you as I touched you that first night, to kiss you again as I kissed you with the entire city glimmering behind us.* My throat tightened, and I cleared it, then drank some of my beer. "Let's do that," I said. It was all I could say.

My soul burned with the desire to never do anything else, but I knew better than to expect such a life. Tristan was right about one thing. I didn't mean to stay here forever. And even if I meant to, I couldn't. Prince or not, there were rules about staying in a foreign country. Whether I wanted it or not, I needed to remember that Verdumont still beckoned me, roped me in, and pulled me back. Sooner or later, Tristan would stay in Hudson Burrow, and I would walk up the steps of the Royal Palace.

Sooner or later, this sweet, unpredictable fling would have to end.

And I wouldn't make it any harder for either of us when the day came to part ways. I wouldn't let myself fall for this wild, beautiful man, and I wouldn't let him fall for me. If I could avoid that heartbreak, then I would go back to the real world a happy man, knowing I'd done something right, knowing I'd spared one beautiful person from falling apart because my life was a mess.

Tristan and I let our glasses touch and drank to seal the plan. Life would run us all over eventually, but at least we could dance all night until then.

CHAPTER 8
Starting Over

TRISTAN

CEDRIC HESITATED. THERE WAS AN ADORABLE frown on his face and a smile that only touched the corners of his lips. If I didn't know how impossible and otherworldly his feelings for me were, I would have swooned.

"Come along, Princess," I said, gesturing down the stone-paved path with my head.

"Uh, Princess? No, thank you. And I'm not four, either, Tristan," Cedric said.

"You're failing to prove that," I teased. "Zoos are fun no matter how old you are."

Putting on a mock pout, Cedric narrowed his eyes and followed me in. "I happen to be one of the patrons of Verdumont's biggest zoo."

"There's more than one?" I asked, genuinely surprised.

Cedric muttered, "There are two."

"How sweet of you," I told him. "And I'm going to show you a handsome fellow you'll fall in love with."

His gaze lingered on me for a moment or two, his expression frozen in that instant. When he looked away, he seemed ever so slightly more flustered. "We'll see about that. Oh, and if it's a snake, I'll just warn you that there's no surer way to send me running home." He glued his feet to the ground, a scared expression washing over his face.

I grabbed his hand and pulled him after me. "I would never do that to you."

He laughed abruptly and hurried after me. As we navigated the maze of this small and intimate zoo, Cedric told me about the efforts in Verdumont to create much more humane conditions for the animals. "It's a complicated situation," he explained. "Most of the animals had been bred in captivity, so to speak, and releasing them into the wild is a death sentence. We limit the number of people allowed inside our zoos at any given time. I wouldn't call them resorts, but the animals have much better living conditions than in a lot of places I visited."

We talked about his travels around the world as he stopped by a few areas with friendly zebras and young, willful elephants. As we neared the destination I had in mind, I said, "We have this sponsorship program intended to rescue and care for the animals." We rounded a corner and climbed over a bridge that connected two sides of an artificial river. "And I'm Pudding's foster dad."

"Pudding?" Cedric asked. Before he could speak the name, we approached the Bamboo Haven, where Pudding lived. It was an acre-large plot of land, walled with bamboo groves and enriched by rising slopes and artificial caves, hosting five pandas living their best lives. Although people moved around the area and observed the pandas that were outside, the place was tucked away for peace and quiet, equipped with specialty walkways for observers wanting a closer look.

At the nearest fence, there were five plaques done in bronze, each stating the basic biological information for one of the pandas, and each had the name of the patron added to the bottom.

Cedric's eyes widened when he saw Pudding's plaque with my name on it. He realized I wasn't kidding. "Tristan, you do odd jobs at a bar. How do you...?"

I shrugged before he could finish. "I'm terrible with money, I know." I wasn't going into the monthly deposits from my parents. It made my heart clench to think of them. Most of it went to Pudding, anyway, except for my portion of the rent.

"Is he here?" Cedric asked. A bubbly, almost childish excitement painted his voice. "I'd love to see him."

My hand wrapped around Cedric's again, yet the sensation of touching him was no less electric the second time around. It raced straight to my heart, but I kept my face smooth and led Cedric down the pathway for observers to an opening that allowed us to see most of the Bamboo Haven's interior.

As we approached the safety railing, I scanned the ground and spotted my friend sitting, his hind legs spread out before him, his back upright, and bamboo sticks scattered around him. He used his front paws to handle the sticks.

"You can tell them apart?" Cedric asked when I pointed at Pudding.

"He's the youngest," I explained. We gazed at the

panda as he lifted a piece of bamboo and started to bend it until it broke. He was careful about doing it, his little arms moving slowly, his teeth baring in an expression of great effort.

Cedric watched with unrestrained wonder. The sheer delight on his face removed the creases of tiredness that were starting to show themselves around his eyes and mouth. "What is he doing?"

I chuckled. I had seen Pudding at it countless times. I had once come here with Roman and asked Pudding's then-carer what it was all about. "He was adopted very young and cared for by humans," I said. "Pandas are very impressionable, especially at such a young age. Pudding obviously has the strength to snap the sticks like toothpicks, but because the girl who cared for him first struggled to break the sticks for him to snack on, he learned to do the same. Or he started doing it to fit in, I don't know. But here he is, two years later, acting like it's the hardest thing in the world."

Cedric laughed out loud. He didn't take his gaze off Pudding since we spotted him.

"You should see him climb," I said. "It's so clumsy and human that it freaks you out."

Cedric shook his head slowly, still looking at Pudding for a few moments. Then, slowly, his head turned to me. The intensity of his gaze never failed to create physical weight when it was on me. "So, this is what you do," he mused. "You go around rescuing and helping."

I couldn't stop the snort that catapulted itself from my nose. "I do nothing, Cedric. Sarah and John care for the bunch; I just send some money every month. It helps keep the misting system running in the summer and heated rocks during winter."

Cedric looked at me just the same. "You act like nothing you do is worth anything, but I've never met anyone who's as ready to give up their time and money for others."

I didn't plan to argue with him. It was nice to be thought of so positively by someone, prince or not, but he had a totally wrong impression of me.

"You're full of surprises," Cedric said, turning his attention back to Pudding.

I waved my hand through the air as if I were doing a sleight of hand. "No surprises for tonight," I promised. "We're only going to dance until we fall off our feet."

There was a sparkle in Cedric's eyes that promised a great night ahead.

Cedric

Although three days had gone by since I first told him the truth of my identity, Tristan acted like we were just two boys lost in New York City's vast cityscape. The first tease I received was long after we had visited Pudding at the zoo and parted ways for a short time. I waited for Tristan at Neon Nights in my best summer clothes. Some unearthly hand had guided me to do all I could to fix my overgrowing hair and spend an hour in front of the mirror as if tonight was anything more than simple fun. My clenching heart and fluttering stomach worried me, but I pushed those thoughts aside.

Tristan entered Neon Nights alone and walked straight toward me. On the way between the door and the spot where I sat at the bar, he greeted several people and a couple of guys who were visibly there together. And when he finally reached me, he batted those long, dark eyelashes at me, making my heart stumble. "Your Highness," he said just loudly enough for my ears as he leaned in to greet me with a hug. I was getting used to being hugged instead of having my hand shaken.

There are many things I could get used to with you, I thought, inhaling Tristan's light, breezy scent. "Is that a threat?" I asked in a low tone.

He chuckled so sweetly that the flutters rose into my chest. "Only if you don't follow me to the dance floor ASAP."

"A drink first?" I offered. "I can get you that radioactive thing you like that makes your eyes glow yellow."

Tristan slapped my shoulder. It was, on its own, just a friendly gesture, meaningless banter, but the feel of his hand on my body, even if the part of my body was a covered shoulder, was as intimate as meeting his Pudding or standing at the top of the Empire State building with him.

What are you doing to me? I wondered desperately. With each moment we spent near one another, thoughts of home crashed on me harder. I figured it was because the more I was near Tristan, the less I wanted to return to it all.

Tristan agreed to have a drink at the bar with me first. Mama Viv hadn't sung her opening number yet, anyway, so the party was hardly warming up. And nothing was as sexy as Tristan biting the tip of his big straw, closing his lips around it, and sucking a bit of the lemony vodka from the glass of crushed ice. He had this flirtatious aura sparking around him that I was finding increasingly more difficult to ignore. Or the shot of caramel rum Roman had served me was extra potent. It was one or the other.

"Have you met my friends?" Tristan asked just as the pair he had greeted neared him again.

I glanced at the couple as I shook my head in reply. They were both tall guys, near my age or slightly older, and clearly in love. It was odd that I couldn't put my finger on how I knew that, but they were so visibly tied together that I didn't doubt my instincts. One was a blond guy with wavy hair and an expression of an introvert's shyness and defiance. The other was slightly taller, his skin like caramel, his eyes warm and brown and full of zest for life, his hair cropped short, and his lips full. "Hullo," said the blond one. "Hey," said the brown-eyed one. They thrust their hands out in turn, and the one who introduced himself as Rafael narrowed his eyes briefly. "Have we met before?"

"Uh, I work here," I said. "But I don't remember seeing you around."

"Sorry," Rafael said lightly. "You just looked familiar from somewhere else. Can't put my finger on it."

"It's your wild imagination," Luke, the blond one with a low fire burning behind his eyes, said.

"You're the one with wild imagination. Mine is perfectly within the limits of reason." Rafael turned to me. "Is that a French accent?"

"Close enough," I said.

"I spent a wonderful night in Paris, oh, ten years ago,

and many not-as-wonderful weeks otherwise," Rafael said. Something about it made Luke's eyes glow.

I sensed more questions coming from Rafael, the conversational one, but a booming voice announced the matron of the neighborhood, Lady Vivien Woodcock, before she appeared on the stage and rescued me from people's curiosity.

There was a cheer that was quickly silenced when the track began to play. It took me a moment to survive the wave of chills running down my arms and recognize the tune. Mama Viv, dancing like a world-class performer about to drop a legendary cover, sang "It's A Sin" by Pet Shop Boys powerfully enough to leave me gasping for air. I hardly noticed getting up from my bar stool and finding Tristan next to me. I was barely aware that we had forgotten all about our drinks and were spinning around the dance floor, lasers beaming at us and at Mama Viv. The world dimmed everywhere but between us. He became the sole figure I could register. And this, with Mama Viv's perfect pitch for the ultimate melancholy threaded through the song, was the moment I knew what it was that I wanted.

I doubted I could have it.

I didn't dare to believe it would last.

But I wanted it. My heart burned in hellish flames with the desire for it. This. This was all I would ever need. I wanted to be consumed by the night, to burn up with a passion that fueled everyone around me, to lose myself in Tristan until all my days passed and I was an old and satisfied man with a lifetime of memories to cherish.

It's never gonna happen, I reminded myself, but it was almost like I was speaking to someone who had long gone deaf to this specific voice. *Your days are already numbered, silly boy.*

But this welling energy that threatened to overflow the confines of my body had to spill somewhere. It had to pour out of me, or I would burst. I grabbed Tristan, this wonderful, impossible guy who never seemed tired, never looked like his life lacked purpose, and never, ever cared if doing the right thing cost him his life. My arms wrapped around his sculpted body, my lips stretched into a broad, uncontrollable smile, and I lifted him off his feet. Some guys would panic, flail, laugh, and ask to be put down, but Tristan stretched his arms above his head and leaned back, spinning in what looked like slow motion to my speeding mind. Beyond the melancholy of the song's iconic tune was something dramatic and urgent, and I felt it in every bone of my body.

Releasing Tristan, I pulled him in again, our bodies smashing against one another, breaths kicked out of our lungs, eyes locked in a fierce battle of wills as we danced.

I had never been this deeply immersed in anything my entire life. How sterile and droll had my existence been before running into this gorgeous man? As the tunes merged with Mama Viv's increasingly more dramatic performance, I sank deep into the well of my feelings. And the explosive final chords brought me back invigorated, reborn, and determined. A catharsis of emotions that lasted a whole five minutes, yet it shifted the ground for a lifetime.

"My, my," Tristan said. "The prince of the dance floor."

"Let's keep going," I said, out of breath and with a thin layer of sweat breaking over my body. "Let's never stop."

When Mama Viv yielded to the thundering requests for

another song, Starship's "Nothing's Gonna Stop Us Now" raised the hairs on my neck and arms. Now, the mix of wild and quirky took over us and we moved as one, almost like every thought that crossed his mind was beamed into mine instantly. It was like we were the marionettes of the lasers cutting through the artificial smoke, moving whichever way they hit us. Tristan was the perfect counterpart, perfect partner, perfect person to be with when you wanted to feel like you were someone's entire world. He knew everything. He knew who I was, who my family was, and what my fate would inevitably be, yet he gave all of himself to me as if none of it mattered.

One song passed, and another came. Mama Viv handed over the stage to a score of queens who lip-synced their souls out, smugly standing by the bar and watching as the night progressed and nobody managed to steal her glory. In the whirlwind of colors and flavors and scents, I spotted glimpses of other people. Roman served drinks from behind the bar, and Rafael ran his fingers through Luke's rich, bright hair. But Tristan and I were inseparable. Nothing could exhaust me. My appetite only grew more ravenous. Every bump, every sweet touch that was gone before I knew it, every glance into his eyes made me want more.

What are you doing to me, you beautiful stranger? I am about to have a terrible life that won't get any better if I forever remember the things that cannot be. But those voices were distant and small, irrelevant, and said to someone who wasn't me. They were said to someone who might listen to them.

"Come with me," I huffed, pulling Tristan into my

arms, his clothes as sweat-soaked as mine. "Let's get out of here." Alternately, I would hold him like this until I felt all of him.

"Are you sure about that?" Tristan asked cheekily.

"Absolutely," I said. I didn't let my doubts creep up.

Tristan and I slowed down. His balled fists rested on my pecs, and his forehead touched mine. "Élodie?"

My stomach hollowed. Yes. There was a real world outside this. How would I reconcile the two? "I'll never belong to her, Tristan. With or without you."

He pulled his head away and looked into my eyes. His teeth closed around his lower lip, and a smile pulled the corners of his mouth. "No, I don't think you will," he said, his eyes glimmering.

"So?" I asked, my hands on his hips, muscles tense as I fought not to pull him in so hard that the impact would unite all our atoms into a single being.

"So," he said, licking his lips, "take me, then."

My heart nearly exploded as his words sank into every part of my body, into my very soul. With a new determination, I released his hips and took his hand. If anyone saw us, they didn't try to stop us from leaving. We moved as one as if we were still dancing, and the crowd parted to let us through.

Whatever came next, I would deal with it. I would fight the fate if I had to. But right now, he was all I could think about.

CHAPTER 9
After the Dance

TRISTAN

I COULDN'T RECALL ANYONE HOLDING MY HAND this tightly. Hardly anyone had ever wanted me so badly. We hurried into the night, Cedric leading the way, leaving a trail of sweet and spicy scent that I could follow anywhere had he not held my hand.

"Where are we going?" I asked, moving as if in a dream, as if leaping from one place to the next, with everything in between blurring.

"The Henriette," Cedric replied without hesitating. He was on a mission. He moved with a purpose. And with the way he had given himself to the beat of the music, he was more alive than I had ever seen so before. "I want to show you something."

A fine layer of perspiration had covered me on the dance floor, and the stuffy air of an August night that was ripe for a rainstorm didn't help, either. Whatever he wanted to show me, it would hopefully follow a good, cold shower.

I didn't doubt His Royal Highness had a little en suite in his apartment at the Henriette.

The hotel was only a few intersections away, but I stopped abruptly somewhere between Neon Nights and the Henriette. The street lamps gave off their orange lights, setting Cedric's light golden hair aflame. "Cedric," I said softly, my chest trembling. Something tugged my heart toward him, but I needed this out of the way. I needed it settled before letting myself leap and fly. "Wait."

He stopped in the very next instant, our arms stretched as far as they would go, hands still locked together. Cedric took a long step back, his grip on me tighter. Even without words, I believed his intentions were purely good for us both. Still...

"I like you," I said, wild, misplaced laughter welling in me, barely held down by the little reason left in my head. "I really do."

His face lit up, eyes wide and so impossibly blue that the orange lights did nothing to affect them. "I like you, too," he said. As his lips stretched into a gentle smile, devastating dimples appeared on his cheeks. "It's the last thing that should have happened, but you..." He lifted his shoulder into a small shrug. "You're the best surprise that happened to me."

My hand tightened around his as I stepped closer. Every bit of me wanted to put my head on his shoulder and feel the same togetherness that I had felt while dancing. I resisted it. "I've done this before," I said. "This flirting, chasing, hooking up."

Cedric pulled on a fake-surprised expression. "You're saying you're not...a virgin? Gasp."

I smacked his broad chest with my free hand. "I'm saying I can't do it again. Not like that. Not with you."

As I moved gently away from him, Cedric abandoned his teasing and straightened his back. He was as regal as if he'd stepped out of a fantasy series. That was what I had noticed about him first, but I couldn't pin it until now. He was so royal, so elevated by life and customs, that I couldn't but gaze at him. He released my hand and put both of his above my hips. "Tristan," he said softly, my name so perfect on his lips. "If you think this is just a hook-up, I did a very good job of resisting you so far."

I pursed my lips against a ridiculously broad smile that threatened to overcome me.

"By all means, that should have been the choice we made," he said, pulling me so gently toward him. It would have been easier to fight ropes yanking me to a bottomless pit. He was so magnetic. My heart would have found him in total darkness, anywhere in the whole wide galaxy, like a compass pointing to the north. "But I met you already, and I fought it only to find myself at the very beginning again. Maybe the right choice isn't right for me."

A chuckle burst out of me before I could stop it. I couldn't tell whether I was relieved or flattered. "You say these things, but there's still an angry prince searching for you and a marchioness waiting to marry you."

"I'm not doing that," he said firmly. "Not to myself and not to Élodie. If I can't have the one I want, the one who wants me—" His body touched mine, and thrills ran through all my nerves. "—then I'll be a miserable husband to a miserable woman, ruining her life as much as my own."

"You'd rather wipe the tables for Mama Viv?" I asked.

He was reasonable enough to shrug and shake his head. "Tristan, I can't promise that this will end well." He took a small step back from me, and his hands found mine. "I can't tell you they won't come after me by force or that we'll just be happy dancing every night, although that's a life I'd choose over Verdumont in a heartbeat. But I can promise you this: I will try my best. And if the worst happens, it won't be because of my lack of trying."

"Okay," I whispered, using his grip on my hands to pull him toward me.

His lips stretched into a broad smile again, the happiness roaring through me visible on his face, too. "Okay?"

I nodded. Our bodies touched again, but the movement brought us even closer. His torso pressed against mine while my left leg fit between both of his.

Something inexplicable appeared on Cedric's face. Something so bright and wonderful that I didn't have a word for it. Happiness was a pale reflection of what I saw when I looked at him.

Cedric licked his lips and controlled his smile. "Can I kiss you now?" he asked. Hurriedly, he added, "I'd really like to kiss you now."

He didn't need to ask—not after all we'd said and done —yet the fact that he still asked made me want him twice as hard if infinity could be doubled.

As one side of my lips lifted into a smile, I rose to my toes. My eyes closed as I leaned in, the warmth of his body and the sweet and spicy scent he wore swirled around me, pulled me in, and embraced me until I felt the softness of his lips on mine. For an instant, it was a sweet and smoldering kiss, but my desire for him fanned it into a scorching, blazing wildfire that would consume us completely if we weren't careful.

I wasn't in the mood to be careful.

Cedric's lips pressed against mine harder, parting to let his tongue venture into my mouth, meeting mine, touching it playfully, and opening an endless well of lust I hadn't realized still existed in me.

I didn't know we were moving. I didn't notice us stumbling back until my back pressed hard against a brick wall, and a gasp left my mouth. He kissed me still, his fingers running through my hair, the other hand sliding down the length of my back. And when he stepped away, fear filled me for a moment. Was he about to run away? Was the Empire State Building happening all over again? Had I misjudged him so terribly that I would fall for the same move twice in a row?

Cedric grabbed my hand, a heated look in his eyes locking on my face and a grin pulling his lips wide.

The relief that lifted the fears off my chest revealed just how heavy they had been. Running after him now, when he set off toward the Henriette, was like floating through the clouds.

CEDRIC

My lips still burned by the time we crashed through the front door of the Henriette Hotel. A sleepy desk clerk had just enough time to spin around and see me passing with the man of my dreams trailing after me. I spoke a greeting, and if he greeted us in return, we were long gone by then.

The lobby was lit softly for the night, although the fine layer of sweat that covered my arms where the rolled sleeves revealed them shone regardless. It didn't matter. If I had my way, we would be much sweatier not long from now. The thought curled my lips.

"Oh, Your Royal Fanciness," Tristan teased, gaze taking in all of the hotel in leaps. "I'd never move out, either."

"Yeah, this won't last," I replied, not particularly regretful. Right now, I felt like I had scored the biggest prize of all. All else faded to unimportance. I'd sleep on his doorstep if that were what it took to be near him. "I'm as good at personal finances as you are."

Tristan laughed. "We're going to dance ourselves to ruin."

"Our money," I mused as if continuing a melody.

"Our reputation," Tristan gasped.

"We'll be the happiest beggars that ever begged," I promised, my free hand pressing the button to call the elevator.

The doors slid open, and we entered the spacious elevator. I wanted to steal kisses; my impatience had never been anywhere near what I experienced now. But when I pressed the button, Tristan chuckled. "Are you in the dungeon?"

"Better," I said.

As the elevator descended to the underground facilities that were available to a certain section of guests at all times, Tristan waited patiently. The door opened to reveal a blue and green-lit area, an oasis of tranquility where only the two of us existed.

"You weren't kidding," Tristan said, stepping into the spa center.

"Massages aren't available, I'm afraid, but I will do my best as a substitute," I said. "Besides, there's plenty we can still do."

"I thought we were going to your room," Tristan said levelly, although not in a disappointed tone.

I laughed. "The night is young, and you are beautiful." I lifted his hand over his head and spun him to some silent tune that lived in my heart, if not in the real world. Tristan turned around and neared me, our bodies pressing together, my arms wrapping around him.

"That is so sweet, Cedric," he said.

His eyes sparkled, and I released him, then led him down the spacious hallway of the underground oasis. The atmospheric noises of raindrops in a rainforest, distant birds, murmurs of hidden springs, and rustling of leaves in faraway canopies were enough to relax my muscles. We passed various sections and hallways, some leading to beauty treatments, others to massage rooms, dark rooms, quiet rooms, and one to a swimming pool. I led the way past all that and into the slightly cooler area that was kept dark for the purpose of total enchantment.

My shirt cooled on my body in a few moments as we passed through the hallway and into a dimly lit locker room. "Grab a towel," I said.

"Aye, aye," Tristan replied. I slipped into a booth to strip and tied the towel around my waist. Flutters filled me to the brim as I realized I would now return to the open space of the locker room and meet Tristan again. As I did, I held my breath. Tristan shuffled behind the wooden door of the changing cabin and stepped out. It made my heart lurch in my chest, and my gaze shamelessly explored all of his visible body. I cursed the towel—it was the enemy of all that was beautiful in the world—and looked at the fine curves of Tristan's muscles, the definition of his torso from his narrow waist to his broad shoulders and firm pecs.

"What now?" he asked, his voice noticeably tighter and more controlled. His gaze dropped to my waist and darted back to my face, his cheeks darkening. He was so beautiful, especially when he was surprisingly shy.

Our towel reached halfway down our shins, and the sweat on our bodies had already cooled and dried. I had to tear my gaze away from his beauty and show the way through another door. We passed a row of spacious showers lit with pale blue light, each separated by a sheet of misted glass and with enough room in each to fit a small crowd.

Yet when we passed the showers, we reached the final door.

Tristan

I was starting to get a clear idea of what we were doing, although getting to watch Cedric's cut definition and broad back as he led me through was enough. I would have done it had he been leading me over a cliff.

His body was like steel, unbreakable, unbending, unyielding. Every bit of him appeared to have immense strength beneath the surface. He moved steadily, almost elusively, as he opened the door to the heat chamber of the sauna. It was lit with bright yellow light and made mostly of wood, separated into three levels. The heat itself suffocated me almost instantly, but I stepped inside and waited for Cedric to shut the door.

The room was small, cozy, and incredibly hot, but to my left was a glass window looking at a high-quality projection of stormy cold seas, gathering clouds, distant rain, and the light of the sun filtered until it was just a pale highlight. With the heat that made my brain spin, I could almost believe we were lost at sea.

Sweat and steam covered me pretty much instantly, and Cedric chuckled. "You're glowing," he said, taking my hand and pulling me back to the lowest bench of the three.

I inhaled the hot oven air, and it burned my lungs. My brain knew I was getting enough oxygen, but my body failed to get the message.

"Relax," Cedric said and leaned back against the second row. He spread his arms wide to each side of the middle bench, his right inches away from my shoulders. It didn't help me one bit to relax, but it was nice to feel him so near me. "I know it feels like I'm torturing you, but it'll be worth it."

Part of me wanted to smack him and tell him I'd rather be kissing him, but another part of me was fascinated to the point that I couldn't do anything other than this. It was a total physical sensation, inside and out. Sweat poured down my face within one minute, but the soothing view of the distant storms and the golden rays of light coming from now setting sun chained me to my spot. Besides, Cedric was inches away from me, and he was just as sweaty and just as naked.

"I'm going to catch fire," I said in a surprisingly soft tone. The sauna mellowed me.

"You're not," Cedric replied. "You're going to stew."

I tried to snort, but I was so relaxed that even that much seemed to require the sort of effort I couldn't find in me. My chest felt empty, and the pressure from the outside felt immense. My hair was matted. I made the mistake of running my hand through it and discovering that it was drenched. I sighed, but it resembled a moan more than anything else. Even so, when I glanced at Cedric, he was gazing out of the window at the realistic projection of the passing storm. His fair skin was red now, and his golden locks were dark with sweat.

"Doing this reminds me that, sometimes, the best things come at a cost," he said in a huff, stretching his legs out. "I won't pretend that this is nice, but it'll be worth it."

I was always in the mood for a catharsis if that was what he was offering.

My towel loosened, and I stretched my legs out before me. My left foot was a fractional of an inch away from his right. With far more clarity than I possessed, Cedric looked at me. "I meant every word, Tristan."

"I know," I assured him. "I believe you."

He put his left hand into his lap, palm up and open, and I put mine inside it. They were wet, although this sweat felt much thinner and cleaner than if I had run a mile.

Our fingers threaded, and he still gazed at my face. "I'll fight for us." He nodded to emphasize how serious he was. "I'll start by moving someplace I can cover without my family's allowance. I'll be near you. And I won't let them tear us apart."

Holding his hand there in his lap, hearing these sweet promises from his lips, and seeing his bare torso glisten like this made me want him more than I ever wanted anything in my life.

I drew a deep breath, although it still failed to register as breathing. "And I'll fight for us, too," I said. I wasn't yet sure how. I just knew I would give us my best shot. Something foolish, something hopeful and optimistic, blossomed inside of me. It felt as though if we wanted it, it had to happen. It felt like there wasn't a royal family tracking him and the burden of a crown weighing his head down. It felt like I didn't carry the baggage of a past I didn't dare look at wherever I went.

It felt like we were two normal boys, falling in love at our leisurely pace, independent from the rest of the world.

Cedric leaned closer in, and I lifted my head just in time to accept his sweet, sensitive kiss on my lips. Even at a hundred and fifty degrees in the sauna, his kiss made everything else seem cold and lifeless in comparison. It was everything and more, giving me hope and life and will to go on, to crawl up from the darkness where I had been hiding. Maybe letting myself feel something wasn't guaranteed to end in a disaster. Maybe the small good deeds I had done meant that I deserved a bit of happiness after all.

He kissed me harder, his right arm sliding off the bench behind us and wrapping around my shoulders. I didn't care that we were sticky and wet. I didn't care that no breath in the last ten minutes felt like it carried any oxygen. I leaned in as well, kissing him back as hard as he kissed me until our mouths opened and our breaths grew shallow and until our arms tangled and our bare torsos touched.

"God, I want you," I whispered over his lips.

"I'm yours," Cedric said smoothly, kissing me again right away.

My hand pressed against his bare chest, feeling that deep strength of his body, the fine muscles that made up his torso, and his smooth, slick skin until I reached his abdomen and the edge of the towel around his waist. "I *really* fucking want you," I insisted.

He kissed me harder, making me moan against his lips, his hand on my leg, rising slowly over the towel to where my hard cock lifted the soft fabric and formed a thick mound. At the same instant as Cedric's hand covered my dick, his teeth closed around my lower lip and bit me nearly hard enough to draw blood.

I gasped, pressing my hand over his, adding pressure until I throbbed so hard that it gave him a smug smirk.

"You really fucking do," he purred against my lips. His hand dragged lazily over my cock once more, and then he turned it around and took my hand into his. "Let's get out of here." As we stood, the sauna spun around me, but I held on to Cedric. At full height and naked, save for the towel, he was the most beautiful thing I had ever laid my gaze on. He towered above me until I straightened and evened out our heights to the difference of those couple of inches, my gaze dragging from the wooden floor over his legs, the rise in the towel where his cock pressed against it— it gave my heart another reason to leap—and the wiry structure of his body. I craved him. I hungered for him.

Pulling me after him, which was starting to become a

habit I enjoyed, Cedric led us outside, where the room temperature appeared freezing, and the air finally filled my lungs. I wasn't only heated by the sauna, though, but by the passionate kisses he had given me and the unspoken promises of a night I wouldn't soon forget.

Cedric paused by the row of showers. "Now comes the best part," he said.

I raised my eyebrows expectantly.

"Go in, throw away the towel, and press that button there," he said, pointing at the round metal button that I assumed turned on the shower.

"Ah," I said, not letting go of his hand. "Come with me."

Cedric paused for only a heartbeat as if surprised he hadn't thought of that and nodded. He wore his confidence plain on his face as he reached over to the knot on his hip and loosened his towel. It dropped without ceremony, quickly followed by mine, and my heart nearly stopped. He was gorgeous, beautiful without comparison, impossible to describe. His excitement was unmistakable, but so was mine, when I dared to look down between us.

My teeth closed tightly around my lower lip as I gazed at him. His cock was completely stiff, spearing upward and extending well over nine inches, swaying gently under its weight. I didn't care for the comparisons, especially when my partner seemed so pleased. "You're so hot, Tristan," he said, his hand reaching near me, then pulling back.

I might have mouthed a *wow* while staring at his surprising length, but then I reminded myself of an old myth about tall, skinny, golden-haired boys always being hung as hell. I just hadn't believed it until now.

Cedric pulled me into the shower booth and positioned us so close to one another that his cock rested against my upper leg and made my blood simmer. I wanted so much more than that, and I was certain he could see it in my eyes.

He wrapped his left arm around my upper torso and pulled me in, our naked bodies pressing tightly together. "Ready?" he asked.

I hadn't realized I needed to be ready until he asked. But before I replied, he tightened his grip on me and pressed the button that sent a flood of freezing water pouring from the showerhead above us. I heaved a lungful of air and bit down a cry as sharp needles pierced my skin all over my body. The pressure was such that we were completely wet and cold in a moment, and the last of the sweat washed away after less than a minute. It was like standing under a waterfall. It was like taking a plunge into the deep, stormy sea somewhere far, far to the north.

But he held us together, and the chills became bearable. With each passing moment, the energy I'd thought long gone was returning to me twofold. It filled me even more when Cedric kissed me softly, water sliding down our bodies.

And when the shower abruptly stopped pouring down on us, we remained in the booth, kissing, holding one another, and experiencing the true catharsis of what he had promised. Not only was the chilly air of the room seemingly the perfect temperature now, but the cloudiness inside my head was all gone. I knew clearly what I wanted to do, and he knew the same.

Colliding with one another, moving in a slow, passionate circle, we turned around until the glass separating our shower cabin from another was hard against Cedric's back. He gasped as he bumped against it, and I kissed him harder.

Without the cold water distracting me and the heat of the sauna dizzying me, I felt like I had never been so present in the moment, so aware of my body and my surroundings. I was completely here; every touch and scent and sight was clearer, more vibrant, and more intimate than any I'd experienced before.

Cedric's innate strength overpowered me with ease, though I hardly resisted. He turned us around, pushing me against the glass wall of the shower cabin, leaning into me, his leg sliding between my legs until I pressed my thighs tightly around it. Every rub and kiss and sigh seemed the loudest sounds and most thunderous sensations; every touch of my fingertips on his body was like touching glowing coals and discovering that they wouldn't burn me. Only me.

CEDRIC

My hands rose along Tristan's muscled torso. Each of my fingers vibrated with the sensation, my hands permanently frozen in this instant before trembling. I drew a forced calm into myself, controlling us so he wouldn't have to, yet inside, I shuddered and fought hard not to be overpowered by the intensity of my emotions.

Throughout my adult life, I had hooked up with guys

who saw me as a milestone, a story to brag about if they were willing to risk the wrath of the palace lawyers or who meant to use me as a tool for their personal reputation. I'd hardly been a victim of some scheming predators. It had always been a clear agreement. *You use me, I use you.* But this...

A shiver ran down my arms, and I pinned Tristan harder against the glass wall, grabbing his wrists and lifting his arms high above his head, crossing and trapping them there with one hand firmly gripping him while the other lightly feathered the length of his ribcage. He tensed and huffed out that he was ticklish.

I grinned and tickled him.

Tristan wiggled under me and laughed loudly, his biceps swelling with the effort to break free of my hold.

"It's useless," I whispered over his lips. "I have you now."

A moan rose smoothly from his chest and through his perfect, parted lips.

My fingers dragged lightly from his hip to his armpit, the short brush of hair dark and wet, his muscles tensing harder, his body rising in protest until he was on the tips of his toes and still in my hold. The back of his head thumped against the glass as he twisted to escape my gentle touch, teeth clenched and bared, air hissing through them. "Fuck," he croaked. "Fuck, that's so..." But he whimpered instead of finishing that sentence. Hot? Devious? Likely, it was both.

He throbbed hard against my leg when I pressed my lips against his. Kissing him was like drinking fresh water from an oasis after a lifetime of wandering through the desert.

Tristan didn't have a secret agenda. I could smell

scheming plots from a mile away, and there were none here. For once, there was a guy who wanted me for the way I was, not for the things given to me by the freak chance of birth. He wanted me now when I was willing to give up my position and live like everyone else lived.

I wrapped my free arm around his waist, holding his wrists tightly trapped with the other, and pulled him closer. To touch his abs with my abs, to feel his chest under mine, to press my hard cock against his lower abdomen and feel his cock pulse against my leg was like nothing I'd ever felt before. Lust had existed in my endless nights for a long, long time, but this was more than lust. I finally knew what the difference was. This was passion.

"You're such a tease," Tristan whispered tightly, tension building up in him to the point of spilling.

I realized that my muscles were just as tight, my breathing no longer so controlled, my chest trembling more with each passing second. "I don't want this to stop," I said between the kisses. I moved my lips over his defined jawline and to the soft part of his earlobe. "Not ever." My teeth closed around his ear, and Tristan sucked a shallow breath of air.

"It doesn't have to," he exhaled.

I released his wrists, and his arms fell around my shoulders, one hand dragging up the back of my head, fingers running through my wet hair.

His fist closed around the tousled locks and pulled my head back. A vicious look in his eyes had me swooning. "But you *have to* fuck me, Cedric, or I'm gonna die," he said. He was serious, too, his voice never breaking, never bubbling with humor.

For once, I was more than happy to do my duty.

Tristan

For a moment, determination came over his face. A trace of excitement, a spark of mischief, but mostly steel-like firmness and fiery passion. He spun me around effortlessly, overpowering my gym-sculpted muscles, half because I let him and half because he simply could. My torso slammed against the glass, open palms pressing it on either side of my head. I thrust my ass out with the sort of neediness some people would call crude or even slutty, but I didn't care what it made me look like. I did need him, or I would burn into smoke and ash from the sheer heat that ran through me.

Cedric wrapped his arms around my body, his dick sliding between my cheeks and reminding me that this wasn't going to be quick and easy. My heart lurched when he kissed the back of my neck, neared my ear, and asked me if I was sure I wanted this. He didn't have condoms, either, but he was on PrEP, just like me, so I promised that I wanted nothing else. "Just have me," I whispered, barely capable of controlling my lungs at this point.

His arms tightened around my torso, lips pressing hotly against the very top of my back. While he moved his hips and slid his cock between my cheeks gently, almost like it was some erotic dance, his lips moved lower and lower along my spine. He kissed the muscles left and right of my spine, licking me and exhaling heated breath over me until he dropped onto his knees and buried his perfect, handsome face between my cheeks.

Cedric was perfectly aware of his size and all that it entailed. He was aware of his strength, too, using it in controlled ways to benefit our mutual pleasure. Now, his hands held my cheeks firmly, pulling them apart and letting him drag his tongue over my tight hole. Yet, for all those ravenous gestures, he treated me with the kind of dignity worthy of a prince. Though I was just a kitchen helper at the best, Cedric made me feel worthy of the royal treatment.

When his right hand moved over from my cheek to the front, taking my hard, pulsing cock into a firm grip, I pressed the side of my face harder against the cool glass. Moans dragged from me despite my best efforts to remain quiet. I knew it was unlikely, but it was possible that anyone might walk in at this hour, just like we had.

It gave such a strong sense of naughtiness that I shuddered and moaned a little louder.

His tongue worked me gently at first, speeding up and adding pressure as time went on. I clawed at the glass sheet and pushed my hips back, relaxing for him as he stroked my dick and rimmed me to blinding levels of lust. When his finger moved over my hole, my muscles clenched momentarily, but I relaxed them after a wave of anxiety washed away from me. Breathing out, I focused on the sensations, his finger gently rubbing around my hole, the rest of his fist resting against my taint.

I reached around with my hand, resting it on Cedric's head, pressing gently to bring him closer. It wasn't enough.

It could never be enough so long as our bodies were separate.

Cedric's finger slipped inside of me, my toes curling madly, my chest pressing hard against the glass as pleasure splashed through my body.

My hand slipped from his head, although Cedric continued to massage the upper rim of my hole while his finger rested inside of me. And when he pulled his head back, I snatched his wrist and worked my hole with his finger for a few irresistible moments.

Cedric pushed my hand away, working me slower, purring that I was his to toy with, and penetrating me quicker, his thrusts firm and determined. He knew exactly what he was doing, his finger finding the right spot with every other thrust. He intentionally strung the tension, never doing it enough to make me soar but always enough to make me beg for more.

My whimpers and moans stretched out from my throat and nose, legs trembling, chest shuddering, chills passing through my thighs. "Please," I choked. "Oh, fuck, please, Cedric."

He understood without the need for more words. His wrist twisted this way and that, loosening me with his spit for lube until I felt near falling apart. Finally, when he judged that I was ready and slick and relaxed enough for him, Cedric let his finger slide gently out of me.

My heart pounded in my throat. Cedric straightened me gently away from the glass and wrapped his left snugly around my upper body, holding my arms pressed to my torso. With his right hand, he spread saliva over his cock, held himself, and let the tip touch the warmth of my hole.

By instinct, it clenched tight, relaxing after I managed to inhale a breath of air.

Cedric was a gentle lover with enough experience to make me jealous and possessive. He was also perfectly happy to be in charge, and I was glad to let him guide us. The pressure he applied let him sink into me, though never deep enough to hurt me. It was like he felt every tremor in my muscles and let it lead his movements.

Breath hitched in my throat. I used my trapped arms the only way I could and reached back to set my hands on his hips, pulling him closer. "I'm ready," I whispered tightly. "Fuck me, Cedric."

He throbbed hard enough that I felt it clearly inside my body. Softly, smoothly, he let me pull him closer, sure in his footing as I thrust my butt back against him. His length wasn't an issue just yet, but his thickness made my eyes bulge for one seemingly endless moment. Though when it passed, I struggled to remember if it had ever been there at all.

Cedric pulled a little back, then leaned in, setting our lazy pace until my body relaxed completely. His other arm wrapped around me, too, and I was trapped in the best place in the entire galaxy. I could stand like this forever if he held me. I could turn into a sentient stone statue and never move for the rest of my days without a single complaint.

With my body accepting him, embracing him with growing ease, Cedric picked up the firmness and the pace of his movement. Each thrust squeezed a moan from me, and each rubbed lightly against my prostate. His dick explored me deeper, and his searing lips pressed hard against the back of my neck.

As he fucked me with growing intensity, we moved against our wills toward the glass. My head rested against it, and Cedric straightened his torso, arching his back and ramming me with much more than I'd bargained for. Even so, it was only a matter of moments before I could surrender myself fully to be his to use however he wished. And when it happened, my deep and secret stubbornness took hold of my body and compelled me to relax, to open myself to him, until he could slide into me with ease. His lower abdomen smashed my cheeks with wet slaps. His fingers threaded on my stomach, arms hooking me and holding me in place as he fucked my brains out.

I no longer cared that my head was bumping into and rubbing against the grass wall. If I noticed it, it only turned me on harder.

My abs tensed as I forced my body to remain open, to welcome his hard length, to accept him entirely inside myself.

"Fuck, Tristan," Cedric huffed behind me. "You're so fucking hot."

Praise me, I wanted to whimper, slamming my hands against the glass and letting his rough moves pin me harder against the wall between the stalls. "Yeah?" I managed to ask, voice tight and pitch high.

"I love fucking your ass," he grunted, his arms yanking me back on him. The movement made me lose control for a moment, my hole tightening around him, making him growl and lust. "Oh, fuck, that feels so good." Cedric released my abdomen and grabbed my wrists. He pulled my hands all the way back until my arms were stretched as far as they could be.

I knew he was leaning back. I could feel him leaning, his cock angled down to impale me as deep as he could go, though not even close to his full length. He knew how to control himself just perfectly, always keeping me at the edge of what I could take, never more, never less.

My biceps knotted as I pulled my arms forward, and Cedric held them back. Legs spread wide, I leaned in, lifting my ass for him, and moaned over each thrust that filled me with his length. Whenever my body allowed it without risking cutting our fun short and spilling my cum too soon, I let myself tighten my hole around his dick, making him hiss and moan just as if our places had been reversed.

I could feel each throb, each flex of his muscles, and each sweet, wonderful word that left his lips. He showered me with praise, telling me how amazing it felt to be inside me, how good I was at taking his dick, and how warm I felt deep inside.

And when my panting quickened and moans rose higher, Cedric jerked my arms back as if grappling me from behind or holding me from running headfirst into a wall. "Do you want to come, baby?" he purred.

Baby, the word echoed through my skull.

"Fuck, please," I begged. "Make me come."

His fists tightened around my wrists, his dick sliding into me with ease and rubbing against my prostate mercilessly.

"I'm so fucking close," I said, frustration and pleasure warring for dominance inside of me.

Cedric twisted my arms until they rested on my lower back, wrists crossed and locked in his powerful hold. Fucking me all along, he reached over with his right hand

and closed his fist tightly around my dick, letting the thrusts of his hips move my body, making me fuck his fist.

He jerked my arms back, lifting my torso seemingly by the sheer power of his will. My trapped hands felt his steely abdomen, and my upper back rested against his defined chest. With his fist firmly around my dick and our bodies grinding hard, it took me a single heartbeat before I let myself soar over the edge.

Every shred of me tightened. My hole closed hard around him, making him groan into the crook of my neck. My dick pulsed hard, and my abs and chest clenched. My toes curled, and my fingers dug into Cedric's sculpted body. In the next instant, cum sprayed the shower glass in long, white ribbons, leaving me a shuddering, hyperventilating mess.

"Fuck," I breathed out. "Harder. Please, Cedric. Fuck me harder." I needed to feel him finish while I still rode the high of my orgasm. As it thundered through me like the crashing waves of the ocean or the eruption of a volcano, Cedric rammed me just like I asked, filling me deep inside and grunting over the tightness of my hole until he warned me he was close.

He released my arms and held my hips instead, pulling me back on his cock. As his breathing grew quicker and more heated, I begged him to fill me with his cum. It was, as I'd hoped somewhere in some still-active part of my lust-clouded brain, exactly what he needed to hear.

Cedric's cock throbbed hard and long inside of me, hot cum filling me so quickly that I could have sworn I felt it. My hole burned and vibrated, sensitive and bruised. I could feel its wetness and the trickle of Cedric's cum as he pulled out, sliding his cock between my cheeks while I clenched my hole to keep the rest inside. Already, I could feel his absence. Already, I wished we could do it again.

Cedric turned me around, one hand resting on the back of my head, the other sliding over the small of my back until his fingers reached deep down to feel my hole. He rubbed it softly, soothingly, and kissed me deeply for a long, long time. "Such a perfect lover. You're perfect." His whispers covered my lips. His touch healed me. His proximity made me feel like I was falling through the clouds, but I didn't fear because it wasn't the solid ground that awaited at the end of the fall. It was something much nicer, softer, sweeter than I had ever imagined could exist. I was glad to fall for him.

Cedric kissed me for a long time before pulling away and suggesting a quick shower. This time, he regulated the flow of the water so it wasn't just the freezing bucket of ice being dropped on our heads. Instead, the shower was hot, and Cedric was gentle and sensitive. He washed my back and moved his hands softly over my body.

Throughout it all, I had that unique feeling buzzing deep inside of my chest like the bass of a really good beat. It was a feeling that only ever came after good fucking, enriched by all my welling hopes that this was more than just sex.

He still didn't think I was no good. He still didn't think I was a single-use guy. Instead, he kissed my lips while hot water poured down on our heads. He kissed the tip of my nose. He kissed each of my closed eyes in turn. He pulled me in and held me, pressing our bodies together and moving to the rhythm of some slow dance neither of us could hear.

The intensity of emotions that ripped through me choked me. I held them back, but every fiber of me wanted to cry and thank him and tell him how sweet it was to feel worthy of someone's attention and care.

How long had it been since I'd first denied myself these things? I didn't want to think. I knew the date far too well. It lived in the darkest, deepest corners of my soul, and I preferred it hidden from the light of day. No. I wasn't going to say anything. Instead, I kissed him back and made him smile.

"You're the best guy I've had in a long time," I whispered.

It made him chuckle and kiss me harder.

I was, for a moment in time, in heaven. I couldn't see the end of it, and even if I could, I didn't try to.

Much later, I lay in a big, expensive bed in a rich hotel suite, staring at the silk canopy while Cedric slept on my chest. I couldn't sleep. Nothing haunted me. In fact, it felt like when I had been a little boy waiting to go to the pool for the first time that summer. It felt like if only I wanted it hard enough, time would speed up, and tomorrow would come quicker. I couldn't sleep because I was far too happy to be bothered by such trivial needs.

I held him closer. His head rested so softly and peacefully on my broad chest.

We might be something if stars align and fate lets us, I thought. But I knew one thing for certain: I wasn't putting my future only in fate's hands. I would fight for us.

CHAPTER 10
The Dressing Room

CEDRIC

Leaving the bed in the morning was far harder than leaving the room and the hotel behind. It was warm in the bed. Sleeping next to Tristan, our limbs tangled and torsos pressed together, was a new luxury that I had never had before. There wasn't a score of handlers queueing to convince Tristan never to speak of this in public. There was no agenda that would drag me away from him. It was just us, naked and drunk on the passion of the previous night.

Morning light slanted through the window and lit Tristan's face and chest. His muscles were irresistible, so I let my fingers trail the hills and valleys of his body all the way to where a thin sheet covered his crotch. A patch of dark, trimmed hair emerged as my hand moved low, and Tristan let out an amused sigh.

"Good morning," I said. What a wonder! I got to greet a boy in the morning and take it easy for the rest of the day.

Alexander couldn't do anything to stop me. The rules that applied only to the royal family didn't apply to me today.

"Mm," Tristan said, closing his hand over mine and keeping them both on the lower part of his abdomen. "Did we fall asleep naked?"

"House rules," I said.

He chuckled and blinked himself awake. When he glanced at me, his hazel eyes were like melting chocolate and a low-burning campfire deep in the wilderness. "What am I gonna do with you?"

My eyebrows wiggled. "You'll wait for me until I move out of here," I said lightly, rolling onto my stomach. The sheet covered the lower part of my body, but it was so thin that there was no pretending I hadn't woken up hard. No wonder since I'd slept next to the sexiest guy on the planet.

"Your Highness is very sure about that," he teased.

"I am," I replied simply. "Because after, we're going on a date."

"Is that so?" Tristan asked, his voice bubbly with humor.

I nodded. "I want to do normal dates. All the normal dates we can think of."

He chuckled softly and nodded, his eyes turning a little sad. "We can do that, Cedric."

My chest rose with a lungful of air. It carried the soft, breezy scent of Tristan's body and an underlying note of sex that I couldn't describe beyond that. It was like having to describe the scent of a strawberry to an alien. Sweet, delicious, rich and ripe and irresistible.

"I can show you what it's like to be a regular old person," Tristan said.

"I hardly believe that," I laughed. "You're very special, Tristan."

He snorted, then turned to me and pressed his lips against my cheek. "Time's running out," he said after.

I wanted to beg for five more minutes. I wanted to be lazy with him in bed for a whole day. I wanted us to eat snacks and fuck and drink orange juice and shower together. But it wasn't meant to be. Not today, at least.

Still, watching Tristan get out of the bed, his upper back broad, his waist narrow, his ass perfectly sculpted to make my heart stumble at every sight of it, and his legs muscled and strong, made the whole thing worth it.

He was still naked when he returned from the bathroom, his face wet, his breath minty, and his hair fixed in that effortless way he sported. I followed his example and dragged myself out of the bed, getting a mischievous slap on my ass as I passed him.

I wasn't ready to start the day. I wasn't ready to give up the world in which only Tristan and I existed. But then, I never would be.

Lady Vivien Woodcock's private apartment above Neon Nights was a spacious place with plenty of rooms in different styles. If I needed any more proof that the queen had an expert taste and a sharp eye for design, this would have sufficed.

Wigless, Mama Viv had already painted her face in bright colors to match a vibrant New York City morning. She wore a red silk robe, and her natural, dark brown hair was short and trapped flat under a tight hairnet. "Darling Cedric," she greeted me when she opened the front door and revealed a brightly lit hallway with hardwood floors and art deco furniture. "Come in, come in."

"Thanks for seeing me so early, Mama Viv," I said. "I hope I'm not disturbing your morning."

"Anything for my boys," she said, shutting the front door behind me. "In here, darling." She led the way down the hallway and into the second room on the left. It was her dressing room with a large dressing table and several mirrors, from a square one above the table to a standing mirror in the corner and one oval mirror mounted onto the wall. A fancy accordion screen separated the changing section from the sitting area. Mama Viv sat down in her big chair before the square mirror and the makeup table. She offered me coffee, which I didn't want, then asked me what she could do for me.

Is everyone here so willing to simply do things for others? But I didn't ask that. Instead, I committed that piece of information to my memory. I could be like them.

"That's just it," I said. "I was wondering if there's anything I could do for you."

Mama Viv methodically dabbed something on her face, although I saw no difference. It was probably what separated an amateur from a professional. I would have skipped the steps that had seemingly no results. "Ah, so you are no longer simply passing by?" she asked.

I lowered myself into a dark green chair with elaborate wooden legs and a tall, straight backrest, knees spread wide and arms hanging between them. "I hope to stick around."

Mama Viv nodded once, firmly. "I'm glad to hear it,

Cedric, darling." She let the silence hang between us for a little while. "Things are going well, I take it."

Aside from running out of cash, they definitely were. I didn't get to say a word, though, because a smile stretched my lips, and Mama Viv looked at me just then, finding her answer painted clearly on my face.

She smiled in return, although not as broadly. I sensed some reservation, but the words that followed dispelled that. "I can offer you a job, darling. A proper one. You're a hard worker and a quick learner. That's what matters in our line of work. But I don't see you staying in that place for long."

I wanted to cut in and promise that I could do it for however long it was necessary.

"No, no, darling. Don't take it the wrong way. It's clear that we're not cut from the same fabric, but that's not a bad thing. You're bright, you're well-mannered, you have a promising future, whatever you choose," Mama Viv assured me. "You're hardly the first runaway I've taken in, and I never ask what it is that's chasing you, my dear."

Something tugged my heart down into my stomach.

"Let's not pretend," Mama Viv said gently. "You're not who you say you are, but I am well experienced in wearing masks, darling. I won't ask what's underneath yours, so long as it doesn't affect Tristan."

My eyebrows shot up. "It won't," I hurried to say.

"Ah." Mama Viv had gotten the confirmation she needed, and I had to admire how efficiently she had done this. With a matter-of-fact posture, Mama Viv wiped her fingers delicately on a handkerchief on the makeup table, put them in her lap, and turned to face me a little straighter.

"Darling, if it's steady work you need, you have it. If you're ready to leave the lavish lifestyle that's above your *current* means, I have a spare room for you. And if it's Tristan's heart you mean to toy with, you have an army to hunt you down and rip you apart should that boy get hurt. Do we understand each other?" The politest of smiles fit for the Great Dining Hall of the Royal Palace of Verdumont touched Lady Vivien Woodcock's lips.

I couldn't hold back the rising laugh and the face-splitting grin if I tried. "I will never hurt him, Mama Viv."

The queen nodded slowly, a touch of sadness shining in her clear, bright eyes. "Very well," she said softly. "You won't hurt him intentionally, but Tristan is...*fragile* is not the word I'm looking for. He's stronger than most people, given the circumstances, but even the strongest people can break and shatter."

"Um...circumstances?" I asked.

"Are you sure you wouldn't like some coffee? I've got a near full pot of it," Mama Viv said joyfully, but I could see it was fake.

"I'm good," I said carefully.

She sighed. "Cedric, this is something Tristan won't tell you, and I may be overstepping more than I'll be forgiven for." She hesitated. "Do you know that Tristan has a standing job offer downstairs?"

I shook my head. "I don't need to know everything about him to feel what I feel," I explained.

"This, you do," Mama Viv said. "Because not knowing it risks Tristan's well-being, which in turn puts your tush on the line should you make an error."

I gulped.

Mama Viv wasn't kidding. Her gentle voice deepened with sincerity. "Tristan won't take the job because he doesn't think he deserves it. Frankly, Tristan won't take anything freely given to him because he doesn't think he's worth your trouble. If you managed to convince him, even for an hour on the dance floor, that he deserved the attention, it's the first time I've seen it." She paused, looking at her hands in her lap.

"Mama Viv, I care about him a great deal," I said carefully.

"As you should," the queen agreed. "He is precious." It tugged the corners of my lips into a smile. He was. "But he has also been hurt, darling. By fate and by himself more than anything else. You see, Tristan is a child of a fairly wealthy couple from upstate New York, but that isn't something he would have told you. And God forgive me for betraying that sweet man to you, but I would rather lose a friend than see him break and hurt." She didn't let me cut in this time, hurrying to tell me everything. "It happened when Tristan was twelve years old. December, I believe, and nearing Christmas. Tristan's father was driving all four of them. He, Tristan's mother, Tris, and Jen, his ten-year-old sister, were returning from a visit to Tristan's grandparents when a truck driver fell asleep at the wheel for just long enough to lean into their lane. Tristan's father tried to avoid the truck, but the road was slippery, and he lost control of the wheel. They drove off the road." Mama Viv's voice trembled a little. "They plunged into the lake, and the car filled with freezing water quickly. Tristan's parents tried to get the children out, but only Tristan made it. You see, Jen died that night. And Tristan..." She shook her head slowly.

"Part of him died with her, my dear. And the part that lived on never really left the shadow." Mama Viv leaned in a little closer.

A rift went right through my heart, splitting it in half. My poor baby Tristan.

"Darling, you need to be gentle with Tristan," she said. "He won't believe your kindness or your feelings. He doesn't believe anyone's. It's hard to make him see he's worth your time and attention on the best of days and impossible on not-so-good days."

It all made sense now. The selflessness, the generosity, the readiness to sacrifice himself for anyone's benefit. He was grief-torn and scarred. A poor little boy who survived and couldn't fathom that he might have been worth saving. "What can I do?" I asked.

"Nothing," Mama Viv said softly. "Don't *do* anything. Just be careful with Tristan because it takes him time to accept that he's worth your effort." Mama Viv gave the smallest gasp. "And, darling, I would appreciate it if you didn't tell Tristan about this unless you truly have to. It's hard to earn his trust, especially if he gets it into his head that you're doing it out of pity. That boy can be as stubborn as a mule." She said the last past so lovingly that it sent a shudder through my chest. "And I care for him very much. I wouldn't want him to hate me for this."

I swallowed and nodded. "Thank you for telling me, Mama Viv," I said. After a moment of processing my thoughts, I smiled a little. "I'd never want to hurt him, you know. He's...very dear to me."

"So I have suspected," Mama Viv said. "I'll have the room waiting for you when you're ready to move in. You'll have to ask Bradley about the bar shift or, if you'd prefer it, Millie for the kitchen."

I nodded, thanked Mama Viv, and hesitated before leaving. Mama Viv was already turning back to the mirror when I dared myself to say what was in my heart. "I think he's lucky to have you," I said. "They—we—all are."

Mama Viv waved her hand nonchalantly. "Darling, I believe Tristan may be lucky to have *you*. And, if I'm not wrong—which I so rarely am in any area of life that it would come nearly as a pleasant surprise—you may be just as lucky to have him show you the way."

I nodded. It was something to think about, but I wouldn't discuss it further with Mama Viv. My head was spinning with information, and my heart was splitting into tiny shards, each sharp and cutting through my soul.

I left Mama Viv to get ready for the day, then went downstairs, through a hallway, and into the bar. Roman was helping open the bar while Bradley refilled the fridge.

"'Sup," Roman said.

I greeted him and slowed down as he flipped a chair over and set it by the table. "Need help?"

"We can handle this," Roman said, but he was no longer doing it. Instead, he looked at me, nearly bristled, and thrust his chin out. "Tristan was with you last night, huh?"

For the briefest of moments, I worried about what I had gotten into. Roman, nicely built, although shorter than me by almost an entire head, with his hair cropped short and giving signs of curling, and with his eyes so full of fire, was undoubtedly attractive. My heart firmly belonged to Tristan, but I wasn't stupid. And I could see Roman and

Tristan sharing intimate moments at some point in their lives if that was what had happened.

For this one moment, I expected Roman to scare me away jealously or threaten me to leave Tristan behind.

But that moment passed when Roman's eyes softened. "I like you, Cedric," he said.

I cocked a corner of my lips.

Roman spoke like it pained him to say these things, but he plowed through. "I like you, but if you wrong him, I'm gonna..."

I lifted my hand. "I got the warning already, Rome," I said, choosing to call him the same that everyone else around here did. He seemed relieved that I had stopped him. "I wouldn't dream of it. I know he has people watching out for him. And now I'm just one more to watch his back."

My significant look locked on Rome's eyes. We gazed at one another for a few moments before he relaxed. There was almost an air of appreciation that he didn't need to pile up threats. He knew me as a hardworking helper. There was a sort of respect between us. "Good man," Roman said with a small smile.

I winked and put a hand on his shoulder. Moving from the bar, I could almost plot out my life. I could see myself here early in the morning—or not so early, like today, when the bar opened late—doing these things with the people I respected and who measured me on what I did and not who my ancestors were. I could see myself walking across the street to take Tristan's hand so we could spend a day together.

Such a simple life, Alexander's voice sneered at me. But

he was wrong. There was beauty in this simplicity, but it was more than that. Underneath all this was a world of opportunities, an endless well of hope, and never-ending optimism. I could drink it until my dying breath. I could bathe in it with the one person who was capable of making my heart lift and my mind spin.

I stepped outside and watched the building across the street. He would be ready by now. And I would tell him that it was all sorted out. I was staying in Hudson Burrow until we figured out how to make it permanent. *Until I figure out how to inform my family*. It would be a scandal.

My heart sank a little. I'd lifted such battlements between myself and the reality, but they were strong. I wouldn't take them down just yet. I wanted to give this thing a try more than I wanted anything in the world. Just for once, I didn't want to be a prince with duties. I wanted to be selfishly in love and to have something that was mine and nobody else's.

The weight of a gaze made me turn my head to my right. At the end of the street, moving away from me, was a slender woman with a tight, angry ponytail, disappearing around the corner.

No, I told myself. I was just paranoid. It was all this guilt that I was keeping down and hiding from myself. The nasty feeling of letting down my parents, my siblings, my people. It made me think there were agents out to get me. But the likely truth of the matter was that Alexander expected me to return when I was ready.

Never, I said silently. *I'm not returning to that life. They will all see me only when I am ready to resign my duties.*

Inhaling deeply, I crossed the street and forgot all about

guilt and agents and distant kingdoms. Tristan was downstairs, in front of his building, leaning against the brick wall with his hands tucked into his tight denim pants and a sleeveless shirt tucked into the pants, revealing his sculpted arms and the low, sexy neckline.

My heart jittered as I neared him, my arms stretching out to him, taking his hands as soon as he offered them. I pulled him in, made our bodies touch, and kissed him deeply out in the open.

"Missed me?" he asked.

"Desperately," I said without telling a lie, though it had been barely an hour. "Now, you have a promise to keep."

"I won't let you down," Tristan said.

Today was going to be a good day.

CHAPTER 11
To Worship and Honor

TRISTAN

AN AFTERNOON PICNIC AT CENTRAL PARK THAT turned into hours of cloud-gazing, kissing, and hand-holding had only been the first of our many dates. To show Cedric what it was to be an invisible old nobody, I took him to a brewery one evening, enjoying the view of the Hudson River flowing by and tasting the various craft beers Mad Hare offered. We watched the stars and walked the streets. We went to underground movie screenings and watched old horror films neither of us expected to like nearly as much as we did. We ate junk food in a parking lot one evening and made love all night long in my bedroom, with Cedric holding his underwear against my lips to stop me from making a sound. We held hands out in the open until they got slick with sweat, and we kept holding them anyway.

Mama Viv needed me to help Millie with the menu for Lady Vivien's 1950s TV Dinner Extravaganza. Cedric worked his ass off that night, helping behind the bar as much as he was helping in the kitchen, yet he kissed me nearly every time he passed through. There was a kindness and softness in the way he looked at me that hadn't been there before the night at the Henriette Hotel.

The TV Dinner Extravaganza had an outrageously delightful lineup of queens depicting the 1950s life, from perfect little housewives to the ruthless survivors of a nuclear apocalypse, their gas masks and bodies seamlessly smoothed with paint that it appeared as if the masks were a part of their heads. It was wild fun, just like every event Mama Viv had ever put together.

Life was good.

Cedric was beautiful, and the moments we stole were priceless. It was almost easy to forget that things were never certain in life, least of all when his time was running out. A decision had to be made, and people had to be told. There would be diplomatic consequences, and there would be paparazzi coverages. I couldn't even imagine the perfect storm that Cedric's announcement was going to create.

But he picked me. Every night, he picked me over everyone else, and he promised he always would.

Somewhere deep within the rotten blackness of the core of my soul, I was beginning to believe him. I was starting to see a bit of light, a bit of life, a bit of recovery where only devastation had existed for over a decade.

Cedric's hand wrapped around mine and pulled my thoughts from wandering. "The Greek and Roman art galleries are a real gem," he said, leading me into a vast area of sculptures, vases, coins, tools, and pieces of walls with frescos or mosaics still on them.

I smiled at him, letting him guide us through the

various galleries. The mission was to find as many homages to Antinous as we could, he explained.

"Um, silly question, but who's Antinous?" I asked, frowning.

"Not silly," Cedric said gently.

"I feel like I should know this," I pointed out.

He laughed lightly. "Never be ashamed of the things you don't know. Only be ashamed of never being wrong." And when I laughed, he led me to Leon Levy and Shelby White Court and galleries, where statues and busts spent their eternity in care and with plenty of visitors to keep them company.

The gallery was rather empty on Wednesday afternoon. Light slanted at an angle from the glass dome, its intensity low enough that the orange lamps were lit throughout the gallery.

One, in particular, was interesting to Cedric, who ignored the perfectly polished, well-kept statues of gods and emperors, of general and philosophers, in order to show me a chipped and chiseled bust of a young man, the marble yellowed and his nose missing, he still had the features of timeless beauty. "This is Antinous. Isn't he beautiful?"

Cedric's eyes were wide with wonder, and the most ridiculous sliver of jealousy passed through me. I envied a piece of marble. The sensation passed immediately, and I tightened my hand around Cedric's. "Do we know anything about him?"

"We don't know much until he appeared in Emperor Hadrian's life," Cedric said. I was giddy with curiosity. This mattered to him, and he mattered to me. "Antinous was born on November 27, and the year was 110. We share a birthday, although I'm of a more recent vintage. He only lived until he was close to twenty, but his image survives to this day. He was raised in Bithynia, today's Turkey, and he met Hadrian when he was twelve."

I sucked a breath through my teeth.

Cedric chuckled. "It's not like that. Hadrian sent Antinous to Rome to be educated and become his page. He invested in the young man and protected him. So when Antinous was seventeen, perhaps eighteen, the friendship turned into something more. He was Hadrian's favorite, which was recorded in 128. I suppose, in modern terms, we'd call him Hadrian's favorite person." Cedric glanced at me with a touch of humor on his lips. "Hadrian was obsessed with the young man so much that he took Antinous on his tour of the Roman Empire. They traveled together until, in October of 130, the couple attended a festival in Egypt when Antinous perished. We don't know for sure, but from what's recorded, it's likely that it was a freak accident that took him. We do know, however, that the contemporaries wrote of Hadrian's reaction. To cite one, 'he wept like a woman.' The local priesthood in Egypt was the first to identify Antinous with Osiris. Others followed, and the young man was deified. Although we don't know much of Antinous' life, we know what he looked like. And we know it because Hadrian did everything to immortalize Antinous. He built a city on the Middle Nile, calling it Antinoöpolis. He commissioned Antinous' likeness to be made into statues and busts. Religions throughout the Empire created cults of Antinous. To some, he was a divine hero. To others, he was the conqueror of death. His name was inscribed on coffins, and his story reached every corner of the Roman domain. Antinoöpolis was a bastion of Greek culture in the region of the Middle Nile, and there were at least twenty-eight temples built to honor the young man. Today, we can find his face on the statues of Dionysus, Hermes, Osiris, the Celtic sun god Belenos, and the divine hero Aristaeus, and many more."

Chills ran down my arms and spine. My vision blurred as I gazed at this chipped bust that only depicted three-quarters of a face, the rest missing. I hadn't known about him, although he had existed for two thousand years.

Cedric turned to me, a twinkle in his eyes from where the tears caught the last of the daylight piercing the dome. "Can you imagine such a love?" he asked, his voice fiery and passionate. "Thirty cities issued coins with Antinous' face, and at least nine cities held games in his honor, including both athletic and artistic components." He smiled. "Hadrian loved him so much and lost him so young. And there's no doubt about that. It's estimated there were over two thousand sculptures created in the years following Antinous' death. Only a little over a hundred survive to this day. Of forty-odd statues found in Italy, half were kept in Hadrian's home."

I shook my head. I could hardly imagine anyone being loved so much.

Cedric shrugged. "I think it's incredible. Two thousand years and we still know who he was because someone loved him enough to make him into a god. We think of the Roman Empire either as this beacon of culture in a barbaric world as barbarians themselves, but people are people. They love, they lose, they hurt, then feel joy and sorrow and pain like everyone that came before them and everyone that followed."

I simply watched him as he spoke, his gaze moving from my face to the dome above us, then taking the entire room before returning to my eyes. "It's easy to be remembered when you're an emperor's favorite," I said.

"You know, I don't think being an emperor makes someone able to love harder than everyone else," Cedric said simply. "Imagine, then, how many people loved just as hard, but we know nothing about it." He nodded. "But yes, not everyone can go around building temples and issuing coins."

I chuckled. "What happened to the temples? The sculptures?"

"What happened?" he mused.

"You said there were two thousand statues and busts."

Cedric shook his head sadly. "Christians happened. They first denounced Antinous with everything else that was pagan and homosexual. Then, they banned all of pagan imagery around the end of the fourth century. The cult was silent until fairly recently."

I frowned. "What do you mean?"

"Oh, the neo-pagan movement re-sacralized Antinous, and he's a gay icon." The cheeky smile on Cedric's lips filled me with such inexplicable hope as though something terrible had been prevented and there was still a chance for good things to prevail.

I put my hands on Cedric's chest and gazed into his eyes. "You're such a romantic."

"I'm a scandalous pagan, Tris," Cedric said with a laugh. He leaned in and pressed his lips softly against mine.

It sparked tingles in my toes when he kissed me. It awakened the butterflies in my stomach. It made me lighter than a feather and clearer than a drop of water from a cold forest brook. And when he pulled back, still gazing into my eyes, I blinked. "You're not scandalous to me."

The smile on his lips was so pure and fiery that I wished to become one of the statues in this room and remain with him forever.

"This one is special to me," he said, gesturing at the bust with his head. "There were queer gods in Hellenic mythology for centuries before Antinous. Apollo, Hermes, Eros. There are Achilles and Patroclus, of course, and some stories about Hercules. Zeus, Ganymede, Hyacinthus, you name them. But Antinous was a mortal man who had never been a great hero or an emperor. People like him simply weren't deified, and it was a scandal at the time." He took my hand and began leading us out of the gallery, throwing one last glance at the bust.

"That's really amazing," I said. "I didn't know any of this." Before this evening, it had only been another bust in a room I'd visited once in my life. I wondered if each had a story as large as his was.

Cedric rolled his shoulders. "I'd like to honor him."

My heart leaped. "How do we do that?"

He grinned at the fact I included myself so gladly. "I'm happy you asked."

Cedric hurried out of the museum, one hand holding mine like he was never going to let go, the other holding the canvas bag that hung from one of his shoulders. We walked fast around the museum, and Cedric found us a path through Central Park that led us straight to Arthur Ross Pinetum, less than ten minutes away.

"I was hoping to convert you," he said mischievously. "Of course, I'm not going to sacrifice you under the full Moon, just in case you were wondering. This is more of a thing I like to do for the purpose of reflection. Antinous was athletic and artistic, according to some rumors, and we know he was educated in Rome, so he's a god of light of sorts. Some modern pagan groups call him a god of homosexuality, but I disagree with that."

I was smitten even without Cedric going on about all these incredible things, but I listened happily. We reached the Pinetum and sat down on a bench just as the last of the daylight set the sky and the wispy clouds on fire.

"To me," Cedric continued, "he's much more than that. Especially because there are many better-known gay gods if you like. I generally don't think of any ancient god as something singular. They weren't seen that way then; they shouldn't be so simplified today."

"Sorry, but..." I winced. He was very much into this, and I needed a moment to catch up. "Do you actually believe he's a god?"

Cedric threw his arm around my shoulders and gazed at the pines before us. "It's unknown if even Hadrian believed it," he said softly. "But that's not important. Who knows what comes after? Who knows if there's anything out there in the universe? We're just one species from a planet brimming with life, and we happen to be a species that exists on stories. Everything's a story, Tristan. History, religion, and nationality, they're all stories we collectively agree on. Or disagree, so we go to war over our differing stories. But stories have lessons, and people need to learn so long as they live. And the story of Hadrian and Antinous is one I like, so I sit down and spare them a thought, and I drink a bit of red wine or read a poem, and that's a way to honor him."

"Red wine? Tell me more," I said flirtatiously.

Cedric smirked. "I knew that would get you interested. You could also go for a swim or, if you're particularly devoted, fight for gay rights, equality of all people, and for peacekeeping."

"Sounds like a lot of work," I said.

Cedric pulled his canvas bag open and produced a bottle of red wine and a corkscrew. "That's why we're starting with something easy." As he opened the bottle, he spoke about his childhood fascination with Greek and Roman religions, as well as most of the world's ancient religions. To Cedric, these things weren't literal, and they had never been particularly organized.

While it might have passed as an eccentric hobby that would surprise nobody coming from a willful prince—a fact I still struggled to wrap my mind around—it was much more intimate, according to Cedric's words.

His eclectic paganism was not an organized thing with a hierarchy or a dogma. There were no rules to follow, but his intuition dictated which gods had a place in his life.

"It's like collecting art," he said. The fact that he was speaking to someone who couldn't even fathom the idea of collecting stamps with how little he owned in life, let alone art, flew way over his head. "It enriches you, the individual. And it presents you to others in a way. So you ask yourself, 'What are the things that matter to me?' And if you're a lover of beauty and peace and compassion, like you are, then you do some little things that affirm those beliefs."

"Like public drinking," I teased.

Cedric laughed aloud and pulled the cork out of the bottle. "Better be quick." He tipped the bottle, pulled a long sip, swallowed, and handed me the wine. I mimicked him and hurried to return the bottle to his bag. Cedric stoppered it with the cork again and leaned back, his arm returning to my shoulders.

I rested my head on his shoulder, and my arm pressed against the side of his torso. "You're wonderful."

"Nah," he breathed. "You are."

My heart filled with so many feelings that I couldn't count them all. They weren't all bright and welcome. Some, like this creeping dread that I tried to keep at bay, threatened to taint the beauty. Fears unfounded and founded, sorrows over the things that hadn't even happened yet, that might never happen, clawed at my heart. Putting a hand on Cedric's chest, I reconnected with the wonderful warmth he sparked in me.

If only time could slow down. If only life weren't as complicated as it was.

I inhaled a deep breath of air and closed my eyes. Antinous roamed through my mind, and I wondered what it must have felt like to be loved so much by someone as powerful as Hadrian. And I wondered if I didn't know the feeling already.

CHAPTER 12

The Phonecall

CEDRIC

PASSING UP THE CHRISTOPHER STREET FROM Marsha Johnson Memorial Fountain, I noticed the Rashid store where Mama Viv sourced her fresh produce. It was in a two-story building, with the ground floor built for the business and the upper floor remaining residential. The faded red awning extended to cast shade across the sidewalk, protecting the few crates of produce still in front. Windows of the shop revealed that the store offered much more than fruits and vegetables. It was cluttered with shelves and aisles, freezers and refrigerators.

The young man sweeping the sidewalk wore a black apron over a white T-shirt and olive cargo pants. His back was turned to me as he worked, but I recognized the mop of black curls instantly. "Hi, Zain," I said, clearing my throat. Passing here had been a fortunate accident, sparking a brilliant idea for my date with Tristan.

My boyfriend was becoming very fond of Apollo, so I

figured we might burn some incense and read a few poems on the seventh. September had rolled in already, but it felt like I had spent a lifetime in Hudson Burrow.

"Cedric," Zain said. "Hullo." He was a soft-spoken young man with big, brown eyes and caramel skin of his mixed heritage. Mama Viv, who knew everyone's story in Hudson Burrow, had told me about Zain's parents; his father, a Lebanese man named Amar, had immigrated some thirty years ago, setting up the shop by himself and setting the foundations for a better life. After meeting a Mexican American woman in the city, the two got married. Mama Viv said she had never seen a more harmonious couple in her life. "Look at Rafael and Luke, darling," she had compared. "They are two lovebirds that fought like hell for one another, but even they disagree more than the Rashids."

"How are you?" I asked Zain, who had directed his full attention to me.

"Sweeping," he said with a shrug. His shoulders were broad, I realized, although the T-shirt was a size too big to show it off. "And you?"

"I'm great. I could use your help, actually," I said. "Do you have any sort of incense I could buy?"

"Oh, sure," he said and rested the broom against the wall. "Come in."

We entered the shop, triggering the bell above the door, and I greeted the person behind the cash register. He was a slender man of middle years with a thick, black mustache and black hair. He had a kindly look in his eyes, although his features struck me as stern just as much.

"I was hoping to find some for a date," I said cheekily to Zain.

"And how is your friend?" Zain asked as he slipped between the aisles.

A frown touched my eyebrows. "We're b..."

"I know," Zain interrupted lightly. "Is he okay?"

I held a breath for a moment, processing his words and his hopeful, innocent smile. "He's perfect," I assured Zain. "We wish you'd stay for drinks sometimes."

Zain nodded jerkily as he paused before a shelf containing various specialty items. There were natural home fragrances, burners, incense holders, essential oils, and trinkets of many different shapes and sizes. I could have browsed through this for the rest of the day.

"I have to help around," Zain explained. "Maybe some other time."

My gaze moved over the incense. "If you ever have free time, consider this an open invitation to hang out with us."

"I know where to find you," Zain said with slightly wider eyes, dark and warm, perfect white teeth sinking into his lower lip. "Help yourself," he said hurriedly and smoothed his features before pulling away from the aisle.

I picked out a few things I would need. Apollo was a fairly big deal for gay men, almost like a patron of homosexuals in the present day. I liked him. I liked feeling a sort of connection to the idea of Apollo. It was something that Tristan was beginning to understand; these gods weren't actually watching over us, and they didn't need to. They were stories, as man-made as any deity in my eyes, but they represented certain qualities, embodied traits and concepts and aspirations. Apollo protected athletes and artists, poets and painters and sculptors, and he was the symbol of light and all that was good in the world. Who could dislike that?

Leaving Rashid's, I waved goodbye to Zain. The incense, burner, and a scented candle, just for good measure, were packed in a paper bag. As I stepped around the corner of Christopher Street and Washington Street, where Neon Nights and Tristan's apartment were facing one another, I stopped dead in my tracks.

Wearing a thin summer blouse and a pair of jeans, the woman with a tight ponytail and a nondescript face hardened by tough training stood still as if unsure where to go. Her gaze landed on me. Unlike every time in the last three or four weeks, she did not slip away.

I grabbed the dead phone from my pocket and pressed the ON button with such angry force that I could have shattered the device into dust. It vibrated in my hand as I forced my feet to carry me closer to the woman. She didn't run. She stood still, acting neither surprised nor interested.

"Hey," I said.

She stared at me.

My thumb slipped over the screen, opening the camera app, and she noticed it. Taking a step as if to turn away from me, I lifted my phone and snapped a shot of her. "Hey, you! Hey!" I photographed her as she turned around and hurried down the street.

A moment later, the floodgates broke, and the queue of undelivered messages and calls set my phone on fire. It vibrated with messages from my valet, my security contacts, my younger siblings, the official representatives from the palace, and, of course, Alexander himself.

I didn't read a single line of text he had sent. Instead, I attached the image of the stalker and sent it to my brother.

As the white heat of rage cleared from my burning face and faded vision, hollowness opened in the pit of my stomach. *Fuck*. But it was too late to consider all the options. It was too late to do anything else.

My phone vibrated, and Alexander's private number flashed on my screen.

My throat tightened. The hollowness in my stomach was filling quickly, and it felt as if I'd swallowed a rock. My guts twisted, my blood chilled, and hairs rose along the back of my neck.

I knew I couldn't argue with my brother. There were no views of the world that we shared. Proving anything to him had always been impossible, so I postponed it. I put it off. I waited for some other time when I would be ready for this, as if it could ever end any other way.

I wish I had more time, I thought before I pressed the green button on my screen and lifted the phone to my ear.

"Cedric. You live," Alexander said calmly. He was so stiff that even his mouth barely moved.

"Like you don't know that already," I said, my voice tight with anger and edged with fear. I hated myself for revealing the latter.

Alexander was quiet for a short time. "Are you ready to return?" Before I could answer, almost as if he could hear me frowning, Alexander continued. "You've had your adventure. It's time to come home."

"Don't..." I choked up and hissed through clenched teeth. "Don't talk to me like this."

"How am I speaking to you, Cedric?" he asked.

"As if I were a child," I accused.

Alexander let a beat pass, allowing me to understand the trap I had entered. "If you wish to be spoken to as an adult, then act like one."

"I wish you'd leave me alone," I said.

Alexander sighed. "Why are you so hostile, Cedric? Do you not understand that I have placed security near you for your own good? However much you wish to pretend otherwise, you are not like everyone else."

"Oh, is that so? I've been doing just fine," I lied.

"Scraping pots and scrubbing floors? It is almost as if you wish to create a scandal. You always were eccentric." Alexander's tone hardly changed from its flat, deliberate way of speaking. "This is not the first time you ran away, and I highly doubt it will be the last. Unless you force my hand, brother. In such case, I will have no options but to assure you remain here."

I barked out a bitter laugh. "You'd imprison me?"

"Life at the palace can hardly be equated with imprisonment, Cedric. You play out your fantasies in some run-down bar, but you know so little of the way the world works," he accused. "It's time to come back before there are consequences."

"Is that a threat?" I asked.

"Nothing of the sort," Alexander said flatly. "You are to be engaged, Cedric, but not even the Marquis de Beaumont will wait much longer. Any disasters that come from this will be entirely of your own doing."

I snapped my mouth shut and let a wave of anger thunder through me. I had been rash enough. It was time to be smart, even if the mention of that ridiculous engagement felt like someone prodding an open wound with a muddy stick. "If you know where I live and what I do, then you know about him."

"He is irrelevant," Alexander said. There was no insult in his tone and none in his mind. He simply spoke a fact the way he saw it.

"He is *not* irrelevant," I shouted. "Don't you dare say that again."

Alexander held his tongue for a moment or two. "Your little affair will not affect our plans negatively."

Same shit, I thought but held back the words. "If you think you're convincing me of anything, you will make a poor diplomat."

"Brother, you misunderstand the nature of this conversation," Alexander replied coolly. "I am not trying to convince you of anything. As far as everyone is concerned, there is nothing more to discuss. This is plain courtesy that I am informing you of what comes next. If you wish, you may pretend you have a freedom of choice."

I laughed and shook my head. "You are rich. Do you know that? I don't have to do anything you tell me."

Alexander waited. It was a particularly potent trick he had. Whenever he didn't speak immediately, he made me question the things I had said. Did I really not have to do anything I was told?

Sighing, my brother stopped me from thinking too deeply about my freedoms. "If you wish to be that way, let me make some things clear. Your latest infatuation is irrelevant to the agreements we have in place. The Marchioness de Beaumont is unlikely to protest your extramarital activities, considering they bring nothing but their name and her good image into this relationship. We need an engagement, but Élodie needs the marriage to secure her family's position."

"Madeleine must be so happy," I squeezed through clenched teeth.

"It will surprise you, Cedric," Alexander said. "I am not as heartless as you imagine, but that is beside the point."

"Have you ever loved anyone other than your duty?" I snapped. The fact that I was getting nowhere in this conversation cornered me and made me desperate.

"What does it matter if I love or not?" Alexander asked, genuinely exasperated. "If you must know, I love Madeleine, but I fail to see how that is relevant."

"Because it just is," I practically shouted.

"Mm." Alexander dismissed me so lightly. "Very well. You think you are in love. And what of him?"

"What do you mean?" I asked. Something clenched my heart and tightened my chest. Some ominous feeling shadowed my soul. He wouldn't hurt Tristan. Even if he was as evil as that—which he wasn't, not like that—he wouldn't risk the outrage.

"Do you really think a common chef has a place in our world?" Alexander asked. It filled me with rage, but he spoke calmly and without a pause. "You might be willing to throw away your royal duties for this...Tristan, but what about his future? Think about it. Once the media gets wind of your affair, Tristan will become the target of endless scrutiny. Every mistake he's ever made, every private detail of his life will be dragged into the spotlight. His career will be over before it even begins. No restaurant will hire him; no culinary school will accept him. He will be hounded by paparazzi and ridiculed by the public, and his dreams will be shattered all because of you. Do you want to ruin the life of the man you claim to be in love with? Do you want his name to be synonymous with scandal and disgrace? End it now, Cedric, before it's too late. Protect him by letting him go."

"That wouldn't happen," I whispered, the horror unfolding clearly before my eyes. "Do you think people here care about us? They don't even know we exist."

"Imagine if they found out," Alexander said flatly, but it sounded far more threatening this time.

"You would destroy someone's life to put me to heel?" I demanded, a sob welling in me so quickly and so hugely that I feared I would explode.

"The question is, would you destroy someone's life because you couldn't let them go." Alexander let the line stay open for another heartbeat, then hung up. He didn't need to say more. The game was set. The pieces were all in place. I had far fewer moves left, and Alexander had every advantage.

My eyes were wet before I realized. My vision blurred, and my mouth opened, but no sound came.

Exactly one minute later, a text message appeared on my screen. It simply said that Agent Duval would have the car ready at the intersection of Washington Street and Perry Street.

Rage boiled in me, but I tightened the lid. I wouldn't let it spill, even if it consumed me instead.

A storm raged through my mind, wiping out every possibility of a clear thought. I hated myself. I hated my brother. I hated the wretched life I was born into, and I hated the man I would be tomorrow.

I squeezed my eyes shut and leaned against the brick-and-mortar wall of the building behind me. I dropped the paper bag containing the gifts, dropped my phone on the sidewalk, and let the weight of it all push me down until I sat on the ground, dirty and devastated, holding my legs tightly together, my head pressing hard against my knees.

I can't do this, I thought. *I can't just go back. I can't. I won't.*

But the future was clear. In the hell of emotions that existed inside my head and heart, I could see our lives perfectly. Everyone loved a good scandal. If the paparazzi got a whiff of a dirty story, they wouldn't care that I was a spare prince of an unknown country. They wouldn't care that my family was nobody to their readers. They'd make us infamous, and Tristan would be at the heart of that storm.

CHAPTER 13

Confrontations

TRISTAN

I CLEANED UP MY STATION AFTER THE CLASS AND headed home. The dusk glow was fading away, and the streetlights were taking over the job of keeping us safe from the dark. As I walked back, I ticked off all the things I needed to do. I needed to shower, I needed to buy some wine, and I needed to tell Cedric about Mama Viv's offer. Something in me glimmered with nervousness and excitement at the prospect. Cedric would be thrilled. I knew that, but I was surprised at how hopeful it made me feel.

Mama Viv had hinted that Millie was thinking seriously about relocating to Chicago to be with her long-distance girlfriend, and there would be a vacancy. "Surely, darling, you're ready to take over," Mama Viv had told me.

"Ah, I'm not sure I'm the right choice, Mama Viv," I'd replied hesitantly, but the thought remained with me for the rest of the day. I couldn't stop imagining what it would be like. I could be in charge of my own kitchen. I could let my heart go wild with creativity whenever Mama Viv wanted something mad.

But I had to tell Cedric first. I had to tell him and see what he thought. Was I ready? Was I good enough to be in charge? He would know the answers.

Oakley was in the kitchen when I entered the apartment. "Hey," he greeted me, his voice thin and soft, just like everything else about Oakley. Although I'd seen him bristle at Lane, so he wasn't as gentle as he appeared. He was a cute guy, short and with a mop of windblown black hair, big blue eyes, and lips that were so red that his naturally pale skin appeared even paler.

"What's up?" I passed through the kitchen while Oakley poured himself a big mug of coffee. "Isn't it a little late for that much coffee?"

"I'd like to see you try studying during the day when Lane's playing games," Oakley said.

I couldn't hold back my laughter. "That bad?"

"Not as bad as he'll have it when he comes back and wants to sleep," Oakley said lightly.

I wasn't going anywhere near that feud. "You show him, soldier," I teased and slipped into the bathroom to shower. We seemed to be alone unless Madison haunted his room with all his moody-broody looks. Roman worked a shift at Neon Nights, which he had been doing more often lately—rent was soon due—and Lane was apparently out.

If Oakley plugged his ears with headphones, and if Cedric kept a hand over my mouth, tonight could be a lot more fun than I'd expected.

After putting on clean clothes, I passed through the apartment again. It was neat enough, and my room was the neatest of all. We didn't need much more than that. So I went downstairs and across the street.

Neon Nights was mostly empty. A couple of tables were occupied by strangers, Roman was polishing the glasses, and Mama Viv was reviewing the books. I waved as I passed through.

"Darling, is that all we get?" Mama Viv teased.

"He's not here for us," Rome grumbled.

"Well, I expect you at the Glitz Galore next week," Mama Viv called after me.

"We won't miss it," I promised over my shoulder as I went through the back of the bar into a hallway that led to the upper floor and Mama Viv's apartment. Cedric had a great deal of privacy up there. His room was much bigger than mine, and Mama Viv spent very little time upstairs. She was involved with a great deal of organizations in Greenwich Village, occasionally did charity performances, and joined many activities to better the position of youth at risk of poverty.

When I entered the apartment, Cedric's room was the first on the right. The door was closed, so I halted before it. My heart skipped a beat, as it often did when I was close to him, and I stifled a smile. Then, holding my breath, I knocked on his door.

I had so much to tell him.

What if he didn't like the idea of us working together full-time? I clamped that fear and shoved it down. It was a useless, irrational fear.

Nobody answered the knock, so I cleared my throat and knocked again. "Cedric? It's me."

Silence.

I wondered if I should turn the knob, then scratched that thought instantly. I might have been falling in love with him whenever he looked at me, but we were still only dating. If he was napping, I wasn't going to sneak in and wake him up. It would be plain creepy.

As I took a step back, wondering if he was out—though Roman or Mama Viv would have told me—a sound came from the other side of the door. "Come in."

My heart leaped, and I pushed right in. The room was clean, aired out, and perfectly tidy. His bed was made like they do it in hotel rooms, his desk was cleared of things, and a small suitcase was in the corner of the room, zipped up and swollen with contents. "Hey, um…" I looked at the suitcase again, then at Cedric. He wasn't looking at me. Instead, he was fiddling with his phone. "It's on? Can't they track you?"

Cedric shook his head. "Doesn't matter."

My heart sank low as I pushed the door shut and stepped back from him. He didn't move. He didn't look anywhere other than the screen, but the gestures he was making with his thumb seemed like he was simply opening and closing apps. "What's going on? Why aren't you worried your brother can see where you are?" I hated how insecure and thin my voice had become.

"He knows where I am," Cedric said. His eyes were dark, his hair a mess, and the shirt he wore was wrinkled. He'd buttoned it the wrong way, missing one, and the sleeves were unevenly rolled up. A sullen expression dominated his face when he directed his gaze to me, but he failed to meet my eyes. "He knew all along."

"What?" I gasped.

"The agent. I kept seeing the agent," he said. After inhaling a deep breath of air, he held it in silence. When he finally exhaled, it felt like a lifetime had passed. It felt like we had crossed the boundaries of this universe and another, stepping from one where there was some happiness and joy to one where we had already lost the fight. "We spoke today, and Alexander made some very good points." He shook his head in frustration. "I was going to leave," he said, his speech a little slurred in haste and his thoughts wandering. "I was going to go, but then you knocked. I..."

Anger and fear clashed in me and lit the very short fuse that led to the explosion of firm action. "You're not leaving," I said. "We can go somewhere where they won't find you. I can help you. I can hide you. I know places and people who will help you, Cedric. You can't go back without any bargaining power..."

"I don't need to bargain," Cedric said firmly. His eyes were red-rimmed and exhausted. "He's right. This...none of this is real. Not to someone like me, Tristan. Kitchen work? Who are we kidding?"

"This is not you," I said tightly. "The real you would rather lose the crown and the palace and all the wealth than marry someone you don't love. And I can save you from that, Cedric."

He clenched his teeth, and something flickered out of him. "I'm not a stray dog to be rescued, Tristan. I'm not Pudding or some kitten you found behind a dumpster. I'm the Prince of Verdumont, and my duty is to my family. If I thought, for a moment, that it can be any different, then that spell is over."

"I didn't mean...that's not..." I shut my eyes and shook my head. "I'm trying to help you."

"I don't need help," he said, a hint of anger coming through the apathy. Who was this person? "I need to go back and live my life the way I was supposed to. This...this was all a mistake, Tristan. And we were blind to think it could work out. For God's sake, I'm a prince."

"Are you?" I whispered. "Because you're acting like any old coward."

Cedric crossed the room to his suitcase and lifted it. "You can say whatever you want. It won't change my mind."

"A coward," I said louder as Cedric stepped toward me and the door. If there was any hope left in me that he would drop the suitcase and hug me and tell me it was all a bad joke, it was gone when he stared at the knob and waited for me to move.

I stepped aside, but panic ripped through me, and I froze in place when he reached for the knob.

"Cedric, don't do this. Don't run away. I know what you're trying to do, and just don't," I blurted.

"Don't talk about running away," he said. "You know better than anyone what it's like to run without looking back."

The words slapped me across the face as Cedric murmured a goodbye and left the room.

I couldn't even run after him.

I couldn't shout or beg him or stop him.

He knew I'd run from home. He knew I'd left it all behind because I didn't dare go back.

Rage and devastating sorrow mixed in me as Cedric's

footsteps retreated from the room that was empty of his things.

The avalanche of familiar feelings crashed on me. I wasn't worth his pain and struggle. I wasn't worth the fight.

I wasn't worth it.

I'd lost everything I had ever tried to have. I had failed at everything I had ever attempted. I was a disgrace.

CEDRIC

I held my breath and smoothed my face as best as I could.

My heart pounded, and I almost wished it would explode and let me be free of the guilt I held down.

The note I had written was still in my pocket, but it was useless to leave it to him now. I had blundered through everything I had touched. And the note wouldn't explain anything. It would only confuse him more.

Forgive me, I whispered inside myself. I wasn't sure who I was speaking to, but I spoke anyway. *Forgive me, forgive me, forgive me.*

TRISTAN

The banging sound of my shoes slamming against the stairs announced me as I burst through and into the bar. Mama Viv was gone, and I was thankful for it. "How dare you?" I demanded as Roman moved into the bar from the front door.

"What happened?" he asked, his face contorting. "He just left without a word. What happened up there?"

"How could you, Roman?" I squeezed through my clenched teeth. "How could you betray me like that?" I crossed the bar so quickly that Roman balked, then dug his heels into the floor and leaned toward me. He caught me and held me, although I wasn't sure what I was about to do. Or had been until he grabbed my wrists.

"What the fuck, man?" he snapped.

"You told him," I snapped. "I know you warned him, Roman, don't deny it. He told me. I know you said you'd hunt him down."

"I never said that," Roman shouted. "What the fuck is wrong with you?"

Angry, hateful tears welled in my eyes as we grappled. "You told him about Jen. You told him something."

Roman was much stronger than he looked, his arms twisting mine and wrapping around me until I was trapped and couldn't move. "Calm the fuck down, Tris. I never said anything to him."

I wasn't thinking clearly, and I didn't need to. Roman had betrayed my trust, he'd scared Cedric off, and he'd made me look like a lunatic. As if Cedric hadn't had enough to tempt him away from me, discovering I was a pathetic mess was just a cherry on the fucking top.

"I told him," a deep, stress-roughened voice came.

Roman held me tighter. I didn't even know how I got bent over and why there were wet drops on the floor three feet under my face. I saw them through a blur before I lifted my head and looked at the drag queen in a purple dress, a matching wig, and distress on her face. The thick, black mascara ran down Mama Viv's cheeks.

She put her hand on her chest, her nails long and fingers spread. "I told him, Tristan."

I exhaled the tiniest breath of air. Cedric had told me that my friend had warned him about hurting me. It had been a sweet moment, followed by a promise that he never would. And I had believed him.

"It wasn't Roman, darling. It was me. Me. You blame me, Tristan. Do you hear me?" Mama Viv's voice quivered.

"Why?" I whispered, Roman's arms tight around me as he lifted me upright. He released me, but he still bristled and stood ready to tackle me to the ground if he had to.

"To protect you, Tristan," Mama Viv said, fear plain on her face and in her eyes. "I didn't want to see you heartbroken."

"Well, you protected me just fine," I said sourly.

"That's not fair," Roman warned me. "Mama Viv didn't make that asshole run away."

"What do you know?" I sneered. I stepped away from Roman and Mama Viv, slowly inching toward the exit. "None of you have any clue..." But I shut my mouth. I would be a traitor like them. Even if he had broken my heart for no goddamn reason, I wouldn't rat him out. "None of you should have meddled."

"Darling, I'm sorry," Mama Viv sobbed. "I'm sorry, Tristan, but I thought it was for the best."

"It's not her fault," Roman said, anger dominating his tone over distress. "Don't be an ass, Tris. You're pretending like it's her fault when it's Cedric's. What the hell happened?"

"This is bullshit," I huffed, shook my head in disappointment, and turned away from them both.

I heard Mama Viv's sob and the beginning of Roman's rant about my manners, but I didn't listen to the rest. I crossed the street without looking left or right, held my breath and the infinite pool of sadness and tears that would be released with it, and hurried into the apartment.

I couldn't stay here.

I couldn't stay around them and around everything that reminded me of Cedric.

He left me.

He left me for a marchioness he didn't even find attractive. He left me after all the promises and all the hopes we had given one another.

But I always returned to the same old truth. I always knew it. If I had thought otherwise even for one moment, I had been wrong. The simple truth was that I just didn't deserve to be happy.

And I wasn't going to find happiness here, in Hudson Burrow.

That was the life of the wretched and the hurt. That was the fate that was given to me when I had wrongly survived.

So I found a duffel and began to fill it with the few things I owned.

CHAPTER 14
Homecomings

TRISTAN

I WANDERED FROM ONE TOWN TO THE NEXT ON MY slow journey north. Every stop I could take, I did. The house where I had grown up was my destination simply for the fact that I had nowhere else to go. The cash in my wallet was thinning fast.

From time to time, I wondered if I should just stop in one of the towns on my way home, get a job, and focus on what was ahead.

You don't dare to look back, a voice whispered. I couldn't assign that voice to anyone in particular. There was a bit of Cedric in there, and a bit of Roman, and Mama Viv holding back a sob, and me speaking to myself with all the hatred I deserved.

I didn't want to go home. Nothing but pain existed there. I was going back to the place where it was the clearest to me that things had played out the wrong way on that fateful night. I was going to visit the people I had abandoned without any way to explain to them that I had spared them by letting them go.

If only they could do the same.

If only everyone could just forget about me.

So long as people knew me, my existence filled them with pity. It wasn't like I didn't know it. And thinking back to all the sweet kisses Cedric had pressed upon my lips and all the words of kindness and support, it became clear to me that he pitied me, too.

It was Mama Viv's doing that Cedric was so kind and gentle with me. But when he remembered the things he was giving up for me, he became aware of how little I was worth in comparison with a kingdom. He might never become a king, but his life would be filled with comforts of the sort I had never been able to imagine.

It was better for everyone that way.

I only wished he hadn't been so nice to me when he thought I was a wreck. I was, but I liked to keep that to myself.

Without much choice in where all the paths were leading me, I continued toward home.

CEDRIC

The mattress swallowed me whole. It was far softer than I remembered. My body sank into its middle, and the duvet rested heavily over me. Eyes open, I barely moved. I barely breathed.

Nobody had come around except Sophia in the last three days. I had returned, met my parents briefly before their visit to the North, exchanged a few cold words with Alexander, and received several angry looks from my little brother, Maximilian. Sophia was the only one who appeared sad rather than angry with me.

Staff entered, checked up on me, and recited my agenda. Small appearances that I had neglected while on the run, others that were up in the air with the uncertainty of my return, and one that towered above them all. Élodie. My airline, as Tristan had put it.

My eyes stung even at the memory of his name.

Would he ever forgive me? Why should he? It wasn't like he would have a chance to see me ever again. And I wouldn't see him.

What could I do, though? Maybe I could let things settle for a bit and pull some strings when I had more bargaining power. I could get him his restaurant in New York through our contacts. I could give him all he needed for a good life. He wouldn't need me.

A little before noon, I attended the opening ceremony of a new wing at the History Museum of Verdumont. It had been closed off for renovations and the new exhibition put together for the reopening focused on the history of world literature. At any other time, I would have been excited. Today, I couldn't find it in me to care.

In the afternoon, my chauffeur pulled the car up by Le Jardin Étoilé, where journalists flocked. The arrival was perfectly timed for them to see me step out of the car and walk up to the big terrace. I ran my fingers through my hair and checked the time. Right on cue, another car halted, and the door opened to let Élodie out.

The lenses turned away from me to her and followed her all the way up the few steps of the balcony until she joined me. The photographers went mad with the flashes, and questions came from all directions. We smiled our practiced smiles as I hugged Élodie.

"It is good to see you, Your Highness," she said.

"And you," I replied in a more casual tone. It wasn't something that would fly with the Marchioness, but I didn't care. She was my prison. She was my doom. She was the end of my life.

I looked at Élodie and saw the ending of everything that was ever good. I saw the beginning of a life of quiet misery.

"Shall we?" I asked, bending my arm for Élodie to take and leading her to the empty table in the middle of the balcony. I had pleaded with the staffers to put us inside and let us speak to one another, but Alexander had been very firm about this meeting taking place in front of the journalists.

"If Your Highness wishes," Élodie said. She was so perfect, so smooth, so flat. She didn't show a single emotion. Her chin was lifted a little high, and her eyes were clear green, locked onto the empty table.

The people sitting around other tables had been handpicked by the palace. Nothing was ever spontaneous, and everything was always a photo op.

"I was so worried over your absence," Élodie said without a trace of worry in her tone.

"Mm." I pulled a chair for her and sat on her left side. We turned slightly to face one another, the positioning of our chairs around the table signaling nothing remotely close to rivalry or antagonism. Everything was friendly, almost romantic. Red wine was served first, and I spared a silent thought for Antinous. "So kind of you," I told Élodie. Her golden, sun-kissed hair was smooth and brushed so that not a single hair was out of place. "I was glad to hear that my brother entertained you."

Had I thought it possible, I would have said that Élodie blushed. "His Highness is kind," she said. "And very entertaining."

"Please," I interrupted. "We know why we are here, Élodie. Call me by my name. And call Maximilian by his. This etiquette has no place between us."

Élodie didn't miss a beat. "If that's what you wish, Cedric."

"It is," I insisted. The perpetual snapping of shutters faded out. It came like waves of the ocean. At every smile and every change of pose, the tide brought it higher, and then it retreated when we stopped being interesting. "I hope my younger brother hasn't been as moody with you as he has with me these days."

"Maximilian?" Élodie asked, the confusion leaving her face as quickly as it came. It was gone before anyone got a decent photo. "Oh no. He was very dedicated and in such good spirits." In controlled movements, Élodie lifted her glass, took the tiniest sip, and let the corners of her lips curl up for me. It was a practiced smile with no warmth in it.

I cannot marry you, I thought.

"I hear the opening of the World Literature exhibition went well," Élodie said.

"Perfect," I replied, frustration rising in me. Was this what we would speak about? Agendas and weather and all this mundane bullshit? "Have you ever broken any rules, Élodie? Ever run away from home?"

Élodie gasped and smiled. "I don't believe I have ever run from home, Cedric."

"You must have had some rebellions that only belong to you," I said.

Her face seemed cooler than ever. "If I have, I must have forgotten them."

"What amazing lives we live," I mused.

I was certain that the temperature around us grew lower by the sheer power of her emotionless gaze. "Forgive me, Cedric, but it seems you find me rather boring."

I waved my hand off. "Not at all. We are going to be married. I would like to know more than what's on the surface."

"Perhaps I am not as willful as Your Highness," she said, the same little smile never going away from her face. We might as well have been talking about the weather for all the press could tell. "Perhaps I have never run to the United States to spend my days in a bar and my nights with a stranger. But please don't mistake my lack of adventures for complete emotionlessness. I am perfectly capable of loving and hurting just like everyone else."

I heard the wave of shutters snapping louder, faster, closer, and I realized it was my face that was contorting with embarrassment and cringe. "Forgive me."

"I already have," Élodie said.

"This...arrangement bothers me, and I never thought that it might bother you, too," I admitted.

"Our kind functions by the rules of another stratosphere, Cedric," Élodie said. I might have heard a touch of friendliness in her voice at long last. "And we simply have to make the best of what we are given. Now, laugh, but not too loudly. I've just said something terribly witty."

I didn't miss a beat. Laughter welled from me, and I shook my head, eyes sparking with joy that I could spend such a fine afternoon in such interesting company. "You've had much more practice, it seems."

"It could very well be a natural talent," Élodie said without a trace of melancholy.

"You sacrificed your heart for this," I pointed out softly, the smile on my face a sharp and painful contrast to the subject we discussed. "I've known you for years, and I never suspected."

"He was not someone I would have chosen had I been given a chance," Élodie said. "But such things simply happen whether we want them or not."

I remembered standing on the top of the Empire State Building, looking into those big, brown eyes, leaning in with the burning desire to kiss him and never stop kissing him. I hadn't wanted to fall for him. I had fought it long and hard, but he was a whirlwind of passion, and he made me feel alive when nobody else could. "It seems to me that you and I have a lot more in common than I had suspected."

"If nothing else, we will understand each other well," Élodie agreed.

I cleared my throat. As quietly as I could and with a

waning smile on my face, I filled myself with the courage to tell her this. "You should know, if we truly do this, I will not object..."

"No," Élodie said politely and chuckled as if I'd made a very clever joke. "Let us not discuss this."

Some wild, crazy hope that I might reach an arrangement with Élodie, go back to New York, explain it all, and claim him as my lover died at the firmness with which she closed this discussion. It was irrational. I could never go back to him. I had broken him for his own safety from scandals. But I had also sealed him from my life forever.

"I'm sorry," I said. I wondered if my suggestion sparked the same sort of uncontrollable hope, the absence of which left you devastated.

We exchanged a sweet, long hug before leaving by our separate cars. A journalist shouted after me, "Your Highness, what was the joke the Marchioness told you that made you laugh so much?" And as the door closed, I wondered why on earth anyone would ever care.

You are not a person to them, a voice reminded me. *You are a symbol, and you live your life as a symbol.*

Back in my apartment, I undressed myself and put on a pair of sweatpants and a hoodie from my last year in college. I picked up a copy of *The Song of Achilles* and prepared myself to cry. I had read it forward and backward. I knew it inside and out. My bleeding heart hardly needed more pain, but this was, at least, a way I could control the pain. I could direct it. If I wept for Patroclus, it had nothing to do with me and the tragedy of Tristan Lawson. It was a safe kind of pain, distant and someone else's.

The knock on my door was followed by the turning of

the knob. The sitting room was empty save for me, filled with subdued lights and deep, sorrowful shadows. Sophia, dressed brightly for the evening and only a little disgruntled, slipped inside and shut the door. "I can't take it anymore."

"Can't take what?" I asked, looking up from a passage that described a wonderful night at Chiron's cave.

"It's a mistake," Sophia said, her voice higher than usual. "All of this. But Alexander is furious with you, and he won't speak about it."

My sister crossed the sitting room and took a seat on the ottoman against the wall. On the small, ornate table between her ottoman and my armchair was a pot of tea, a blend of soothing herbs built around nettle at its core. I was about to offer it, but Sophia continued speaking.

"You really made a mess of things when you ran away, Cedric," she said, teary-eyed as I had never seen her. "You're so goddamn romantic. You thought running away would solve your problems. Did you imagine you would earn your keep by playing a harmonica in the old Wild West?"

I would have chuckled were she not so hurt by it. "Why does this upset you?"

"Because you could have fought it before," she said. She wore her dark brown hair short and stylish. Her makeup was minimal and always on point. She had been the last mischief-maker in the family, together with Maximilian. Her rebellion had gone out earlier, and it seemed that Maximilian's was settled, too, in my absence. That left me. The sole troublemaker. Sophia shook her head jerkily. "Alexander won't speak of you. Mother and Father allowed him to handle the situation, and he is taking it far too seriously. Not even Madeleine can get him to bend enough to just listen."

Listen to what? It's settled, I thought. "Sophie, you are upset over nothing," I said dully. "What's done is done."

"You don't listen," she accused me, a sob bursting from her. "You never listen, and that's the problem."

I shook my head slowly. "Because it won't change anything. Élodie and I understand each other. We..." I shrugged and faked a smile. "We have a lot in common, it turns out. I don't know. Maybe marrying her won't be that bad after all."

"Cedric, you are rambling," Sophie warned me coolly.

"But I'm telling you," I assured her with a fake calm. The truth was, I wanted to cry and rave and rip everything around me to bits and pieces. "It's all just for show, Sophie. She doesn't expect me to love her, and she won't love me back. We'll...manage."

"Because she loves Maximilian, you dummy," Sophie said, her voice a thin sob that cut right through my heart. The world tilted on its axis. "And he loves her, too."

I didn't know if it was heartbreaking pain or crazy hope that I felt. There was no hope. Nothing could be done. I had been photographed with her just today. It had been rumored that we would be engaged for months, years. "W-what do you...?"

"Just listen," Sophia said firmly, getting back the control over her voice. "You left on the night Élodie was supposed to arrive. Alexander put Max on the task of keeping her occupied and properly honored. She doesn't care about museums or history or art. She loves jazz, just like Max, and they're crazy about vintage vinyl records.

When they bonded over that, they became inseparable. But Alexander was too busy and too angry with you to notice a solution right under his nose. And if he suspected it, he now refuses to let you off the hook."

"He'd ruin all three of us just to prove a point?" I heard myself ask.

Sophie raised her hands and shrugged. "A month ago, I would have told you not to be an idiot. Now? I don't know anymore."

"What about Mother and Father?" I asked urgently.

"What about them?" Sophie asked. "They are watching all those anti-monarchy parties rising in popularity, and they aren't allowed to say a thing. Grandmother is ill, and Mama is with her almost all the time. Father's too stressed to sit through dinner. If you had any misconceptions about who is in charge of your life, you weren't paying attention."

I covered my face with both hands, the book forgotten in my lap. Leaning back, I sank deeper in my chair. "They never would have fallen in love had I not left," I whispered.

Sophie was quiet for a moment. "It crossed my mind. I think they would have. Eventually. Would it have been too late, I don't know. But your absence went for too long, and Alexander won't forgive it."

"He can't trap all of us," I said, looking at Sophia hopefully.

She shook her head. "Max thinks he's being chivalrous. And Élodie does what she is told. And you do whatever the hell you like. I seem to be the only sane person in this palace, and I don't know what to do."

"They're in love?" I whispered. I couldn't wrap my mind around that. It seemed so impossible. Maximilian was immature. Other than his fascination with jazz, he was just a college prankster with little interest in anything else. And Élodie was prim and proper, the spitting image of regal perfection.

"Oh, they're in love," Sophie assured me. "I've never seen Max so gutted as the night Alexander announced you would return."

No wonder he refused to speak to me. I had accidentally ruined his happiness together with everyone else's. I closed my eyes as if to mourn the loss of someone dear to me. I had broken all the hearts, but all I had ever wanted was the freedom to love whoever I wanted to love. "I'm sorry," I whispered.

"Don't be sorry," Sophie said. "Think. Think of something and change the ending."

Although I nodded, hoping to put her mind at rest if I couldn't do it for everyone else, I doubted there was anything I could do. If Alexander were so spiteful, he would want to see me step up no matter what. He would gladly pay the price with Max's and Élodie's hearts just to see me brought to heel.

Sophie left me alone, and I tossed the book to the ottoman because my focus was in tatters. I covered my face and wondered if I should have hidden with Tristan for longer. Could I have drawn it out until Max reached a breaking point and declared his feelings for Élodie? Or would it be all the same to Alexander? Would he still seek to bring me back at the cost of ruining Tristan's life and everyone else's?

Too many questions and no time to answer them.

But in the end, hardly any answers mattered.

I was never getting Tristan back. Why shouldn't I simply let my brother dictate the course of my future? That way, we could all relax and pin all the blame on him.

It was a sweet, hateful thing to contemplate, but a spark of rebellion had returned to me. Something had to be done.

CHAPTER 15
A Time of Healing

ROMAN

I DIDN'T SPEAK TO ANYONE AS I PASSED THROUGH the living room. Ever since Tristan picked up and left, the guys looked at me as if I had any answers. I didn't want to get involved. Screw this shit. Madison got the message and stopped looking. Lane frowned whenever I was around, as though on the verge of asking me a question, but he knew better. Oakley was clueless; he could not read the room. So he peppered me with his curiosity like he dissected a frog in biology.

I didn't want to talk about it. And I didn't want to meddle when Lane growled at Oakley and Oakley snapped at Lane. I let them work it out however they wanted and skipped over the awkward questions about what the hell had happened to Tristan.

I don't know, I muttered after Oakley had first asked, and the same three words roamed through my head whenever I was here.

Anger remained at a low simmer, never fully going away but never reaching the boiling temperature. Still, the steam filled the pot, and it had to go somewhere.

The night was warm when I stepped out of the building and crossed the street. Entering Neon Nights, I spotted Mama Viv. She had this unbearable and frustrating new habit of looking at me as if we shared something nobody else did. We did not. It was just the randomness of the universe. We got hurt by a hurting guy. *Screw him for taking it out on us. Screw everyone.* "Gimme a shot of vodka," I told Bradley.

The fucker had the nerve to cock an eyebrow at me.

"What? Am I supposed to serve myself on the one night I'm off?" The growl warned him that I wasn't kidding. And at my bristling, Mama Viv lifted herself out of the chair and carried the books to the back of the bar, slipping through the door and retreating to her apartment.

"Dude," Bradley said.

"Don't," I said tightly. "Just...don't."

But if Bradley could keep his mouth shut, Luke Whittaker couldn't. He entered with Rafael and spotted me. "Hey, Rome," he greeted, making his way straight to me.

Will everyone just leave me the fuck alone? I wanted to plea for some peace.

"Any news?" Luke asked just as Bradley moved his hand over his throat hastily, signaling to Luke to stop.

"No." My answer arrived at the same time my vodka did. I emptied the glass and sent it back to Bradley. "Another."

"Easy, cowboy," Bradley said as Rafael put an arm

protectively around Luke as if I were a threat. The two retreated to the nearest table and sat down.

I glared at Bradley. "I need to get drunk, dicked, or rested. And since I can't sleep and nobody's dicking me, give me another."

Bradley rolled his eyes and kept his opinions to himself. He poured me another shot, took cash, and let me sit in silence. I turned my head around and checked out the crowd at the bar. Not a big one, I saw, but enough to notice a few new faces. There was a DJ on the stage, warming up for the night, and a few people caught the rhythm with their bopping heads.

Rafael and Luke were engaged in a heated debate. Rafael was winning. Batman was, apparently, the superior hero, no matter how you cut it.

I looked the other way and spotted a face that wasn't so unfamiliar.

He was tall and broad, and he wore a hoodie with the hood halfway over his head. Not exactly party attire. The baggy cargo pants with many pockets that he wore were faded black. He stood along the long, high table against the front window, leaning his back against it and resting his right elbow on it. I had seen him at parties before. There was no forgetting that hoodie. Or the wary look on that handsome face.

I picked up my vodka and carried it over. The rest of the long counter against the window was unoccupied. "Can I join the brooding table?" I asked.

"I'd rather if you didn't," the guy said.

I sucked my teeth. "Sharp. Straight to the gut."

"Not interested," he said.

I shook my right hand in the air as if I'd just touched glowing coals. "You don't know what I'm proposing."

The handsome stranger snorted and shook his head. His gaze avoided me fully. He scanned the room.

I inhaled a deep breath of air. I wasn't one to surrender. Especially not when someone disregarded me so easily. "You don't look like you're here for fun."

The stranger exhaled and turned to me. His eyes were green like summer grass in Central Park, and his jawline was so defined that he looked like a chiseled statue. *I might get dicked after all*, I thought. It would be extra fun if he stayed angry throughout. "Pardon me, but you don't exactly bring fun with you."

"You haven't seen me naked," I told him, my mouth forming a pout against my will.

"And I don't intend to," the stranger said, his frustration heating up his face. "I'm not like you."

"Everyone's a little bit like me," I said.

That got him. "Not me," he said with surprising firmness. "You should back off, buddy."

"You do realize this is a gay bar run by a drag queen, right?" I frowned. No straight boy in a gay bar was this defensive without hiding something. I liked a good fuckup. They could be a lot of fun.

"It's not your fucking business what I'm doing here," he said.

"Alright, alright. I'm not judging. I've seen you around and got the wrong impression." I shook my head. He turned me on with devastating precision. "Ever tried it with a guy to make sure?" I teased. The words felt wrong even to my ears. I was always rash and forward, but not this rash and forward.

He set his drink on the table and brought his face to mine. Minty breath mixed with the citrus from his not-so-straight cocktail. He gripped my white T-shirt and pulled me in. Now that his back was straight, I realized that he was taller by a good four or five inches. I stared up into his eyes, bristling and ready to fight him.

If only it didn't make me horny.

"You're sick," he spat, then shoved me away.

Before I could catch my breath, heat erupting into my face, the hot fuckup stormed out of Neon Nights. I smoothed my T-shirt and took a sip of my vodka. It was vile, and it only added to the burning sensation in my head.

I guess I'm not getting a piece of that, I figured quietly. A sliver of shame passed through me, if for no other reason than because I'd gone all-in and got *that* in return. I had already pictured us coiling in the bed. I had already felt the sweet, ruthless pain he could inflict. *Pull yourself together*, I snapped at myself, but it felt like I was grasping for shadows whenever I tried to take control of my thoughts.

I glanced around. Bradley stared at me with disbelief painted on his face. Luke cringed. Rafael, on the other hand, seemed upset. He got up and shook Luke's shoulder, showing him something on his phone, then hurried from the table to me.

I wasn't in the mood for a lecture, but Rafael was completely determined to round on me now. His eyebrows were arched and high, his eyes wide, and his breath shallow. "Rome, you've gotta see this," he said. "I knew he looked familiar."

Rafael wasn't going to lecture me at all. Instead, he turned his phone around, and the ground slipped from under my feet.

Tristan

Mom and Dad forced me to join them for dinner. It was Mom's special casserole with the fluffiest mashed potatoes and savory gravy. It was such a simple recipe, yet I had never been able to recreate it. No matter how many times I'd tried to make it, following the exact steps I'd seen Mom take throughout my childhood, it never smelled as good or tasted as delicious.

The lights in the house were all on. It was bright, and extra so with all the furniture being white and cream and light gray. The dining table was covered with a white tablecloth, and Mom's dishes were all pastel.

We ate in silence, although Mom and Dad exchanged glances every now and then. They looked at me expectantly, as if they waited for me to deliver some great news of my successes and make it clear that I was putting my time to good use. I wasn't. I was wasting it left and right like I had done my whole life, and when I was gone someday, there wouldn't be a hair of difference in the world.

The last time we had spoken at any significant length, I had informed my parents that I had left college.

Since then, my parents tried to get in touch, but I knew

what was best for everyone. It was better if they didn't know how I failed them every day.

"Darling," Mom said softly as I tensed my muscles to get up and carry my plate to the sink. I stayed where I was. "We're happy you're home."

I nodded and muttered my agreement.

"We really are, Tris," Dad said, his voice a little gruff.

"Yeah. Me too," I said in a low voice. I wished they would let me go to bed. I was an adult, but they acted like I was more fragile than an egg.

"I wish you'd come more often," Mom said.

Great. More guilt, I thought. "I was busy."

"I know, baby. That's not why I'm saying this," Mom explained.

"We don't want to bother you callin' all the time, Tris," Dad chimed in.

I shrugged. "It's no bother."

They exchanged that look again, and it made me hold my breath. Mom folded her hands on the table. "Tristan, you are not a child anymore, and it's not fair to treat you that way. But we're your parents. It's our job to be worried."

"Why are you worried?" I asked for the lack of anything else to say. They probably worried about my future, which was uncertain at the best of times.

Dad exhaled through his nose. "Don't you think it's odd to keep us at distance, then just show up in the middle of the night?"

"The bus broke down," I said. "I didn't plan to come so late."

"That's not the issue, darling," Mom said, the gentleness in her voice never faltering. "We're happy to have you here as much as you'd like to stay. This is your home, Tristan."

"You'll always be welcome here, son."

"But," Mom said carefully, "it worries us that you seem so...depressed, darling."

"Not depressed," I said tiredly.

"We're not tryin' to send you away, Tris," Dad said.

Mom took over. "It's only that we fear something happened to make you come back like this."

I inhaled, held my breath, and fought the oncoming tears. Damn them, they always brimmed in my eyes when I least needed them. "I..." My voice snapped, and I pressed my mouth shut, but grief contorted my muscles. Exhaling, I let a shudder pass through me before I tried to speak again. To their credit, my parents didn't overreact. They hurt for me, but they kept their hurts limited to their faces, their eyes. They didn't let them dictate their behaviors. "I failed."

Silence.

I had hoped it would have explained everything, but the word simply wasn't big enough to convey the depth of my failures.

"I...I failed at everything," I said.

"Darling," Mom said in a pained voice that she barely controlled.

"What did you fail at, Tris?" Dad asked, just as concerned but better at keeping it down.

I shook my head. "Everything, Dad. I failed at everything. College, friendships, work. Love. I...I can't win." The words tumbled out of my mouth despite my rational wish to shut up and keep it all down. "Everything I ever touched turned to dust. I left you guys because I couldn't make myself look you in the eyes after dropping out." Mom and Dad both pressed their mouths shut, but their heads shook a little. They didn't interrupt me, though. "I ruined my friendships and hurt the people I love and lost the one guy I thought loved me back."

"Oh, sweetheart," Mom said.

But the dam was broken, and the entire lake of admissions was starting to pour out. "I lied to him. I lied by omission, never telling him about...the accident. Keeping it hidden so he wouldn't act all sad with me. I know full well how people look at you when they know something tragic about you. I've seen it. They offer you their friendship. They offer you jobs you're not ready to take. And for what? Because something bad happened to someone you loved? Bullshit. I didn't want his pity. I wanted him to love *me*. But...he couldn't. Not when it cost him so much. So I ruined everything. He left, and I destroyed all my friendships like I destroyed all the chances you gave me." My tears were no longer satisfied with brimming. They spilled down my cheeks, and I wiped them away angrily. "I've made such a mess of my life. Why am I even here? I'm not ready for any of this." Then, my gaze darted through the blur of tears to the wall where my first-grade portrait was hanging. Next to it, there was Jen's. "She was smarter," I whispered, my throat closing. "She was so much smarter. Don't say she wasn't. She wouldn't have failed so bad at everything." Mom's chair scraped against the wooden floor loudly, and Dad's followed. "She would have been brilliant," I said, choking, though I couldn't tell if it was a sob that choked me or the tears. When arms wrapped around me—and I couldn't see whose arms and where they came from—a final gasp filled my lungs. "It should have been me," I cried.

Words of comfort swirled around me, none sinking into my mind. I heard them, though I didn't memorize them. I couldn't repeat them. I could hardly reply to them. I bent forward as they held me and cried like I hadn't cried in years. I wished, with all my heart, for a window in time to open and for our places to be swapped. I wished Jen had survived instead. She had always been so brave and bright. She would have known what to do. She would have grown up to be a genius. Not like me, a dropout with mediocre cooking skills and little else.

"...son, do you hear me? You're already everythin' we..."

Mom's drowned out Dad's as she whispered into my ear. "Darling, you are amazing just the way..."

But I heard neither of them, really. Not until the sobs that rocked my body had long passed, and I remained drained of everything, empty, exhausted.

I didn't remember us moving to my room. I didn't remember going to bed. Yet when I blinked, my parents sat at the edge of my bed, and I lay on top of the comforter, still dressed in the same clothes. I hadn't slept, although I had skipped a certain amount of time.

My head hurt. My eyes stung. I was so tired that I thought I could sleep for an eternity, and it wouldn't be enough.

Mom ran her hand through my hair, and I was embarrassed to realize it had gotten sweaty. She didn't seem to notice or mind. "...and we love you," she whispered.

"I love you, too," I murmured.

Their eyebrows rose high. "Hello," Dad said.

"Was I...sleeping?" I frowned.

They brushed it off. "You're safe, baby," Mom said. She looked at Dad, who cleared his throat. "Tris," he said, "you'll get over that young man, okay? And if you don't, you'll get him back. Hearts have to be broken from time to time, or we'd all forget we had them."

Mom brushed my hair with her finger. "But you need to remember that your father and I love you. And we're proud of you, baby. You're the sweetest person. Do you know that? We couldn't be more proud of you if we tried."

Something tugged the corners of my lips down. Something else tickled my heart gently and made it rise.

"You always knew right from wrong," Dad said. "And you were always the first to help anyone who needed it."

I failed to help everyone, I thought.

"We can't change the past, darling," Mom went on. "What is gone is gone, and Jen's not coming back. She was a beautiful girl. And she was smart, you're right. And when she died, a bit of light went out of the world. But all we can do is go on, baby."

"You can't let that tragedy shadow over your whole life, son," Dad explained. "It's not right."

"And it's not fair to compare yourself to something that simply doesn't exist," Mom said.

"Especially when you're such a fine man already," Dad finished.

A small, stubborn part of me woke up and believed them. And when it did, there was no shutting it down. That night, and the next day, I believed they were proud of me. We spoke more, and I told them about Pudding the Panda and where most of their money was going. They laughed and shook their heads in disbelief. We visited Jen's grave and left flowers. I cried.

By the end of the following day, I began wondering if I should return to the Hudson Burrow and start making things right with Roman and, even more so, Mama Viv. My parents thought I had overreacted, but they didn't blame me for it. Not when every deeply buried trauma had resurfaced in an instant.

I failed to tell them who Cedric was and what he left me for. It didn't matter.

He had picked the comfortable life of a young royal instead of the calloused hands of a kitchen helper. I couldn't blame him for taking care of himself. I only blamed him for kissing me in the first place.

That thought was followed by regrets. I didn't mean that. I wanted all his kisses, and I didn't want them to ever stop. But if they had to stop, I wanted to remember the kisses as clearly as I could.

Roman called me one evening, and my heart climbed into my throat. I didn't feel ready to face him, but I wasn't going to make things worse by ignoring him.

"Um...hello?" I shut the door of my room and sat on the edge of my bed. Only a reading lamp was on, and an old book about Apollo and Hyacinthus was on my bedstand, procured from my mother's collection the day before.

Roman cut right to the chase. "I know you don't want to hear from me. I'll respect that, even if I don't get it. But this is important. More important than whatever we're fighting about, alright? I need to tell you something..."

Mama Viv's voice came from the background. "Is he alright?"

My heart ached. I was such an asshole.

"Hush," Roman replied to her in frustration. "Let me tell him."

"What does he sound like? Does he sound well?"

"Tris, you there?" Roman asked. I sucked in a breath of air; it was most I could do now that the emotions threatened to overwhelm me again. "Look, Tris, it's about Cedric. You better be sitting down." For a moment, panic spiked in me, but the controlled laughter in Roman's voice removed the fear that something bad had happened to him. "Oh boy, I don't know how to..." The sound was filled with static, and something clicked and clacked.

"He's a prince, darling," Mama Viv said far too loudly. "Some Vermont place in France, Tristan. Rafael recognized him and saw the news."

"Verdumont," I corrected her, then frowned at myself. That was the least important part. Rafael? News?

"Ah, yes, you see, you know better than...hold on. Tristan, darling, did you know this?" Mama Viv was scandalized.

"What is it? He knows already?" Roman demanded in the background.

"Darling, you never said," Mama Viv cried. "I made that boy scrub pans twice because he didn't remove the grease well."

A laugh pealed from me toward the ceiling. I could imagine Mama Viv quivering with anxiety now that she knew all the things she had asked a foreign royal to do in Neon Nights.

Roman stole the phone back. "Tris, you knew this?"

"I...yeah, I knew that," I said softly. "But how did you find out? What's the news?"

"Oh, well, Rafael follows these French magazines, and some duchess or whatever was photographed with Cedric a couple of days ago. They say they're getting engaged." Roman said, bewildered.

"Who says?" I asked, my heart sinking lower than I had expected.

"The magazines," Rome clarified.

The ridiculous relief at finding out that it wasn't Cedric saying it lifted me off the bed and made me cross the room. But it was useless. He would announce it in due time. "If he's meeting with Élodie in public, it must be true. His family wants to announce the news before the elections."

"Dude, what the fuck?" Roman demanded. "You know *everything*?"

I cleared my throat and pushed all thoughts of Cedric aside. "Rome, I was an ass. I'm sorry. He left me, and I couldn't do anything about it. I couldn't even blame him. Hell, I'd leave me for a crown, too. I couldn't take it out on him, so I took it out on you and Mama Viv. I...I hope you can forgive me."

"Hold on," Roman said. "His family wants the announcement?"

"Um, yes, but Rome..."

"Did he tell you he wanted to marry her when he left?" Roman asked.

"What's going on?" Mama Viv cried.

"Hold on," Roman said. A moment later, the quality of sound changed, and I knew they'd put me on the speaker. "Tris, did he tell you that?"

"Well, no, but it's obvious," I said.

"You have to tell us what he said, Tris," Roman insisted.

So I did. I wanted to protest it, but they deserved to know the whole story. It would be great gossip to tell people forever, hiring a prince and criticizing him when he dropped a tray full of beers and cocktails. I told them, however much I hated remembering it, everything from the moment I knocked on Cedric's door. I told them about his phone and about Cedric's fears that he could be located. I told them that they had already found him and followed him. The story wandered back into the past to everything Cedric had told me about the marriage, election, tradition, and his older brother. And then, I told them about Cedric saying we simply couldn't be together because his duties were elsewhere.

"And you believed him?" Mama Viv demanded.

I rolled my eyes but didn't let that enter my voice. "It's the truth. You know who he is."

"Darling, he ran from them," Mama Viv.

"No, but he changed his mind," I said. "He realized he was better off without me."

"Don't be silly, Tristan," Mama Viv said.

Rome hijacked the conversation. "It's so clear, but only you don't get it. He told you before that he wouldn't marry her for anything in the world. That he doesn't love her. Tris, they must have threatened him real bad to make him go back. If they were following him here, then they probably knew about you."

"Darling, can you call him?" Mama Viv asked.

"No. He never had his phone on," I said. "I don't even have his number." *And he won't want to hear from me.*

Silence. They were thinking. Roman spoke after a while. "I think they blackmailed him, maybe. Or worse. I think they forced him to go back. It makes no sense that he just flipped around and decided he was done. That guy *loved* you, Tris."

"He did," Mama Viv said softly. "When I told him we would hunt him down if he hurt you, he beamed. He was so happy to know you had loyal friends, Tristan."

"This smells rotten to me," Rome said. "We need to get in touch with that guy."

My soul was torn out of me, and an abyss opened up in my chest. Had I let him go on some stupid, self-sacrificial quest because I couldn't believe that he loved me? Had I doomed him to a forced marriage just because I didn't think I deserved love? Oh God. Oh, all the gods that listened. Apollo and Antinous, Hyacinthus and Dionysus and Hermes. "We have to save him," I whispered.

Whatever they threatened him with, I could protect him from it. I could help him get out.

"And I have a plan," Mama Viv said.

It took Mama Viv three days to arrange the flight. Her text message to me said, "I have always stood by your side. And I always will. Get that boy back."

The return to the Hudson Burrow passed in the blink of an eye, and the flight that followed was restless and sleepless. Its significance clutched my heart and filled me with anxiety.

How would I ever find him?

How would I ever come near him?

Would he even want to see me?

It turned out I didn't have to worry at all. As soon as my passport was scanned, I was detained, and two agents in black suits appeared some minutes later.

"Mr. Lawson, welcome to Verdumont. We have been told to expect you," the older one said.

"Good," I said, a hopeful smile touching my lips, although I knew everything about this was absolutely wrong. I forced out a laugh. "I hope I didn't keep you guys waiting."

They didn't smile back.

CHAPTER 16
Heroes and Lovers

TRISTAN

THE ROOM WAS THE BIGGEST AND MOST luxurious I had ever seen. It was the size of an entire floor of a regular residential building, or perhaps bigger. The walls were covered in wallpaper with elaborate design patterns. The southern side had a row of windows looking over the summer gardens that sprawled endlessly behind the Valois Montclair home. Two fireplaces stood on the opposite ends of the room. The northern side wall was cluttered with portraits of men with mustaches and beards, women in ridiculously padded dresses, and youngsters with stiff, regal postures. A large number of young men and women resembled Cedric. There was a clear theme running through the generations. They were all blond in various degrees; most were blue or grey-eyed, and those that smiled had prominent dimples on their cheeks. The high cheekbones that I knew so well and had explored with my fingers and lips ran through the generations of royals in this small country.

The furniture was positioned as if this room served ten different purposes. I was told to sit on a sofa that had elaborately carved mahogany legs and soft padding. It matched the armchairs that were positioned precisely on the other side of the elegant coffee table. If someone had erected walls around these items, this would have made a nice little living room. As it was, however, the space resembled a hotel lobby. Similar sets of sitting furniture were scattered around the hall, and there was a desk with a high-backed chair, both made of the same sort of dark wood. The chair had murky crimson upholstery that matched the carpet under the office furniture in that corner of the room.

I had not been welcomed warmly. Nobody brought warm cookies or a glass of lemonade. The two agents who had escorted me here from the airport wouldn't answer any questions. When I mentioned that I had never before been kidnapped, one looked at me with an expressionless stare and informed me that I was to be introduced to His Royal Highness. Based on the level of politeness and mirth in the agents, I stifled the hope that the highness in question was Cedric. Maybe he had really chosen to toss me aside, but he wouldn't have done this to me.

I allowed some optimism to shine through. "At least I'm at the palace," I whispered to myself as I stood.

Light slanted lazily through the windows from the west. The last rays of sunshine had a dim and tired quality to them. There were no specks of dust I would have expected to see in an antiquity showroom such as this. So I explored the portrait of a young man above the western side fireplace. Locks of golden hair fell over his dark, defined eyebrow. He was the spitting image of Cedric Philippe

Valois Montclair, except that it was dated two hundred years ago.

Just looking at the portrait made my heart clench and my muscles knot with tension over all the uncertainties. I didn't know what the next five minutes would bring, let alone what the rest of my life would look like, yet it felt as though such decisions would be made here and today.

The door creaked open and shut.

Footsteps crossed the space with a firm click of the soles of the wearer's dress shoes. Where were they taking me next?

"Those hinges could use oiling," I said. I didn't care if I offended a butler or a security detail. I was far beyond caring at this point. My requests to see Cedric had been met with absolute silence during the ride here.

The figure approached me and halted a few steps behind my back.

I kept my eyes spitefully on the young man wearing Cedric's face in the painting.

"Louis Montclair," the voice behind me said. I regretted my remark about oiling the hinges when I heard the regal control of the vocal cords. It would have been funny had the future of my love not been in Alexander's hands. "Our seventh great-granduncle was a patron of the arts and poetry. Louis passed away at the age of twenty-seven, taken by a cough, leaving behind a collection of letters he received from his lover, Théodore de Montmorency. You have a keen eye, Mr. Lawson, and a type, if you don't mind me saying."

I turned around, smoothing out the ripples of emotions on my face. In the span of a second, I had cringed, and doubted myself, and felt a leap of sorrow in my chest, and wanted to laugh hysterically. "Your Highness."

Alexander was as tall as Cedric, although his body exhibited none of Cedric's easygoing relaxedness. In fact, only now, I saw how relaxed Cedric had appeared at his stiffest, most royal postures. His gaze was on the portrait of Louis Montclair. His hair was much darker than Cedric's, and his suit was pressed and smoothed to perfection. There wasn't a wrinkle or loose thread on it. And there wasn't a hair out of place on his handsome head. Were all royals blessed with devastating beauty? It didn't seem fair that they should have everything.

Cedric's eyes are brighter, warmer, more intense, I thought. They were like burning ice, like oracles made of sapphires, like clear skies on a summer day. Alexander's were pale and cool. The ice in them was deep and frosty and sharp.

"I wonder if there is something beyond our understanding, picking through our past and bringing our old characters into new lives," Alexander said, looking at his brother's image on another man's face. "And I wonder if we share the same fates with those that came before us."

"I can answer that, Your Highness," I said with enough cynicism that he didn't need to hear the rest.

Alexander Louis Valois Montclair, as his Wikipedia page named him, lowered his gaze from the portrait to me. It chilled my spine to meet those cold, blue eyes. "I expected you to be much more romantic, considering you flew here on such short notice."

"I'm not so easily swept away," I replied.

"Very well," Alexander said. His hands were behind his

back, his shoulders squared, and his chest puffed out. Only the top button of his shirt was undone. The dark blue suit jacket matched his pants, and the brown belt around his waist went well with the darker brown shoes. He was very much a modern-day prince; there was no mistaking him. Cedric had been a delicious mystery, but Alexander might as well have worn a crown. "Mr. Lawson, your presence here is my personal courtesy for the foolish attempt to keep my willful brother safe. Although I do not appreciate that your actions were designed to keep him away from his family, your dedication is commendable."

"Call me Tristan," I said. "We can drop the pretenses."

Alexander blinked once and stared at me from under flat, unmoving eyebrows.

"Basically, I am here to see Cedric," I said.

"It is my understanding that Cedric does not want to see you," Alexander said coolly.

"And my understanding is that he isn't allowed to," I replied with just as little emotion, except that I could feel my eyes flaring with anger.

Alexander curled those perfect, pouty lips and cocked his head. "Why would he not be allowed to see anyone?"

"I'm pretty sure you have the correct answer to that. Your Highness." I held my breath. This was a dangerous game I was playing. I didn't think the odds were in my favor.

"Mr. Lawson," he said, "I could have had you on the next plane to New York. Is this how you express gratitude for a private audience?"

A laugh rose from me and almost choked me as I tried to hold it back. "Your Highness, I come from a place that celebrates the day we divorced our monarch. You should visit. Nobody does a better barbecue than Mama Viv's Neon Nights on the Fourth of July. And though I'm grateful for the ride from the airport, I'm not here for an audience with you. I'm here to see your brother."

Alexander's face seemed to get stiffer. Muscles in his cheeks knotted, and he poured all his strength into freezing me on the spot. It didn't work. Rage burned far too hotly inside of me. I didn't care if King Ferdinand himself stood in my way. I didn't care if the entire Royal Guard surrounded me.

"Let me make something perfectly clear to you, Tristan," he said, towering over me. "Cedric will not see you. He will not speak to you. He does not want you here or in his life. And we would all appreciate it if you left quietly. The gratitude of a Crown Prince is worth a lot, even in New York. I took the liberty of preparing a generous agreement for you to sign."

"Let me return the favor, Alex," I said casually, but I glared at him just as if I were shouting. "I wouldn't take your gratitude if it came with millions of dollars. And I won't accept your words, either. The only way I'll ever be quiet is if I heard all this from Cedric's lips."

Alexander's cheeks grew hotter, but so did mine.

I was, after all, a very stubborn mule when I was in love.

Cedric

Sophia's summer dress fluttered in the wind she created when she ran into my quarters.

"Cedric," she huffed, catching her breath. "You have to come."

"What is it?" I asked. "What happened?"

She had a worried look on her face, but she was not devastated by a tragedy. I had been trying to think of a way to speak to Max without setting him off or insulting him. The tricky part was not to lift his hopes too high, either. Nothing any of us could do was guaranteed to succeed.

"You have to come. Now." Sophia almost tripped over her own words. "It's Tristan."

My heart dropped into the deepest pit of my stomach. "What about him?" I whispered, too horrified to think. "What happened to Tristan?"

Had I misjudged my brother so poorly that I had just opened more risks for Tristan?

"He's here. He's in the yellow sitting room," Sophia said, practically bubbling with excitement. "Alexander is with him. Go."

I was on the move before she finished speaking. It didn't feel like it was my body that carried me there. It felt like I was walking through the thickest mist with no direction. It felt like something lifted me off my feet and pushed me to float down the hallways of the palace until I reached a guarded door of the yellow sitting room. "Let us through,"

I demanded. I realized that Sophia was not there when the guard frowned.

"Forgive me, Your Highness, but I cannot let this meeting be disturbed," the man replied.

Where the hell was my sister? "This meeting concerns me greatly, Gaston."

"I have direct orders, Your Highness," he replied, his eyes regretful. He had known me since I was born. He was assigned as the head of Alexander's personal security team just before I had had a chance to request him for mine. Gaston was loyal and smart and kind. I didn't want him getting hurt because of this, but if Tristan was on the other side of the door, I would have no choice.

"Gaston, I swear to you, this meeting is for me to attend," I said seriously.

It seemed to hurt him deeply. "Forgive me, Your Highness, but your name is at the top of the list. I cannot let you through."

"Ah, then I'm very sorry about this," I said and meant every word. In the next instant, I bellowed my brother's name from the top of my lungs.

Gaston seemed stricken.

I yelled again, louder, and again, and again. I shouted Alexander's name so loudly that the kitchen staff must have heard me. And at last, the door flew open. Gaston begged Alexander to forgive him, but my brother had a tired expression on his face. "Enough," he said, and we all fell silent. "You might as well join me." He shot Gaston a look of reprimand, then moved from the door to let me through.

I had been so focused on entering the room that I had completely forgotten to prepare myself to see Tristan. He stood tall and broad and beautiful under the portrait of Louis Montclair.

My hands trembled, and I closed them into fists. Air drained out of my lungs, and my gaze locked onto his face.

Tristan's lips quivered, and he pressed them tightly together. The corners of his mouth moved just enough to form something like a smile to greet me. He gazed at me across the long sitting room, his chest rising and falling lightly as he breathed in and out. He wore that sexy sleeveless shirt I loved and a pair of light brown pants with a darker brown belt around his waist. His bare arms were tense, his biceps swollen like he was holding something heavy.

"Tristan," I whispered, barely in control of my voice. It was on the verge of cracking. It took all the strength I had in me to stop myself from leaping toward him and hugging him. He had come all this way for me after everything I had said and done.

And he had walked right into a trap.

I gave you up, I thought. *I gave you up so you wouldn't be crucified by the press, so you could live your life freely and away from all the scheming that is so natural to my kind.* Regrets welled in me. Perhaps I should have stayed and risked my brother's wrath. Perhaps Tristan's arrival had changed his mind.

"Tell him," Alexander said.

I clenched my teeth, never breaking the eye contact with Tristan. He wore a pleading look that broke my heart.

"Cedric, you need to tell him," Alexander warned me. "Tell your lover you don't want to see him."

My gaze snapped to Alexander's face.

"And tell him what will happen if he doesn't leave," Alexander said.

So, the threat stood just as tall and unbreakable.

A little smile touched my lips. It was total defeat, and the fight hadn't even begun. I'd lost everything. But I smiled regardless. Tristan was here. I had expected never to see him again, but he was here, in this room.

I turned to Tristan and kept that soothing smile on my face. It was more melancholic and apologetic than bright and loving. "Tristan," I said as I made my feet carry me closer to him. I crossed the room, and Alexander followed until I stood a couple of paces away from my beautiful boyfriend. "Why are you here?" I asked softly.

"I came to get you," Tristan said simply. "To...rescue you." He laughed very softly when he said that. "I can't help it. It's who I am."

I nodded, holding back the tears as best I could. "It really is." I made another step toward him. "I hope you never change."

Tristan let out a little laugh, his eyes glimmering, his fists shaking like he had to fight them to remain still. "Are you ready to run away again?" he asked, but he didn't mean it. Some part of him maybe hoped I would say yes, but we both knew that this was a goodbye.

"Tristan, I'm sorry about the way I left," I said, pretending Alexander wasn't in this room at all. "I thought that if I could just make you hate me for a little while, it would keep you from doing something stupid. Like flying all the way here." We both laughed at that, and the sadness that gripped my heart rightened. "I should have told you."

Tristan nodded. "You should have."

"But I know you wouldn't accept a defeat," I said. "Because that's what this is. We lost."

Tristan nodded. "You're right." He glanced at Alexander behind me, then returned his gaze to me. It was so dark and fiery. It was a chocolate fountain with big, black pupils and brimming tears that he blinked away. "I don't accept it."

I had expected as much.

"Cedric," Alexander said warningly.

I snapped my head around. "I'm doing it, dammit."

My brother took a step back in total silence.

"What's he talking about?" Tristan asked with absolutely no respect Alexander expected. It entertained me madly.

I opened my hand and offered it to Tristan, who took it carefully. My fingers threaded with his, and he waited. "Alexander is right," I said. It made Tristan wince, but he listened. "He knows what's going to happen if we are together. The media will...they'll pull you apart, Tristan. You'll never be like everyone else again."

Tristan rolled his broad shoulders. "I'd have you."

It shredded my heart. "You don't know what paparazzi are like, Tristan. They'll look for drama, and if they can't find it, they'll make it. They'll dig up everything about your life until they make you fight them. And when you do, they'll win because it'll be their headline."

"I don't have anything to hide," Tristan said.

It hurt me more than I could say to remind him of it. "Are you sure about that, Tristan? That you would want them speaking of...?"

"I'm sure," Tristan said. "They're welcome to dig

through it. I made my peace with everything that happened."

"What of us?" Alexander demanded, and it only awakened the deeply buried spite in me. "What of the scandal?"

"What scandalizes you more?" Tristan asked without a sliver of patience, his hand tight around mine. "That a Montclair prince left for an American or that he is gay?"

Alexander lifted his chin defiantly.

"Tristan, are you sure about that?" I asked. The last sparks of hope fanned to life somewhere deep inside of me. "Are you sure you could face seeing your entire life bared open? Every scrap and bruise and loss? For strangers to read and gasp?" It choked me up to even imagine it. His loss was so incomprehensibly large that I couldn't wrap my mind around it.

"Is that all that's in the way?" Tristan asked hopefully. "Because I went home. I visited her. I'm ready to move on." His voice had gone low, just for my ears.

"Cedric, you are doing more harm than good," Alexander reminded me. "Don't feed him hopes. You know that you must marry Élodie."

"Perhaps I should have a say in that," announced a regal and controlled voice from the distant part of the room.

I spun around to see Élodie leading a small procession. Sophia was behind her, arms folded on her torso like she was holding herself together against the worry that threatened to pull her apart. The final member of Élodie's party was my slender and tall younger brother, Sophia's twin, Maximilian. His mop of aged golden hair was ruffled and stylishly messy, his pointy chin lifted, and his gaze direct. The animosity he had exhibited toward me had barely softened in the days since I had returned, but now, he looked at Alexander with something far colder and more menacing.

"Is that her?" Tristan whispered, holding my hand and standing next to me.

I quickly told him all their names.

"How are you all so beautiful?" Tristan murmured sourly. "It's crazy."

I wanted to laugh, but Alexander was crossing the room with purpose in his stride just as Élodie, Sophie, and Max were moving toward the middle.

"You will forgive the intrusion, Your Highness," Élodie said in perfect diction and in clear English because Sophie must have told her that Tristan was here. "But if my future and marriage are at stake, then I believe I should be present when they are discussed."

"Élodie," Alexander said carefully. "I am merely trying to prevent any changes to the plans our families have agreed on."

Max looked at Élodie, and all the cool composure shattered. He loved her.

The Marchioness spoke on. "Then you should be aware that there have been some changes in the arrangements, Your Highness. Perhaps you should attempt to protect the new agreement. My father has listened to my wishes, and yours has listened to the wishes of his children."

Alexander glared at me as if I had done something.

Sophia spoke up. "It was me, Alex. I'm sorry. I spoke to Father."

Alexander laughed bitterly. "I seem to be the only person who has any interest in preserving the reputation of our family here. Very well. We can continue this some other time. Until then, Cedric, you have a scheduled appearance with Élodie at the Modernist Verdumont exhibition, and you are not ready."

"I'm not leaving Tristan," I said. The battle lines had shifted tremendously. Tristan's hand in mine gave me strength. "I swear to God, Alexander, you can't make me." I looked at Tristan doubtfully. "Are you sure about this?" I whispered.

He gave a single, deep nod.

Fear rocked me, but it wasn't the fear of Alexander. I realized, a moment before they were out, what were the words that welled in me and fought to be free. "I love you," I said.

Tristan's eyelashes batted, and a grin split his face. "I love you." He tightened his hand around mine.

I wanted to kiss him right then, but Alexander slapped his hands together and ruined the moment. "This is irrelevant."

"Don't be an ass," Max said loudly, bristling and standing shoulder to shoulder with Élodie. "It's no longer your job, Alex. Retreat."

"Father allowed it," Sophie said. "Just now. I spoke to him, and he agreed."

"I will marry Élodie," Max announced bravely.

Élodie's perfect composure wavered momentarily. She loved him, too. "And we have my family's blessing."

"Wasn't she forced to marry you?" Tristan whispered, appalled.

"She never protested," I whispered back. Poor girl had never thought she had a choice. Almost like me.

"That is all very well and fine, but how will we explain a

prince running away with a common chef to New York?" Alexander demanded.

"How dare you?" I snapped. "Tristan is so much more than that. Do you hear me? He is the finest, noblest person I have ever met, and you *will* show some respect."

Alexander turned to me impatiently as stillness settled in the room. "That may be so, but he is still an unknown man who shares an apartment with four men and does odd jobs when he needs to. Even if you do not marry Élodie as had been agreed, you are going to destroy this family's reputation by sweeping floors and living with drag queens. And I will *not* allow that."

"My, you've done your homework," Tristan said in a peculiar tone. "Maybe it'll make your family more relatable if people see you're capable of washing dishes and sweeping floors."

"Thank you, but we do not need input on how we manage our image," Alexander squeezed through his teeth.

"But he's right," Sophie said. "We don't need to explain it. Let Cedric go. Let him be in New York. He would hardly be the first royal to relocate away from the palace. He can continue his studies in the States or focus on research."

"He can spend his days in museums like he always wanted," Max said. He looked at me with those grey-blue eyes, and an old spark of kinship returned to him.

"If he dates Tristan, that is entirely his choice," Sophie said. "And we can supply plenty of reasons for his prolonged visits."

"He can attend everything that is important when he is invited," Max added. He looked at Élodie, and I knew what important event he had in mind. I noticed that they held hands.

Alexander took a step back, shaking his head. His gaze crossed the entire room, taking each face in carefully. "It would appear that you have all made up your minds."

My older brother was not someone I felt an obligation to reassure that things could continue smoothly. Even so, I had a word of warning for him. "The only problems that I can foresee are those that you create, brother."

"Oh, I am afraid that you have very little foresight, Cedric," he said calmly as he straightened, his hands resting on the small of his back, his gaze downcast. "I will not create problems for you. Problems, you'll learn, have a tendency to create themselves no matter what we do. More so when we are careless." He directed his gaze at me as a warning. After nodding once, he did that stage trick where it appeared like he was looking into everyone's eyes at once. "It seems there is nothing I can say to dissuade any of you from making avoidable mistakes." He sighed, straightened his suit jacket, and marched out of the room.

The sun had waned and left the sky, leaving only the afterlight of a day gone by. The door shut, and a collective sigh of relief seemed to occur at once. By instinct, I turned to Tristan. I held his hand just the same, but now I looked into those chocolate eyes. "Do you really love me?" I asked. "After all I said."

"Yes," he said, a smile barely contained to his face. "I love you. After what you said and because of what you said."

I raised my eyebrows.

But Tristan frowned and released my hands. He rested

his hands on my chest and looked into my eyes. "Don't ever be the hero like that," he said. It would have been a grave warning had he not grinned so freely. "Silly sacrifices are my job."

"I'll never do anything so stupid again," I promised.

"And do you know what?" Tristan smiled as he rose to the tips of his toes and leveled our gazes. "Neither will I from now on."

Our bodies melted into one another as our arms wrapped around each other's torso. As I leaned in and pressed my heated lips against his, life returned to the darkest corners of my tired soul. He healed me. He saved me.

I kissed him softly, then harder, holding him with all I had. I hugged him so close that neither of us could inhale a real breath of air. I loved him. I loved him so much that the intensity of my emotions would have terrified me had it been anything other than love.

"Hey, boys," Sophie said.

Tristan pulled away from me first, licking his lips and blushing. His eyes were glassy and glimmering when he blinked. He cleared his throat and lowered himself to his feet.

I looked at Sophie, who seemed relieved like everyone else. Behind her, Max and Élodie held each other's hands, but their impatience was clear because they practically trembled with the desire to kiss.

"I don't want to interrupt, but we should go somewhere cozier," Sophie said. "There's a lot to celebrate."

I looked at Tristan. "What do you think? Should we celebrate?"

"I'm never one to miss a party," he said softly, his pupils so big and black that they pulled me in.

I turned back to Sophie. "You heard him. Lead the way, sis."

And she did. Gesturing at the door, Sophia led all of us out of the yellow sitting room, down the hallways of the palace, where Tristan stopped every so often to look at portraits and other landscapes of Verdumont's most famous artists. Busts lined one hallway, and Tristan paused a few times, pointing at some that resembled me. "It seems you have a very Valois Montclair face," he observed cheekily. "I love it."

He would get to kiss it however much he wanted. Later. And I would kiss him back.

Sophia led us to my apartments, where the sitting room was sizeable enough for a party of five. Books were scattered around the furniture, and my little shrine to Antinous was the first thing Tristan noticed. I wondered how strange it was for him to be here and how intimate it was to show him the rooms where I had grown up. This space had so much of me, more than any other, and letting Tristan in gave the rooms some higher meaning. It gave them heart and soul and life.

"Blessings to Antinous," Tristan said, looking at the small bust I had commissioned some years ago. The altar was an elegant thing, containing the bust, a small bouquet of red flowers of various kinds, candles, an incense burner, and a small porcelain dish with a few golden rings I had outgrown to symbolize his light.

I leaned in from behind Tristan, arms sliding around his torso and hands resting on his abs. I pressed my front against his back and kissed the length of his neck. "You are an impossible man, Tristan," I whispered. "I never loved anyone the way I love you."

Tristan turned his head and looked at me. "I believe you."

It was a leap. From the hurt boy who couldn't fathom anyone could love him to someone who was willing to risk it all for a shot at being with me, he had flowered and bloomed. He had stepped into his true self, and I loved him more than I had thought was possible.

"And I love you, too, Cedric. So much." His words were spoken in a quiet voice, just for me.

Sophia made a cheerful sound and announced that there was wine. Maximilian and Élodie seemed excited about it, so Tristan and I turned to them, glanced at one another, smiled, and joined the celebration.

CHAPTER 17
Happily Ever After

TRISTAN

ALTHOUGH IT BEGAN QUIETLY, ALMOST WITH AN awkward silence, the little party of five warmed up as the first round of drinks came and went. Sophia recounted the events of the afternoon, saying she had resorted to calling their father when it seemed like Alexander wouldn't back off. For days, their eldest brother had been holding fast against Sophia's attempts to discuss the marriage arrangements. "'He needs to learn how to do what he is told, Sophie,'" she imitated in a deep, mocking tone, sitting on the floor with her back against the chair in which Maximilian sat. The young prince's back was straight and his movements elegant. According to Cedric, that was not very much like him, but Élodie's proper conduct inspired Maximilian to act the way he was taught.

My gaze moved from one face to the next until I reached Cedric, sitting next to me on the ottoman, holding his wineglass in both hands.

"Hm?" he said quietly, his gaze never far from me. And when he looked at me, I couldn't believe he was this beautiful. I couldn't believe it had worked.

"You're all nobility," I said, looking around the room. "I'm sorry," I said, laughing, "but I never processed this completely."

"Almost all of us," Sophia said. "Max doesn't qualify."

"Hey," the young prince said as everyone laughed.

"He lost that status when he set off a stink bomb in school," Sophia explained.

Max seemed on the edge of arguing but then nodded in surrender. "That's right." He chuckled like he had revisited a fond memory.

Élodie asked me about cooking and my ambitions, and I talked about Neon Nights. A job waited for me there, which made Maximilian and Sophia exchange a look that drew my attention.

"They're assuming you're going to be a socialite from now on," Cedric explained.

I laughed. "Me? At soirees? I'd sooner jump out of the window." And when that provoked a laugh with an underlying note of bewilderment, I spoke again. "I love preparing food. It's when I'm the happiest. And when people eat what I made with my own hands, that's when I feel real pride. I feed people."

They wondered if I wanted to have a chain of restaurants, but I said I only wanted one, eventually. Until then, I was happy with Mama Viv's Neon Nights.

"And is that the place where Cedric worked?" Maximilian asked with a cheeky smile, barely containing the snicker that visibly tried to escape him.

"Hey, at least I worked," Cedric said. "Sure, I wasn't the employee of the month, but I did my best."

"You should have seen him drop a tray full of drinks," I gossiped.

Cedric poked me in the rib cage, then pressed a kiss on my face. It was enough to derail my thoughts completely and leave me fighting for air. I loved him so much. I couldn't shake off this feeling of having won something immense and incredible tonight.

The party slowed down after another round of drinks. Élodie invited Max to her sitting room to listen to music. Sophia wondered if she should visit this bar where Cedric had worked, saying she would adore seeing her brother pour a beer with the right amount of foam. After that, she yawned and got up from the floor, kissed Cedric on the cheek, and then did the same to me. When she left, silence settled in the sitting room.

I took a sip of my wine under Cedric's loving gaze. Inhaling, I dared myself to check if everything was still true. It was too big, too impossible to believe right away. "Are you sure about moving to New York?"

Cedric chuckled. "Absolutely," I said. "I'm not sure I'll survive visiting Neon Nights. Mama Viv might welcome me with a firing squad."

I shook my head. "I'm pretty sure she's still freaking out for criticizing a prince."

"They all know?" Cedric asked.

"Rafael figured it out," I said. "He knows the weirdest facts, like European royalty, you know?"

We shared a laugh. Cedric inhaled deeply. "What made

you come here? I thought I did...pretty well...turning you against me."

"Oh, you did that just fine," I growled. I couldn't stay mad, though. "Rome made me rethink everything. He made me realize that what you did was out of love."

"It was," Cedric hurried to assure me.

I smiled and took his hand in mine. "I know that now. And I won't doubt it again."

Cedric stood, pulling me up with him. He pressed a kiss on my brow, then each of my closed eyes, and finally, on my lips. It was soft and loving, heating up with the lust that never failed to appear between us. It existed like an eternal ember, only ever needing a small gust of wind to create an all-consuming fire. And the fire roared.

I kissed him back harder, touching his hips and pulling him close. I could never have enough of him, body and soul. Shivers ran down my arms as something inexplicable rocked my chest. Was this what pure happiness felt like? Like climbing the highest peak of the highest mountain, like rising to the top of the biggest Ferris wheel, like sitting in a magical rocket and flying into space.

Cedric pulled back from me, his eyes glimmering with happy tears and his deep dimples accenting his smile. He took my hand and led me through the sitting room into his bedroom. There, when I asked, he showed me where the en suite was behind a discreet door that looked like part of the wallpapered wall.

I showered, feeling the tiredness of this extraordinarily long day wash away and leave down the drain. When I was done, I tied a big towel around my waist, Cedric's initials embroidered over a corner of the soft, white fabric. The shower had energized me and cleared my thoughts, but it didn't dampen the desire that ripped through me.

As I stepped into the bedroom, all the lights were out. Instead, Cedric had prepared candles that glimmered from every surface in the room. The nightstands held porcelain plates with candles of various sizes, and so did the shelves, the surfaces of both of his dressers and the windowsills with curtains wide open and tied to the sides of the tall windows.

Cedric wore his white shirt and dark gray like before. He stepped toward me and gazed at me shamelessly, taking in every inch of my body.

"I should have put something nice on," I said.

Cedric shook his head. "You are perfect exactly the way you are."

My heart stumbled. I put a hand on the middle of Cedric's chest, my stomach filled with butterflies and my head spinning. When had he done all this? To be fair, I'd taken my merry time, and I hadn't exactly planned to go to sleep right away.

"And so are you," I said, popping a button of his shirt. "Although I can see a few ways we can improve your appearance."

He let out a low, deep chuckle, his hand resting on the fold of the towel on my hip. "I have a few ideas, too." His fingers slipped the fold open, and the towel parted like a curtain, sliding from my waist.

I gasped, but Cedric put his hand on my hip, the other hand resting softly on the small of my back. His lips covered mine in the next instant, and the other half of my gasp turned into a gentle moan.

These were the heated kisses of the lovers who had been

separated by forces beyond their control. I hadn't known that such kisses existed, but I could recognize them clearly now.

It didn't take long for the fire in me to become apparent. My cock grew, swelling to its full size. Our bodies pressed tightly together, my dick trapped between our legs, throbbing and begging to be touched.

Cedric was hard, too, although the dark grey pants contained him mercilessly.

As he kissed me, I undid his buttons, feeling his heated body and smooth skin until he could shrug the shirt off. It flew somewhere behind him, and he unbuckled his belt for me. When the belt was off, I turned us around and pushed Cedric back. He let himself fall flat on the big, soft bed, sinking into the mattress and grinning like it was his first time.

I'm going to ride you until you go mad, I thought, my brain spinning and my heart thundering.

Cedric's gaze locked onto my hard cock, and his perfect teeth closed around his lower lip. "Come here," he said after a moment, but I hesitated just to torture him a little more. My left hand rested on my chest, sliding slowly down the length of my torso. The pull of attraction I felt between us was like sliding to the eye of the horizon of a black hole. It was inescapable. It was unbreakable. My course was charted for me, and there was nothing I could or would do differently.

It pulled me toward him until I knelt on the bed between his legs. Leaning in, I rested my hands on his chiseled abs and dragged them down to the last button that needed undoing. Once I finished, I leaned in deeper, pressing my lips against the middle of his chest. I kissed and licked him all the way down to the waistband of his underwear, pulling his pants to his knees as I kissed him. And when my lips found the soft, tight fabric of his boxer briefs, I held my breath against shivering and moaning, and I pulled his underwear down, too.

I didn't know how he did it. It was swift, and it relied on his strength. I only knew that he was lifting his torso in one instant and that our places were swapped in the next. I gazed up into his deep, blue eyes as Cedric towered over me. His legs moved, and I heard his pants and underwear falling off the bed. His arms were tense as they supported the weight of his torso, but he was lowering himself onto me slowly. His hard cock pressed lightly against my abdomen before he sank low and melted into me. Our bodies, naked and warm, touched everywhere at once. The air left me, but I kissed him instead, and it was enough to keep me alive.

"I thought I lost you," he whispered.

"You'll never lose me," I told him, my hands on his hips, sliding to his round ass and pulling him closer.

Our mouths pressed together, Cedric's tongue sliding to explore my mouth, teasing me, toying with me, driving me crazy with all this desire I had nowhere to spend. He moved quickly and trapped my hands high above my head, locking my wrists in the hold of his left hand. His right hand moved gently up the side of my rib cage until he closed it around my neck. It turned me wilder than I had thought it ever could.

My eyes rolled back, and I whimpered with a desperate need to do more.

Moments merged and blended until they were indistinguishable. It was like the soft glow of the countless glimmering candles in the room erased the space between one second and the next. Touches and sighs and kisses all melted together until I didn't know the order in which things happened.

We coiled and rolled and turned, limbs brushing against limbs, my legs wrapping around his waist, us rolling until I was on top and holding his arms trapped. We kissed, we licked, we sighed against one another's mouth. And when I lowered myself down to take him into my mouth, I could sense the tingles running through his fingers and toes. I felt the same sort of thrill when we disregarded all sense of shame and politeness. This was the ultimate intimacy between two bare souls.

I sucked him slowly, taking him deeper and deeper into my mouth until it felt like even a little more would choke me. The sounds I made and the tension in Cedric's muscles were only distant facts of the physical world. Our souls were converging and twining across the stars, far beyond anything our bodies could experience.

Cedric stopped me abruptly, laughing nervously that I had nearly finished him before we started. He turned us around and told me how much he loved me, then kissed the length of my back until his warm breath graced my sensitive hole. His tongue was hot and wet and soft at first, growing harder with each lick. He ate me, sucked me, kissed me, and probed me gently with his tongue and his finger, massaging me mercilessly and for a long, long time. And when I whimpered and pleaded with him to feel his cock inside me, he told me how much he liked hearing me beg.

With that otherworldly strength, Cedric lifted me until

I was kneeling, my elbows and forearms sinking into the mattress, my ass perched for him, and my hole bared and ready for taking.

Cedric brought us lube from a drawer in one dresser, poured it over his length, and rubbed himself, then my hole, while I held my breath and shivered with desire. I relaxed myself by force of will and allowed him to enter me with one finger, then another, moaning into the thick duvet that covered his bed.

My love pressed one hand on the small of my back, the other working me loose with two and then three fingers, opening me slowly and deliberately until I couldn't remain so patient anymore.

"Please, oh fuck, please, Cedric," I growled against the bed. "I'm ready. Fuck me, please..."

His fingers twisted and slid out of me, quickly massaging my closing hole with soothing softness. And when he thrust his cock between my cheeks, sliding it until his balls settled against my hole, I exhaled roughly.

Come on, I begged silently. *Do it. Fuck me. I'm ready for you, just take me.*

Cedric was slow, but he was precise, and when he pressed the tip of his bare cock against my hole, he waited for me to make the next move. Relaxing once again with all the force I could summon, I thrust my ass back and impaled myself on him, his body never moving.

The first inch hurt, the next one felt like heaven, and the third made me feel complete. After that, I never wanted us to be separated again. Cedric swung back, letting me breathe out and in, then thrust his hips forward, sliding deeper into me.

Each thrust sent a small whimper from my mouth and nose, my fingers clawing the duvet, my face rubbing against the soft, clean fabric. And every other move he made caused my dick to throb and my hole to clench around him. Those were my favorite; he hissed and grunted whenever I tightened around his cock.

Cedric's fingers dug into my hips, and he knelt on the bed, ramming me harder, faster, with such force that it pushed me further along the bed, making me slide away from him. My legs spread wide, the intensity of his movements making me lose control over the very basic control of my own body. My eyes rolled back in my head, and my mouth opened wide, but all my cries and moans were trapped in my throat. Occasionally, I heard myself hiss or whisper my pleas for more or to keep going just like that.

My arms spread around the bed, hands digging deep into the duvet, fists closing around it as if I was holding myself against some force that would lift me up and carry me away.

Cedric dictated our movements; he decided on the pace and on the intensity with which he rammed into me, his dick pushing against my prostate and sending these wild, impossible sensations through my entire body.

I felt myself lifted off the back without quite understanding it. In my state of bliss, I might as well have been floating through the clouds. He had lifted me up, dragging me down his length and holding his hands firmly on my groin, sliding deep into me and huffing with exertion.

He told me how good I felt, how warm, how wet, how perfect. He told me how he loved fucking me and how I was his.

When he let my knees sink into the mattress again, his hands moved up my back, grabbing me and pressing me wherever he reached. And when his hands rested on my shoulders, he gently nudged them around my neck.

I knelt up, angling my body so that every thrust of Cedric's thick, long cock hit me exactly how I wanted the most.

Cedric's arms wrapped around my body. One coiled around my torso, and the other moved up until he had his hand around my throat.

I grabbed that hand and held it fast, not letting him let me go. It felt terrific. It felt so good to be without control, without shame, without sins, and without freedoms. They were all his. He held me, and he owned me.

When I wrapped my right hand around my swollen cock, it was wet with precum. I knew that his dick was, too, although deep inside of me. And the thought was enough to start the eruption of sensations deep inside my chest. It exploded like the universe had exploded from a single, incredible dot, spreading in all directions in a heartbeat. It consumed me, and I moved my hand away from the one holding my throat tightly to touch Cedric's hip. I pulled him in, closer and closer, wanting him to finish deep inside of me just as my hole pulsed and tightened around the base of his cock.

Hot cum spilled over my fingers and across the bed in white strings, landing on the clean sheets and staining his royal bed.

The throbs inside of me came after Cedric attempted to pull back, whispering a hurried warning.

"Inside," I gasped. "Please. Need you..." And then, it

was too late to change anything. Cedric pressed himself deep into me, his cock shooting loads of white heat into my body, filling me and sending waves of tingling down my limbs with each fresh throb.

"I love you," he huffed, his forehead sweaty and hot and pressed hard against the back of my neck, his hand around my throat relaxing, his cock pulsing more softly and slowly until it stopped.

Although some small part of me said we would be smart to shower, my body gave in to the temptation at the first hint from Cedric, and we collapsed in an exhausted and happy heap on the bed. We held one another, limbs still tangled and sweat cooling on our bodies.

Cedric found my hand and threaded our fingers together on my stomach. Our hands rose and fell with my abs as I breathed deeply. "You are..." I whispered, out of breath again.

Cedric inhaled and exhaled just as deeply, catching his breath. "And you." He managed a grin, his eyes bright but his eyelids drooping slightly with exhaustion. "I love you, Tristan."

I looked at him. He was glowing. Sweat and joy combined on his face and lit by the many restless candles in the room, softening his sharp features and making him look like an angel. Or a god, one I would worship for the rest of my days. "I love you, too."

We lay there in the lazy bliss that followed great sex. We held each other, listening to the other one's breaths and heartbeat, my head resting on Cedric's chest at one point and his on mine later. I looked around, tremors of disbelief battering my consciousness.

This is a royal palace, I told myself, not quite believing it. *And you love a prince who loves you back.*

Laughter tickled me deep inside and bubbled to the surface.

"Huh?" Cedric asked drowsily.

"I...I'm happy," I said, my hand sliding up and down his muscled arm. "I'm just so happy."

He smiled and tucked his head under my chin. His palm was open on my left pec, and he caressed my naked torso lightly. "I promise I'll make you happy for as long as we live."

And I believed that he would.

Epilogue

Three Months Later

Cedric

Thick snowflakes filled the evening air, catching the bright lights of the streetlamps. Despite a dark blue wool scarf tied tightly around my neck and the screaming orange beanie Tristan had produced from his wardrobe when I had left his apartment in a hurry, snowflakes found their way to my neck.

The morning had been slow and lazy. Tristan had been warm and beautiful, reluctant to leave the bed, and with an appetite for hot chocolate on a gloomy winter day. I had given him all that, and in return, he wouldn't let me leave. So we cuddled, and then we did much more than cuddle, and we cuddled some more. But then I needed to hurry to the museum as a representative of the royal family. Thanks to the fact that I practically lived in New York, certain artifacts found their way from the Royal History Museum of

Verdumont to New York. Conveniently, I was asked to attend.

When it all ended, I insisted on being let out of the car a few blocks away from Hudson Burrow. "I don't mean to be driven around, and I do not want to be followed," I told my chauffeur. And if my security team could allow me to walk, they certainly didn't let me walk alone. At a distance, two agents followed me discreetly.

Life wasn't as liberating as I had hoped, but it was far better than what I had expected just a few months ago.

Instead of going straight to my apartment, I circled the neighborhood. I expected Tristan to be working tonight, so I wandered the streets. As I passed by Rashid's grocery store, I noticed that the lights were all out and the store shuttered. They had probably gone somewhere together with nobody left to mind the store.

When I reached the corner of Hudson Street and Christopher Street, I let myself into the tall, luxurious building my team had deemed appropriate. I had wanted an apartment deeper in the neighborhood, in a redbrick building like Tristan's, but they had dismissed it for security reasons. I couldn't win all my battles.

Someone moving attracted my attention to the far side of the lobby, their black curls slipping out of my view as the elevator doors closed. I muttered to myself as I pressed the button to call the next elevator. While the one that had just escaped ascended high to the top of the building, another one arrived, its doors sliding and letting me in.

Up on my floor, I reached my door, swiped my key, and walked in. The lights in the spacious living room were on, and the sound of feet lightly touching the hardwood floor made me smile. He wasn't working after all.

I took off the beanie and scarf, then shrugged off my coat before Tristan walked into the living room shyly from the study.

"Hey," I said. "Got a night off?"

"Yeah," Tristan said, crossing the room carefully as he approached me. He smiled at me hopefully, then pressed a hot kiss against my mouth. The chill of the night had cooled me down much more than I had realized.

"I wouldn't have wandered if I knew you were waiting," I said.

Tristan and I spent most of our free time together. My duties were very relaxed, especially since the elections passed favorably to my family. The moderate parties swept another victory in Verdumont, and the talk of firing my family from the job had subsided. I had plenty of time to focus on things that mattered to me. Not only did Mama Viv put me to good use whenever there were crates to be moved around and I was nearby, but I got to begin my research of queer motifs in Hellenic and Roman mythology.

Tristan's schedule was less forgiving, but he spent his free hours either with me or planning something to do with me. The sexy lip bite he was performing now was not the same as those he made when he wanted us to undress quickly or die. This was something closer to guilt. "So, the reason I'm not at work," he said carefully, "is because I couldn't take Biscuit with me."

"Biscuits?" I asked, frowning.

"No. Biscuit. Singular. It's loud at Neon Nights, and Biscuit's frightened," Tristan explained hurriedly. "And my place is overcrowded and loud, plus our landlord never agreed to...erm, letting Biscuit stay with us. I figured this would be a great place for him. It's not like anyone will complain to the Prince of Verdumont. And it's only until we figure something out..."

"Tristan?" I asked, trying to keep my voice cool and firm, but it bubbled with humor and happiness. I knew. I always knew. This was who Tristan was, and I wouldn't want him to change if it spared me a thousand headaches. "What is Biscuit?"

Right on cue, a whimper-bark of a puppy who was only discovering his voice reached us from the bedroom.

Tristan blushed, and I tried not to set a precedent by leaping with joy. I failed. I grabbed Tristan's hand and practically ran to the bedroom. "You didn't," I whispered in disbelief as I carefully opened the door. A mixed-breed golden cocker retriever stumbled around our bed.

If any frost had remained in me after the chilly stroll outside, it was gone now. Warmth spilled through me as if my heart couldn't contain all its blood and all these feelings. They overwhelmed me. I hadn't had a dog since I was a little boy, and even then, the dogs had been selected and cared for by other people.

"Are you going to kill me?" Tristan asked.

"What?" I heard myself ask, my gaze on the light brown, furry thing making itself comfortable on my pillow. Biscuit barked, then grew alert as if he hadn't been the one barking, cocked his little head, then made circles around my pillow.

I saw myself moving carefully toward the bed, Tristan trailing after me and kneeling on the edge of the mattress. I lowered myself carefully and extended my hand far to Biscuit to sniff. His big, black eyes were smart, his fur clean because Tristan had, no doubt, bathed the puppy.

"You impossible thing," I whispered, not sure who I was talking to. My love. I was speaking to the love of my life. "You incredible thing."

The puppy sniffed me carefully, then immediately decided we were friends and abandoned his work on my pillow in favor of getting to know me.

Tristan joined me on the bed. "So, you're not mad?"

Biscuit sniffed my face and licked my cheek, his excitement so typical for a puppy without a care in the world. He quickly became too happy to hold still, welcoming ear scratching and belly tickling. "Mad?" I asked, my throat closing as I felt the oncoming happy tears. "Are you crazy? I'm happier than I can tell you."

Tristan's face split with a brilliant grin. "You're gonna help Biscuit?"

"Oh, my love, I'm going to keep Biscuit. For us." I teased the puppy thoroughly, then let him get away and catch a break from my fingers. When I looked at Tristan again, his eyes glimmered. "He's ours, Tris."

My love bit his lip and leaned in. As he released his lip, his mouth pressed against mine, and we kissed deeply and passionately. An inexhaustible pool of love existed in me. However much I dived through it, exploring its depths, I always knew I was far, far too close to the surface, and there was no end to it, no matter how deep I went.

"I love you," Tristan said.

"And I love you," I replied.

As we kissed, Biscuit decided he wanted more scratches.

He tucked himself between Tristan and me and got a belly rub of his life.

This was who my love was. He went through life picking up strays, fixing what was broken, and making the world a little better with every new day.

Thank you for reading The Cinderella Prince. If you enjoyed it, please remember to leave a review on Amazon and/or GoodReads to support Hayden's work. For timely updates from the author, consider subscribing to Hayden Hall's newsletter. You will receive two complimentary novels. And for exclusive works, art, and more, consider becoming a Patron.

The next novel in The Boys of Hudson Burrow is Romeo vs Romeo. Keep reading for an exclusive preview.

THE END.

Romeo vs Romeo

The sexy newcomer at Neon Nights hates me. I'm not too thrilled about him, either, except that those hungry eyes full of hateful desire do wild things to me.

I know I shouldn't meddle with a closet case. Good Catholic boys are nothing but trouble and heartbreak.

Except that this Catholic boy is a foot taller and a foot wider, with dusty blond hair and piercing blue eyes. My legs turn to jelly whenever he comes near me. And all of a sudden, I'm messing around with the exact type of guy I should avoid. My time would be better spent protecting our safe space from demolition, but my obsession with Everett consumes my body and my soul.

If only things were as simple as all that.

Just when I think that Everett and I could have something a little like a future together, I discover who he really is. Everett Langley is the son and heir of the very man who is trying to build a luxury hotel after he ruins our neighborhood.

Neon Nights is at risk and I am never scared to be the

first line of defense. But this time, standing up for the bar that shelters all the outcasts and runaways in the neighborhood means fighting the very person I am falling in love with.

You can find Romeo vs Romeo on Amazon.

Acknowledgments

Hopefully, this book has given you a taste of what the series will be like. More drama, spice, and dancing are on the way. That's guaranteed!

In the meantime, I would like to say that no book is written by one person alone. While typing the manuscript may be seen as a lonely job, authors depend on a score of people to make all of this possible. My huge thanks to Sandra from One Love Editing for reading this book and giving it a thorough polish.

As always, I am in debt to Angela Haddon for her spectacular cover design. And to Xram Ragde, thank you for providing me with the best photos ever.

My patrons are a crucial part of my process. They are the first who see my chapters. They're the cheerleaders when things are hard and when things are good. Your support is priceless.

Thank you too all the readers who ever read one of my books. Especially if you decided to stick around. You give my life meaning.

And finally, thank you to Xander for being the love of my life. I love you.

Hayden
July 10, 2024

Also by Hayden Hall

The Boys of Hudson Burrow
The Cinderella Prince
Romeo vs Romeo
Beauty and the Billionaire
Arctic Titans of Northwood U
Crossing Blades
Scoring the Keeper
Big Stick Energy
Icebound Rivals
Rebels of the Rink
On Thin Ice
Coaching Prince Charming
Frat Brats of Santa Barbara
The Fake Boyfriends Debacle
The Royal Roommate Disaster
The Wrong Twin Dilemma
The Bitter Rivals Fiasco
The Accidental Honeymoon Catastrophe
The Bedroom Coach Contract
The Office Nemesis Calamity
College Boys of New Haven
The Nerd Jock Conundrum

The Three Hearts Equation

The Two Stars Collision

The No Strings Theory

The Geeky Jock Paradox

Standalones

Rescued: A Hurt Comfort Novel

Damaged: A Black Diamond Novel

When We Meet Again

For more information about books by Hayden Hall, visit www.haydenhallwrites.com.

About the Author

Gay. Sweet. Steamy.

Hayden Hall writes MM romance novels. He is a boyfriend, a globetrotter, and an avid romance reader.

Hayden's mission is to author a catalog of captivating and steamy MM romance novels which gather a devoted community around the Happily Ever Afters.

His stories are sweet with just the right amount of naughty.

You can find out more and get in touch with Hayden through his website at www.haydenhallwrites.com or one of the links below.

- amazon.com/stores/author/B08R5CSXYS
- patreon.com/HaydenHall
- instagram.com/authorhaydenhall
- facebook.com/hayden.hall.773